I0645053

St. Annie's Corps

Mollie held out her hand and he pushed the small but flawless diamond ring on her finger. "It fits. I made a good guess." He lifted her hand and kissed the ring.

"A seal of our pledge." Mollie stared at the ring, her eyes misting. "Thank you for waiting until after the perfect night, darling. First the deep feeling, then the public expression."

The clock on the dash loomed giant sized. Its hands pointed to seven. "I eagerly accept Lieutenant Van Ness, with one condition."

His arm about her loosened, and his expression changed. "Not another one!"

Taking both his hands, she spoke softly, "If either of us decides differently when we are separated by oceans and half a world, we wait until we can tell each other in person. I've heard of sad things about Dear Johns...or Rons."

Ron whistled his relief. "A remote possibility, Sweetheart. I've already tested my passion for you a year. I do agree about rejection by mail. I promise there will be no Dear Mollie's. We have another hour if you drop me off and take the car back to your house. Did you ever get your driver's license?"

"Dad took me over to the state patrol station about a month ago. He insisted I might need a license when I'm in the Army. Why, I have no idea. I doubt I'll be driving anything but gurneys wherever I'm going."

His arms tightened around her, and she could feel the bandage on his shoulder. "Be safe. I pray God you won't be in one of those carts."

She could stem her tears no longer. They spilled over her face and dampened the blue serge on the chest she leaned so tightly against.

Other Works From The Pen Of
Mary Brockway

Persimmon Bayou, a murder mystery set in the south in 1868 during the difficult reconstruction period , was published by Wings April 2010. It is included on Amazon.com, Fictionwise and other markets.

St. Annie's Corps.

Mary Brockway

A Wings ePress, Inc.
Historical Romance Novel

Wings ePress, Inc.

Edited by: Jeanne Smith
Copy Edited by: Joan Powell
Senior Editor: Pat Evans
Executive Editor: Marilyn Kapp
Cover Artist: Richard Stroud

All rights reserved

Names, characters and incidents depicted in this book are products of the author's imagination or are used fictitiously. Any resemblance to actual events, locales, organizations, or persons, living or dead, is entirely coincidental and beyond the intent of the author or the publisher.

No part of this book may be reproduced or transmitted in any form or by any means, electronic or mechanical, including photocopying, recording, or by any information storage and retrieval system, without permission in writing from the publisher.

Wings ePress Books
http://www.wings-press.com

Copyright © 2010 by Mary Brockway
ISBN 978-1-61309-989-6

Published In the United States Of America

Wings ePress Inc.
3000 N. Rock Road
Newton, KS 67114

Dedication

To nurses everywhere for their dedication to caring for us all

One

The Plebes:

Mollie McAllister and her best friend, Barbara Andrews, panting from the steep climb up Seattle's Marion Street, stopped at the corner of Third Avenue to catch their breaths.

Barbara closed her umbrella and pointed it across the street. "There's a bus."

"The sign says 'Mount Baker'. Let's ask if it goes anywhere near St. Anne's." Mollie pushed through a crowd boarding an electric trolley and Barbara tilted after her on three-inch heels. With suitcases bumping their legs, they entered and climbed the steps.

"Sorry," Barbara said when her umbrella poked a fat man's blue serge-covered behind and he said something obscene.

The door closed and the trolley pulled away, sparks snapping from its wires.

"Wait. Where does this bus go?" Mollie yelled, trying to make the driver hear over five chattering people gathered around the fare box. "We need to go to St. Anne's School of Nursing on Hospital Hill."

A woman with frizzled henna-tinted hair, her eyes circled in green shadow and smeared mascara, clung to a strap near the driver. "Goes up Jackson, kiddo. Opposite direction. You'd better get off at King. There's cabs around the train stations. I'll pull the cord when it is time." She deposited a couple of bus tokens into the slot for them while Mollie searched her purse for quarters to pay for the generosity.

"Thank you, ma'am," Mollie said, shifting her right leg to the top step to balance the left one sandwiched between two people behind her.

When the trolley stopped at Jackson, the two girls pushed past disgruntled boarding passengers and stepped onto the sidewalk crowded with hurrying pedestrians.

Mollie stumbled over a sleeping old man sprawled against a trash can, his ragged coat sleeves cradling an empty wine bottle. "Creeps! Let's get out of here, Barb. Dad told me to stay away from Skid Row. He said people carry knives and cut each other up even in daylight. There's another trolley headed the other direction. Hurry, let's make the light!"

Barbara sucked in a noisy breath. She cast a sideways glance at the derelict, hefted her luggage and ignored the cacophony of honking horns to follow Mollie across the street just as the light changed.

As the girls hurried toward the bus stop, a freckled redhead, Navy bell-bottoms emphasizing his bowed legs, blocked their path. He whistled through his teeth and reached for Mollie's suitcase, sending her tennis racket scooting over the walk. "Carry those bags for a good screw, baby."

Mollie scowled at him and bent to retrieve the racket. "Someone's picking us up." She pointed toward the bus stop where the trolley had just pulled away.

The skinny dark-haired sailor bared overlapping teeth in an assessing smile and rolled his eyes at Barbara. "I'll take yours, any little thing of yours, blondie."

Barbara's fair skin flamed as she turned away, then she glanced back to see if the sailors were still there. "I'm not sure what they meant by 'screw.' Too bad they weren't better looking."

"I think it's something like heavy necking," Mollie said. The word had to have a bad meaning, because her mother had called her brother, "Joseph" when he used that word, and she only did that when Joe made her mad.

The girls settled down on their suitcases and opened umbrellas to protect their curls from the drizzle.

"There's a Yellow Cab just turning the corner. Catch him, Shirley!" shouted a girl with short brown hair, her pleated skirt whirling and saddle shoes scattering rainwater.

The tall girl behind her took long strides toward the curb, jabbed two fingers into her mouth, and forced out an earsplitting whistle. "Got him, Ginger. He's pulling over."

Mollie and Barbara scrambled to their feet.

"Going up town?" Mollie asked of the whistler.

"St. Anne's Nursing School. Don't know where it is. Just got off the train from Idaho," answered the girl wearing the glasses.

"We're headed to St. Anne's too." Mollie yelled. "Can we share the cab?"

"Sure," the one named Ginger said.

The four girls squeezed into the cab, holding their excess baggage on their laps while the driver shook his head, grumbling aloud. "Of all the fares in town, I get four goddam girls." He tied down the overflowing '39 Ford trunk lid with a piece of frayed rope. "Bet they haven't two bits between 'em for a tip," he muttered loud enough to send all four searching coin purses.

~ * ~

At St. Anne's nursing residence the four girls, ignoring the impatient cabby, counted out change for each tab.

3

Mollie hefted her luggage and walked to the entrance of the square four story brick building. Two large camellia bushes dripped raindrops from shiny leaves onto three wide brick steps leading to the entry. There were no other plants except ivy clinging to the walls. A tingle of apprehension touched her spine. "Guess this is our home for the next three years, Barb."

Barbara reached for the bronze latch. "Yes, but right now I just want to get out of the rain."

The other two girls caught up with them and the four entered. Just inside, a roundish, pink-faced nun's soft voice greeted them. "I'm Sister Anne. Please leave your bags here. Sister Marie needs to explain procedures before you go to your rooms."

The odor of fresh-brewed coffee wafted from somewhere as the nun ushered the four into the nursing supervisor's office.

Mollie wasn't sure whether to sit in one of the four straight-backed oak chairs facing the desk, and decided to remain standing. The others followed her example.

An older nun, dwarfed behind a large oak desk, turned slightly in her squeaky chair and scanned them through round metal-framed glasses.

"Welcome to St. Anne's. If memory serves me correctly, you are Miss Margaret McAllister," She smiled at Mollie's nod. "And Miss Barbara Andrews."

"Yes, Sister," Barbara said, fidgeting with her handbag.

"And I'm Shirley Britton. You've met me and Ginger only through our applications, Sister Marie."

"And I'm Ging...Virginia King. We're from Boise."

Smiling, Sister Marie pulled a sheaf of papers from a drawer, rose and handed a copy to each girl. Returning to her swivel chair, which emitted a nerve-tingling squeak, she continued. "These regulations are designed to assist you through your nursing training, and keep you in good health." The tiny nun adjusted her glasses and read.

"Curfew will be strictly enforced. You must sign in by nine each weekday evening and lights must be out by ten. If your grades are passing, and you are not assigned duty, a weekly late leave until twelve-thirty will be granted on request. You may smoke in your rooms if it is agreeable to your room mates, and play radios and records quietly. I am always available to help with problems." Sister Marie rose to her full five foot two, smiled and asked, "Have you questions?"

"When will we get our uniforms?" Shirley asked.

"Tomorrow afternoon." Sister Marie scanned Shirley's figure towering eight inches above hers. "Of course some will need altering. Your first classes will begin tomorrow morning at nine, and directions about how to reach the college are included in your printed instructions."

"When are meals served?" Ginger asked.

"You will find meal schedules and menus posted in the lounge. I might add that students are encouraged to attend chapel at six, a good beginning for the day whatever your religious preference. Breakfast follows in the nurse's cafeteria, which closes mornings at eight. You will also find schedules for college and floor work on the bulletin board in the nursing residence lounge. Coffee, tea and juice are always available there. Plebes...new students, are housed on the fourth floor. The elevator is just around the corner. Thank you for choosing St. Anne's School of Nursing for your training." She extended a hand to each girl.

Mollie lifted her baggage and followed the three girls across the tiled entrance foyer to the elevator and loaded it with luggage. Crowding in, she pushed the fourth floor button. The aging lift creaked and grumbled to the fourth floor and she punched the stop button until the girls and their assorted suitcases were carried out.

Barbara scanned the diagram of St. Anne's Nursing School dormitory. "There is ours, four-o-one, across the hall, Mollie."

"Ours is four-ten. Must be four rooms farther on," Shirley said. "See you later."

"At least we are close to the elevator." Mollie scooted her suitcase over a shiny tile floor and reached for the door knob. "It's locked! Sister didn't give us a key."

"Try again, maybe it's just stuck."

Mollie turned the knob again and pushed her shoulder against the door.

"Hey! Hold it!" A girl with hair in pin curls opened the door. Clad only in a tight rubber panty girdle with rolls of unbound fat escaping over the top, she struggled to fasten a full-figure bra straining over her generous breasts. "I'm Dorrie. You must be our roommates."

"Roommates?" Barbara looked at Mollie.

"Yeah. Cozy, huh? St. Annie's accepted so many applications for this new three-year program; they had to double us up. There are ninety in our class!" Dorrie said.

"But Barbara and I paid for a double room, not a barracks!" Mollie sputtered.

"So did we. I'm Carmen." A pretty olive-skinned girl with a mole on her left chin and deep dimples in both cheeks, poked her head from the end of a double bunk.

Mollie scowled at the bottom bunks, obviously the territory of Dorrie and Carmen. Several stuffed animals decorated one of them and scattered satin pillows were strewn over the other. On the two top beds were thin mattresses showing new blue and white striped ticking and a pile of blankets, sheets and pillows.

"Looks like we don't even get a chance at a coin toss for beds."

"First come, first served," Carmen said. "We're lowers, you're uppers. Nothing to do with social status."

"I slept upstairs at home." Mollie climbed the ladder to survey her scant private territory barely three feet from the pale green plastered ceiling. "Where are the clothes closets?"

Dorrie jerked her head to the left of the entry door. "That one's for you gals. And you get those two desks." She pointed to new, thirty-six inch unpainted pine desks between the window and the end of their bunks.

Tucked into the two-foot space between the desks and window wall was a white lavatory with towel racks on the side and a mirrored medicine cabinet above. Mollie opened the mirror to put away her toothbrush and scowled at the assorted makeup, combs and two huge tubes of toothpaste."Looks like you two have already filled this up. Don't you expect us to brush our teeth?" She pulled out the makeup and combs. "Everything's gotta be divided into fourths."

Barbara tugged open a sticky desk drawer. "This is where we put everything? No dressers?"

Carmen and Dorrie shook their heads.

Mollie grunted to lift her favorite high school graduation present, a portable typewriter, to the top of the desk nearest the window, wondering when she could type without disturbing the other girls. She opened a suitcase and began to sort out the contents. "I'll ask Dad to build us bookshelves for under the window, Barb."

"Phew." Barbara settled into one of the hard oak chairs, kicked off her three-inch heels and wiggled her toes.

"We're supposed to get lamps and shelf units for over the desks next week. They're being shipped from some government storage place," Dorrie said, "and like everything government, probably painted that hideous puke color."

After packing the four-foot closet solidly with bare essentials, Mollie frowned at the remainder. "What'll we do with our shoes, boots, luggage and tennis rackets?"

"How about under the bed?"

"Good thinking, Barb." Mollie shoved her racket under the bunk, dislodging two flat boxes. A volley ball rolled across the floor. She squinted at the assortment of stuff crammed in the ten inch spaces. "Good golly! You two solved your storage problem!" She glowered at Carmen, who lounged on her bed blowing smoke rings.

"Come on, Barb, we might as well find the lunch room and see if the food is better than the sleeping quarters." Mollie slammed the door, and then felt guilty. Her mother would say, *"Mollie, your manners."* She turned the knob and stepped back inside the room. "Wan'ta join us, gals?"

Dorrie buttoned her blouse and tied a kerchief over her hair while the others waited at the elevator. They followed directional signs and appetizing food odors to a long line of white uniformed nurses scanning the entrees displayed on steam tables in the center of the large room. Two plump women were dishing up the food.

Barbara brightened. "Chicken ala King! I love it." She held her plate forward to receive a big helping spooned over two hot biscuits.

Behind her, a nurse wearing a white cap with a black senior's stripe, raised thin penciled brows and grinned. "I wouldn't take too much of that at first. The creamed stuff gives you trots until you get used to it."

Mollie shrugged and moved on to the meat loaf. "Barb, remember our room's a block from the toilets."

~ * ~

After two days of procedures classes, Mollie donned her new, stiffly starched uniform, feeling so proud she imagined God and her mother would frown at her inflated ego. Sucking in her stomach, she buttoned the twenty-two inch belt, rubbed an imaginary spot from her white shoes and twisted to straighten a slightly askew seam in the required white cotton hosiery. She'd planned to become a nurse since she was ten and her brother, Joe, had his tonsils out. Smiling, she remembered how babyish and helpless he'd acted.

Mollie savored her ten minutes alone after Barb left with Shirley for her first day of duty, and Dorrie and Carmen headed to morning college classes. She poked the cluster of dark auburn ringlets over her forehead with a rat-tail comb, turning her head slightly to push an escaping strand into place in her new upswept hair style Barbara had arranged. The rules said no hair over the collar. She patted the back of her head. In December, a stiffly starched white cap would be pinned there. "You'll look real 'nursey' then, Miss McAllister," she muttered, fastening her name tag above the left pocket and glancing at her watch. Ten minutes to seven.

On the south end of the hospital's fifth floor, Mollie stopped in the chart room. Miss Emerson, the charge nurse, assigned her to do four bed baths in room 517. She squeaked down the white tile corridor in new rubber-soled shoes, trying to ignore a slight rumbling in her stomach.

"Hello. I'm Mollie McAllister. I've been assigned to give you baths today." Her voice sounded weak and shaky, not at all confident. Nervous smiles from two of the patients proved they knew she was a plebe; didn't do much for her courage either.

Struggling to keep a pitcher of hot water from spilling on the stack of clean linen piled beside it, Mollie cautiously wheeled the squeaky cart to the first bed. "I guess you're first," she leaned to read the chart on the foot of the bed, "Mrs. Russell."

The woman in Bed One, her head swathed in bandages, opened swollen eyes and blinked. "Why're you wearin' grapes in your hair, honey?"

"Grapes?" Mollie's hand went to the little ringlets over her forehead.

Bed Three giggled. "She had brain surgery and is loony as a clown. We don't pay no attention to her."

Mollie dodged Mrs. Russell's octopus-like arms band clutching hands long enough to get her bathed and dried. She slipped a clean gown over the rag-doll head, and then changed the bed. A glimpse at her watch revealed that Bed One had taken twice as long as it should. She'd never finish by eleven. "Rats," she muttered aloud. "Forgot about the catheter." Fumbling in the night stand for the bed pan, she pushed it under the sagging hips and released the rubber catheter, feeling smug that she remembered how.

Bed Two's sheet was streaked with smelly drainage from the tubes in her abdominal incision. Mollie swallowed, remembering Sister Anne's warning that sensitive noses were misplaced in the nursing profession. Lack of time to dwell on it closed her nostrils to the odor.

Bed Three gave her no trouble at all and she had caught up on time. She turned to Bed Four, a dark-haired woman in her forties. "Guess you're my last lady this morning, Mrs. Novak." She peeked at the chart on the end of the bed. "And you're scheduled to get up in a chair today."

After finishing Mrs. Novak's bath and helping the gall bladder surgery patient into a leather armchair, Mollie wheeled the cart to the utility room to sterilize the bed pans and empty the wash basins. She stacked the steaming pans onto the cart and hurried along the corridor toward the room.

The light over the door of five-seventeen flashed impatiently.

"Nurse, something's wrong with Mrs. Novak. I can't see her face from here, but it looks like she's slumped over in her chair. I heard her sort of grunt. Did she faint?" Bed Two twisted, trying to see around the dividing curtain.

"Holy cow!" Mollie wavered, knocking a bedpan clanging to the floor. She bit a knuckle to stifle a scream as she ran to the charge desk. "Hurry, Sister. It's Mrs. Novak! She looks like...she's dead!"

Sister Agnes drew the curtains tightly to partition the room, but it wasn't easy to disguise the morgue gurney.

Mollie leaned against the charge desk. "She...she seemed just fine, Sister Agnes. Well maybe a little wobbly. The last thing she did was ask for a book to read." Mollie felt tears dampen her face and fumbled in her pocket for a handkerchief. "How can anyone look perfectly healthy two minutes before dying?"

Sister Agnes patted her shoulder. "An embolus can develop and dislodge rapidly after any kind of surgery, Miss McAllister. Some patients are especially prone to clots and we turn them at regular intervals to avoid their formation. You should never leave patients alone when you get them up the first time." Her voice sounded firm, but a soft sigh escaped. "Sudden death of a patient is terrifying for all of us. How unfortunate it happened on your first day on the floor. Don't allow this to discourage you. Most of our patients get well."

Mollie squeezed her eyes tightly to stop tears, and drew in a deep breath. "If I'd known about the chance of an embolism..."

"Instructions on this surgical complication are found in chapter forty-one in your *Principles and Practices of Nursing* textbook." Sister Agnes tilted Mollie's face with a slender finger. "Perhaps it should have been emphasized before you worked on the surgical floor."

Mollie nodded, forcing out a weak smile. "Yes, Sister Agnes." She felt the nun's hand squeeze her arm.

"Miss King needs help finishing her duties in room five-ten. Since yours are completed, perhaps you might assist her."

Shrugging, Mollie pocketed her handkerchief and walked slowly down the corridor, wondering how she could face another patient. She shut the door of 510, grimacing when she saw Ginger, tongue clenched between her teeth, struggling to pull a twisted sheet under an enormous patient. The elderly man filled the bed like a grounded dirigible.

"I think I can pull this through if you tilt him a little, Mollie."

Mollie hurried to the other side of the bed. "Mr. Phelps, I'm pushing your shoulders forward a bit so we can finish changing your bed." She grasped the mountain of slippery flesh while Ginger tugged hard to pull the sheet across the damp smelly rubber one beneath him. After repeating the operation at the patient's hips, sweat glistened on both girls' faces.

Ginger smiled nervously, looking embarrassed. "Thanks, Mollie." She backed around the bed. "Maybe I can return the favor sometime."

Mr. Phelps, who had lost his power of speech because of a stroke, chose that second to cough loudly, startling Ginger.

"Yikes!" Ginger uttered a high squeaky cry as she tripped over the tubing draining his urine into a gallon jug under the edge of the bed. It toppled and the dark amber liquid sloshed across the tile floor of the small private room. "Oh no!" she moaned, shaking the stained limp hem of her uniform and watching the leaking odorous fluid saturate her white stockings and trickle into her shoes.

"I'll get a mop." Mollie raced out while Ginger stooped to reconnect the tubing and right the jug.

Miss Emerson grinned at Mollie when she hurried past. "Got your initiation in room five-ten, I see. Old Lardback Phelps gives plebes a real test."

Mollie's deep sigh whistled through the room when they finished with Mr. Phelps. "The cafeteria closes in five minutes, Ginger. I'll run and grab a sandwich for us while you hurry over to change. Meet you on the steps outside Anatomy class."

Ginger sniffed, rubbing her eyes with her handkerchief. "I...I'm so humiliated, Mollie. Don't bother with a sandwich for me. I couldn't swallow a bite of lunch. I just want a nice hot shower. Tell Doctor Sauder I'll be a little late."

~ * ~

Mollie gulped a ham sandwich while running down the hill to the college, her thoughts skimming back over four hours she hoped never to repeat. And poor Ginger, who she suspected couldn't stand doing less than a perfect job, had to feel worse. Why were Ginger's standards aimed so high? "Guess if Dad was a college professor instead of a carpenter, I might be afraid of not being perfect," she mumbled. "But only Ma Perkins on the radio solves everyone's problems. Wish she could make me forget Mrs. Novak." She shuffled through dry leaves covering the sidewalk. It had been a scary first duty day for two of St. Anne's plebes. "Bet none of them can top my story, at least I hope they can't," she muttered as she hurried into the building.

~ * ~

After dinner, Mollie scanned the letter she had begun to her brother the evening before. She and Joe had always shared triumphs, secrets and a good many arguments. They were the two oldest children in the family, a three-year difference between her and Sally, then four more to her little brother, Mike.

Joe, twenty-one, had been a junior at U.C.L.A. before joining the Army Air Corps. He would have been an aeronautical engineer in another year. War raged in Europe and threats of involvement loomed for the United States. A lot of guys were interrupting college classes to join reserve units.

She yawned, trying to keep her mind on writing to her brother, a duty neglected longer than usual because the frantic pace of her first two weeks at nursing school had proven exciting and downright scary. She sensed an inner clock advancing her life by years instead of days, like the girl in *Lost Horizon* who turned into an old woman when taken from the sheltered atmosphere of Shangri-la. She touched the skin on her arm, vaguely fearing it had grown flabby and wrinkled, but the smattering of hated freckles looked eighteen, not eighty. Her head felt swollen with newly injected knowledge, yet each day revealed how little she knew about life outside her warm tight family cocoon. Chewing the end of her pen, she reported the beginning of her metamorphosis to her brother.

~ * ~

St. Anne's Nursing School
September 15, 1941
Dear Joe,

While you practice three point landings without smashing cactuses at Kingman Air Base, Barb and I try to give hypodermic shots to patients without sending them out of their beds. Every day, we plebes (that means amoebic life around here) work four hours on the floors and have four hours of classes at the college. I feel kind of scared doing so much nursing I know practically nothing about. After just two weeks at St. Anne's, we're taking patients' temperatures and blood pressures and giving bed baths they like, and enemas they don't. Other things nurses have to do, you wouldn't want to hear about if you happen to be eating when you read my letter.

Yesterday, we practiced giving saline hypodermic shots, poking oranges, then ourselves. Barb may never get above plebe status if she doesn't learn to stick needles into real arms without causing screams of pain. Mine!

We drew roommates who are about as tidy as the Lower Slobovians in the comic strip L'il Abner, but did meet two nice girls from Idaho the day we arrived in Seattle. Ginger King, one of them, is assigned with me on the surgical recovery floor. Ginger has the edge on brains at St. Anne's, but our first day on duty was awful. Mine was worse than Ginger's. One of my first patients died!

As you know, studying in such crowded quarters takes real concentration. The gals tease me about wearing those red ear muffs you gave me last Christmas, but they help. You know I can't stay in school if I lose my scholarship.

Mother needn't worry about me having dates with big city men. Our schedule doesn't leave time, and if war jitters continue, there won't be any men around. Like you, the guys are all joining one of the services. I hear there are some cute R.O.T.C.s at the U.

You surprised Dad when you left college to enlist in the Army Air Corps, but he acts kind of proud. Mike and Sally think it's keen. Mother is another story. Golly, Joe, I miss home already. How did you stand being away three years? Bye now. I must write to Wally and Don. Love, Mollie

P.S. Barb vows never to touch Chicken ala King again. She spent the first two days at St. Anne's racing to the can.

P.P.S.S. Hope you don't mind me borrowing your radio.

Two

Barbara opened the door of 401 and plunged headlong over a mound of blankets, pillows, and assorted clutter from the unmade lower bunks. "Judas Priest! Dorrie and Carmen must've overslept. Looks like an earthquake struck this room." Struggling to stand, she shook lint from her uniform and stepped into a small open space.

Mollie slogged through the tangle of bedding, and then heaved it onto Dorrie's bunk. "Sleeping in didn't make them slobs. They left the room this bad yesterday and I cleaned it up when I came up to change after duty."

Barbara scooped assorted paper from the floor, stuffed it into the trash basket and gingerly lifted a pair of panties between two fingers. "I'm sick of tripping over their junk but what can we do about it? They don't even pick up their dirty underwear. Ugh!"

"Crammed in here like stacks of lumber is bad enough, without drawing a couple of real pigs for roommates. Maybe we ought'a tattle." Mollie ran a sheet of paper into the typewriter. "Anonymously, of course."

She quickly typed a note.

Miss Koski and Miss Morales. You must make up your beds before you go to class or duty. Please take care of this right away. Sister Marie.

Mollie pinned the note to the pillow on top of Dorrie's bedding. "Hurry, Barb. We've just enough time before chemistry class for a coke at the drug store. I need some sanitary napkins." She frowned, counting out change.

"Carmen and most of the rest of the girls swipe those nice soft ones from OB," Barbara muttered.

"Sister Marie would assign Carmen a few penances if she caught her. Besides, you have to pin them to your panties because they don't have tabs."

Mollie donned her coat and tied a bright rayon scarf over her hair, thinking how much she and Barbara had learned about female behavior in two months. Two hundred girls crowded together yielded fascinating lessons in sociology.

Her dad's most profane word in the presence of women was 'rats' and Joe swore only to shock his sisters and with expletives far less blue than those echoing through St. Annie's dorm. Dorrie's language fit right in. Nude girls parading from room to room and telling lewd jokes that Mollie didn't quite understand, made her struggle to cover blushes. Why couldn't she become sophisticated like Joan Crawford in the movies and not be shocked at such different moral values?

She smiled, noting Barb's mouth still flattened in distaste at the messy room. "Maybe they'll take our hint. We'd better hurry."

At the drug store, Barbara's straw bubbled noisily at the end of her lemon coke. "Too bad we didn't get to room with Ginger and Shirley."

"Yeah," Mollie mumbled, stifling a giggle at the reminder of Ginger's Puritan-like wrinkled nose and Barbara's brown penciled eyebrows often lifted over some new shock. All the two needed to complete the strict moral image were close fitting caps and long gray dresses. A tinge of conscience nudged at her complacency. "Hope we don't regret leaving that note."

~ * ~

When they returned from the college at four, Barbara listened at the door while Mollie, standing slightly aside, turned the knob and entered. "Ulp." She ducked a hot water bag hanging by a string too late to miss being drenched. "I'll kill Dorrie!" Grabbing a towel, she rubbed her bedraggled hair, grimacing at red dye from her sweater dripping down the front of her white blouse.

Barbara helped her pull the sweater off and hung it over a chair by the radiator. "They took the hint. Look at those neat beds."

Mollie unbuttoned her stained blouse and ran cold water in the lavatory to soak it. She turned around and gasped. "You bragged too soon, Barb." She jerked her head toward the upper bunks. They were torn apart, the pillows opened and feathers drifted everywhere. Wastebasket contents had been carefully divided between the two bunks and cigarette butts ground into the mattresses. Mollie snatched a note from the pile of bedding.

Good thing you locked that damn typewriter or it would never work again.

Barbara sighed. "We'd better get this mess cleaned up fast or we'll miss dinner." She climbed to her bunk, turned the mattress over, and gagging at the cigarette odor, began to remake her bed. A light tap at the door turned her head. "Probably Carmen and Dorrie, afraid to just walk in and face us."

Mollie opened the door and uttered a little cry when Sister Marie swished into the room.

"Girls! What is the meaning of this? At St. Anne's, we do not tolerate destruction of property. You will mend those pillows and have no late leave this week."

"We...we..." Both girls stammered.

Mollie felt tears sting her eyes. She stood stiffly as the note from Carmen and Dorrie sailed to the floor from the edge of her bunk. Sister Marie picked it up, scanned it without changing her expression and tucking it into the pocket of her black woolen habit, turned on flat heels and rustled out with her rosary rattling.

~ * ~

A strained quiet existed between the two levels of bunks for the rest of the week. On Friday, the four girls were summoned separately to Sister Marie's office.

Mollie faced the nursing director, feeling like she had in the fourth grade after plagiarizing a poem from the *Ladies Home Journal* and reading it as her own before the class. Sister Marie leaned back in her squeaking chair, sending tingles up Mollie's spine.

"Miss McAllister, there seems to be a misunderstanding between you and your room mates. Can you tell me about the problem and what you suggest might be done to resolve it?"

"I apologize for writing a note and signing your name, Sister." Mollie glanced down at a smudge where her sweaty hands had touched her uniform. Was there a fleeting hint of surprise in the nun's bland expression?

Sister Marie shuffled a stack of papers on her desk.

"I realize we are overcrowded, but your class is easing the shortage of nurses at St. Anne's."

"Thank you, Sister." What a stupid thing to say. Thanks for what? Overcrowding? But Sister Marie had given a veiled compliment. Mollie shifted her feet, impatient for the little nun to get to the real reason she had been summoned. Sister Marie appeared to be in a good humor. Maybe her late leave would be reinstated. But she had learned you could never tell about the nursing director's moods. The puzzling woman never showed strong feeling, her face a mask of tranquility. The starched white coif over her forehead, and the black serge habit, drew the image of a perfect nun.

"Miss McAllister, I know you are past due for a late leave." Sister Marie paused and glanced toward the window as if awaiting a comment.

"Yes, Sister. I rather counted on going to a movie."

"I'm sorry, but I insist you, Miss Koski, Miss Morales and Miss Andrews abide by the rules at St. Anne's. You must wait until next week end."

Mollie swallowed disappointment without comment and turned toward the door, thinking the interview was over. "I understand, Sister." She turned the knob to leave.

"I have asked your room mates to exchange beds with you and Miss Andrews. From now on, you will take monthly turns sleeping on the top bunks."

Mollie smiled. "Thank you, Sister." Couldn't she think of any other reply? Sister Marie would be sure her vocabulary was limited to *thank yous*.

A hint of humor flickered in the nun's eyes when she tossed a crumpled piece of paper into the waste basket. "And Miss McAllister, Sister Anne and I look in rather often to see how our student's rooms are kept."

Mollie could see Dorrie's scrawl on the note.

By the middle of the week, the girls were speaking again and had exchanged beds. Mollie turned off her desk light, yawning. Funny, how you get accustomed to going to bed by ten. Barbara, Dorrie, and Carmen were also getting ready for bed.

"Leave the light on, Mollie, 'til we get up to our perches," Dorrie said.

Mollie glanced out the window and saw a group of soldiers coming down the street. "Hurry up. The nuns are out for their walk and some soldiers are heading for the bus stop. They might be able to get quite a view." She went to the light switch by the door and waited until the two uppers were under cover, then turned off the ceiling light, wondering if she really heard laughter from below the window.

~ * ~

After eighteen hours of attempting to shape two hundred young women into registered nurses, Sister Marie and Sister Anne pulled their cloaks about them and began their habitual evening stroll.

Sister Marie nodded toward a girl scurrying into the nursing residence. "I suspect they know our walk is not only for health, but to see if our new students are turning their lights off by ten."

Sister Anne laughed. "I've heard them call it St. Anne's bedtime story." As they walked past the auditorium entrance, not quite hidden in the door alcove, a couple was kissing. She glanced at her watch. "Peters should be inside by the time we circle the building if that goodnight kiss isn't much longer."

The nun stopped a moment, reached in a pocket for a handkerchief and blew her nose noisily, smiling as the shadows moved from the alcove and around the corner of the building. "Peters doesn't concern me. She will graduate next spring and is engaged to that young soldier. This September class does worry me a little. So many of the girls are from poor families and are younger than those of our previous entering classes who had a year of college behind them."

"Government aid is a two-sided proposition, I suppose," Sister Anne replied. "It has allowed us to cut our tuition to help the less wealthy girls become registered nurses. I wonder when the program will be fully funded?"

"We have written promises, but will be deeply in debt if we subsidize these students much longer. They are easing the nursing shortage at St. Anne's, a financial bonus in labor costs." Sister Marie glanced toward the fourth floor windows and smiled as two rooms darkened.

When the two nuns rounded the corner to the south side of the building, Sister Anne tugged at the nursing director's sleeve.

"What could those young men be watching?" She pointed at six soldiers stretching their faces toward an upper floor of the nursing residence.

"Whatever the attraction, they like it." Sister Marie tilted her head upward. "Holy Mother of God!" Her hand covered her mouth. "Sorry, Sister." She allowed a giggle to trail into a funny little choking cough.

Sister Anne couldn't stifle hers. She laughed softly, casting an apprehensive glance toward the gathered soldiers. They were far too engrossed in watching a command performance on the fourth floor to hear.

"I'll take the skinny one with the curvy gams and the nice pink butt." One of them slapped his thigh. "With that equipment, you wouldn't care what she looks like from the waist up." He made suggestive circling motions with his hips. "Hot damn! I'd give ten bucks for a tall ladder!"

A thin corporal adjusted his wire framed glasses and rubbed his chin. "The fat gal has nice jugs. Wouldn't they be heaven to squeeze? Gotta get Ed to have Peters arrange a meeting with the rest of her." He turned to hiss. "Jiggers! Company, guys."

Sister Marie's face wore its noncommittal mask once more and Sister Anne smiled sweetly and muttered, "Good evening," as if she hadn't seen anything at all unusual.

The soldiers hurried to the bus stop around the corner of the nursing residence and the two nuns resumed their walk looking a shade paler under their tight-fitting caps.

"What shall we do about our fourth floor nudist colony?" Sister Anne asked, laughing so hard she had to search for her handkerchief to blot tears from her eyes.

Sister Marie's mouth widened into a broad smile too.

"I suppose we can't blame the girls. They must sleep in the top bunks and there aren't any shades on this side yet."

"If the girls keep attracting an audience, it will cast a most unsavory light on our pristine school," Sister Anne said. "What will we do if those young soldiers come back for tomorrow night's show? And we haven't checked to see if the other rooms..."

Sister Marie chuckled. "Those two girls were bare as Father Patrick's head. They ought to wear night clothing, but I note less modesty each year among our students. Yesterday, a nude girl hurrying from a shower to answer the phone nearly toppled me. We allow no visitors anywhere except the lounge, but we can't restrict the streets."

"I remember sleeping just that way myself in hot weather...before I entered the order of course." Sister Anne crossed her fingers in the folds of her skirt.

~ * ~

After duty the next morning, Mollie burst out of the elevator and almost collided with two workmen carrying tool boxes.

One of them nodded toward her open door. "Hope you girls like your new blinds. Sister Marie had us install black out shades in the whole building. Guess a lot of you nurses have to sleep days." He nodded at the notice on the elevator door Mollie hadn't seen. *Workmen On Fourth Floor.*

Dorrie stood grinning from the door of 401.

"That isn't the real reason, Mollie. I'm surprised you haven't heard the buzzing. Carmen and I had an audience when we climbed into our bunks last night. Dotty Peters' boyfriend's buddy just came by to ask me for a date. Me! Old tug boat Dorrie!"

"Gypsy Rose Lee will have to compete with Dorrie Koski!" Laughing hard, Mollie rolled onto her bunk. "What a treat you must have been when you climbed up the ladder with your rear end winking at those guys down below."

Barbara couldn't resist a lecture, "I told you gals you ought'a wear robes until we turn off the lights. I saw people staring at Mollie and me when we lived up there."

Dorrie laughed. "I've decided to keep the shades up and see if we can get a better assortment tonight. I must admit though, the curly haired Jewish corporal is kind of cute."

"How do you know he's Jewish?" Barbara asked.

Dorrie wagged a finger. "By my superb deductive powers, Doctor Watson! His name is Jacob Swartz for one thing, and he has a decidedly Jewish angle to his nose. He talks in pure Jersey, practically like a foreign language."

"You aren't going out with him?" Barbara's voice rose a measure in shock.

"No. I am going in. He's coming over Saturday night. I promised to make him a big bowl of popcorn and we'll listen to the *Hit Parade* on the radio in the lounge."

"At least you have a date." Mollie said. "Seems like years since I was near a man not covered with surgical bandages or casts."

~ * ~

Dorrie spent all Saturday afternoon getting ready for her date. She pulled so hard on her favorite rubber girdle, an inch gap opened over her right hip and threatened to slice to the top from the strain of the mound of complaining flesh beneath it. Blinking tears, she pinched the pink skin oozing through the rubber. "I can't get into my blue dress without it. God, why did I have to be born fat?"

Mollie reached in her uniform pocket and pulled out a roll of adhesive tape and her bandage scissors. "Hold it closed while I try to tape it." She cut several small strips and two longer ones. "I've never put a butterfly bandage on a girdle, but if you stop breathing and stand up all evening, it might hold." Holding up crossed fingers, she giggled. "Can't you just picture Corporal Swartz running for a fox hole if it pops?"

After Dorrie wiggled into her dress, she preened in front of the mirror trying to coax her unruly naturally curly hair into a chignon. "Does the *rat* show, Barbara?"

Barbara, the foremost authority of hairstyles in the group, spoke through a mouth full of bobby pins. "Here, let me tuck another pin or two into it." She poked the bun-shaped brown cotton roll until it weighed as much as Dorrie's whole head of hair.

"Go on down, Dorrie. Turn off most of the lights and Jacob Swartz will think you're Rita Hayworth." Carmen strolled into the room with her own hair askew and lipstick smeared. "Dr. Tolan showed me a very interesting supply closet on the OB floor." She wiped the smears on a cotton ball.

Mollie shrugged. "Dr. Tolan has every nurse at St. Anne's drooling."

"Jealous, Mollie?"

"Not of you, Carmen. Maybe of Dorrie. The corporal is cute. You should have seen her blush when she got the white carnations he sent from Sullivan's Florists." Mollie rolled over on her bunk, tilted her lamp and opened the new Hilton book *Random Harvest* she'd received for graduation.

Mollie, Barbara, and Carmen made their own dull evening brighter by finding excuses to go down to the lounge while Dorrie Koski entertained Corporal Swartz from New Jersey. Carmen, smiling sweetly, brought an ashtray for the Corporal, and Barbara carried ice cold cokes from the drugstore. Dorrie glowered at them until they crept out, yet there was a look of smugness when she thanked Mollie for maple bars from the bakery.

Later when Mollie sneaked back down for a look from behind the door, she sneezed just as Corporal Jake kissed Dorrie goodnight. She scurried toward the elevator, expecting a string of blue words. As the door closed, she saw Dorrie wave goodbye to Corporal Swartz with one hand while shaking her fist behind her back with the other.

Dorrie stomped into room 401 livid. "Okay, gals. Just you wait until your boyfriends come to call for you! Holy cow! You'd think it was Grand Central Station down there." A pillow flattened Mollie's book.

She tossed the feathered missile back. "Didn't you want us to see you snare him?"

"Are you sure he's a Jew?" Barbara asked.

Dorrie giggled. "Yeah, Orthodox he says, whatever that means. My mother is likely to croak. A Polish Catholic going out with a Jew boy is some kind of cardinal sin, and she likes to forget she was born in Jersey herself."

"I never knew any Jews except that rich Rachel Cohn in the class ahead of us in high school. Remember how everyone connived to get a ride in her red convertible, Mollie?"Barbara brushed vigorously at imaginary tangles in her blonde hair.

"Yeah. It's a wonder we didn't flatten it when we all piled in to go to football games."

"Why should it make a difference anyway? You aren't marrying him," Carmen mumbled from her pillow.

"And neither are you, Carmen. Stick with your Arab doctor," Dorrie said.

"What a group," Mollie said. "I'm a Scotch/Irish, Barbara's English, Dorrie Polish and your parents were born in Mexico. Our own little world is right here."

"And all allies, except poor Dorrie. Poland has been invaded." Carmen was buried by a well-aimed pillow.

"Haven't been yet, kid. But give me a week or two. Jake did check out my boobs and pronounced them enticing." She thumped the right one before loosening her bra. "Damn!" A loud pop marked the end of her rubber girdle.

"Turn off that light, Mollie." Dorrie mumbled after crawling into her blankets.

"When you write to Joe, ask him to find a big hunk for me down there," Barbara muttered drowsily.

~ * ~

St. Anne's Nursing School
November 7, 1941
Dear Joe,
I'll bet even you Air Corps guys don't use language as dirty as Dorrie's. She's got me swearing too, and I'll have to watch it around Mom.

I think Sister Marie handled our sloppy roommate problem well. Somehow Dorrie and Carmen don't seem quite as tiresome or else I am finally getting used to living in a crowd. Today, Sister Marie told the students about a government program to pay for nursing education. I think it is sort of like a branch of the armed forces. Barb and I plan to fill out the papers Sister Marie gave us. Love, Mollie.

Three

"Hurry, Mollie. We'll be late." Barbara gave her stiffly starched abdomen a cursory pat, sucked it in, and shortened her belt a notch. "Look at that, twenty-four inches. I've lost five pounds."

"It's probably the Chicken ala trots," Mollie mumbled, leaning to the left to straighten a stocking seam. "Can't wait until we can wear silk hosiery again. Do all white cotton hose come with built-in crooked seams?"

Dorrie, twisting to rescue a broken bra strap, hissed through a mouth full of pins. "I hate both of you. You look positively undernourished and I've gained five on that doctored chicken. Doesn't give me the runs, just blows me up. Jake says they probably use saltpeter to keep food from spoiling like they do in the Army. GI's say the stuff makes them lose the urge to screw."

"Sounds like saltpeter hasn't bothered Jake. You two must be getting really chummy to talk about sex," Carmen said.

"Don't be so damn nosy." Dorrie struggled into her stiff uniform and bent with a grunt to tie her shoelaces.

While waiting for the elevator, Mollie bent to give her shoes a quick wipe with her handkerchief. "Second helpings of cake and pie and maple bars from the bakery you snack on between meals don't help keep your weight down, Dorrie. Come on gals. It's five to."

Extra folding chairs had been set up for the crowd in the auditorium. The student nurses filed in to reserved seats in the front while Sister Anne played piano selections from Bach, barely audible over the squeaks of chairs and muted conversations.

"There are Mom and Dad and Sally and Mike," Mollie whispered to Barbara.

"I see Pop, Alan and Evelyn and..." Barbara uttered a muffled whistling sound. "I can't believe it; Mother's here. She must have flown up from California." Barbara fluttered a discreet wave to them.

Mollie noted that at one end of the group sat Barbara's mother, as always, fashionably dressed. The former wife and the new Mrs. Andrews were tactfully separated by Barbara's brother, Alan.

One of the seniors droned a poem in a singsong chant. "Good thing she came first," Mollie whispered to Barbara, "or everyone would fall asleep." She winced as another girl sang a selection from *Madama Butterfly* a trifle off key.

Finally, Sister Marie came from the wings to the center of the small stage, her black skirts swishing over the floor and a rosary rattling in a cadence to her lively steps. The nursing director leaned on the podium, coughing slightly to silence the audience.

"It is heartwarming so many of you came for this important occasion. We are proud of our first three-year nursing class. The program is new to us and to our students. I confess to pleasant surprise that these ninety girls have done so well in college discipline and nursing duties. Two of them have made perfect scores in their classroom work. Will Miss Virginia King and Miss Margaret McAllister please come forward?"

Mollie heard a piercing whistle from her little brother's direction. Others joined it and cheers erupted from the crowd.

Sister Marie continued. "The nursing and teaching staffs have chosen these two girls for special honor." She handed over scrolls and cellophane envelopes containing tiny red pins in the shape of "A" for their caps. "Miss King is from Boise, Idaho and her parents were unable to attend, but I wish to welcome Miss McAllister's family." She nodded toward Mollie's folks.

She placed Mollie's and Ginger's caps on their heads, then the other girls filed to the stage and leaned to receive theirs. Some of the hair fashions posed a challenge for the petite nun, but she carried it off with aplomb.

Sister Anne played a recessional march and the girls, followed by the crowd, funneled into the lounge for refreshments.

"What happened to Gloria?" Barbara puffed from scurrying to catch up with Mollie. "I saw her come in with us, but the next thing I knew, Sister Agnes had her by the arm leading her out the side door."

Mollie had a suspicion why Gloria got sick, but decided to keep it to herself. "She was sitting at the end of our row. I saw her head droop and her face turn lime green."

Dorrie inched closer to them. "Wasn't sick. Drunk. Gloria's out of her mind drunk. Must'a got some of that pure alcohol from surgery, probably with help from a few bills. I think Dr. Alexander has been slipping it to her."

Mollie frowned. "I hope you're wrong, Dorrie." She crossed her fingers. "And if he's giving her that stuff, that Sister Marie doesn't find out."

"I hear if you drink a swallow of vanilla, you can't smell it," Barbara murmured.

"Like my pop, Gloria hits the booze too much. She oughta quit drinking before she lands on Skid Row with the floozies down by the station." Dorrie pushed through the crowd to the buffet. "Look at all those scrumptious little cookies."

Mollie ran to hug her dad and kiss her mother and Sally, but Mike turned his blushing freckled face away.

"Stop it, Mollie."

"I haven't seen you in nearly three months. And when did you get so bashful you won't let your big sister kiss you?" She poked a finger into Mike's ribs, causing a grin to crease his face.

Mollie steered the family to chairs along the wall and passed plates of cookies and punch to them.

"I hope Casey misses me more than you do, Mike."

"He must. He goes to your room and drags stuff out."

"What stuff? Mike! Are you letting that dog sleep on my bed?" Mollie rumpled his thatch of red hair.

Sally frowned. "He would if we didn't keep your door closed."

Devil lights sparkled in Mike's brown eyes. "You should have seen Sally's face when Casey dragged out one of your bras and brought it to her new boyfriend last week."

"What were my bureau drawers doing open so Casey could get in them, Sally?"

"I just sorta borrowed your pink sweater and I guess I might have left one drawer open a little."

"Hush! Don't argue in public, girls." Mrs. McAllister said. "Joe wrote that he'll be home for Christmas. Talks of a special surprise. Do you know anything about a new girl, Mollie?"

"He hasn't mentioned anyone special." Mollie blinked back tears. With Joe in the Army Air Corps, this might be the last Christmas the family would be together for a long time.

She settled onto the folding chair beside her father. He looked tired, and coughed hard to clear his throat before speaking.

"The world news doesn't sound encouraging. Radio says a Japanese named Kurusu is in Washington talking to Roosevelt. I don't trust Japan and hope the President doesn't. We're going into the war, Mollie. Soon I think."

"Maybe not," her mother said quietly. "Talk is a lot better than bombs and bullets."

"Chamberlain's talk didn't keep England out, Lou." Ian McAllister pulled out a pack of Lucky Strikes and reached for a standing ashtray two chairs away.

"This is a celebration, Dad. Let's forget that awful war for one night. Have more cookies and coffee. You look thin, like you could use a few extra calories." Mollie interjected her new wisdom from nutrition class, enjoying Sally's questioning look. "How many hours a day are you working at the Navy Yard?"

"It's been twelve hour shifts all this month. Makes a mighty long day with the home chores."

"Guess everyone's working longer these days. Be sure to get some rest when you're off weekends, Dad."

Mollie turned to her mother. "Now for my surprise. Because of this," she pointed to the little red pin on her cap, "Sister Marie gave me permission to go home with you if I promise to be back by tomorrow evening at ten. I'm all packed, just have to run upstairs and change out of my uniform." She nudged her sister. "Want to come up and see where I live, Sally? You can come too, Mother if you like." She crossed her fingers, hoping Dorrie and Carmen had picked up their underwear.

~ * ~

Sunday morning, December Seventh, Ian McAllister brought the thirty-nine Plymouth around to the front door and leaned out to wipe a smattering of dust from the windshield. The rest of the family climbed in for a trip to church.

Mollie enjoyed the familiar scenes on the four-mile drive to Bremerton from the little seaside community where their comfortable frame house, surrounded by five acres, stood. It felt good to be home, yet different. Her family hadn't changed, so it must be her own view of the world after three months of living in a completely different environment. Or maybe the quiet. She had found it difficult getting to sleep last night without the sound of traffic, squeaking elevator doors and the breathing of three other people.

The pastor's sermon dwelt mostly on the horror of war and the turning of the other cheek. Mollie saw her father rub his chin, and frown several times in disagreement. Although the sun shone brightly through the stained glass, a somber feeling penetrated her own mood and she shivered slightly, causing her mother to squeeze closer.

"Are you cold, Mollie?" she whispered.

Mollie shook her head. Her chill was inside. She could sense something about to happen, like a thunderstorm brewing, but it was December not July. She fought to shake the disquieting tension, relieved when they stood in the sunlit doorway to shake the pastor's hand.

After the family settled into the car, Lou McAllister opened a window to wave at two elderly ladies. "See you at the Potluck Wednesday."

Ian pulled the car into a parking place on a nearly deserted street. "I want to get the Sunday paper. Need anything from the drugstore, Lou?"

"You're about out of Alka Seltzer."

Mollie rolled down a window, wondering why the drugstore had a radio on a chair outside the entrance. An announcer's bass voice came through the speaker. Her breath caught.

Japanese planes struck Pearl Harbor in a surprise attack at seven-fifty-five Honolulu time this morning. Japan has declared war on the United States! Please stand by for further bulletins.

Her father leaned to hear the details, shock and disbelief twitching his mouth into several expressions. He talked with the druggist while paying for the paper and antacid, then hurried back to the car. "I expect we'd better get home. Mr. Todd says all military forces have been called to their stations and that we'll have a blackout here tonight. They're holding a Civil Defense meeting at four. I'd best be back here for it."

No one spoke on the drive home. They concentrated on the car radio sputtering more bulletins between recordings of somber classical music. Mollie ran into the house to turn on the big Philco console in the living room, adjusting the dials to tune out static.

When her mother announced dinner was ready, Mollie pushed her chair to the table to join the family in eating the good Sunday dinner she had been missing for three months. Now, she fought hard to swallow food at all. Excitement and alarm mingled. Her mind spun out thoughts. How would this affect the McAllisters and every other family in the nation?

Lou McAllister sighed as she spooned gravy over a little mound of mashed potatoes. "Will this keep Joe away for Christmas?" She directed the question as much to Mollie as to her husband.

Mollie swallowed a bite of pot roast. "I hope not, Mom. Joe's finished his first flight training session. Right, Dad?" Something in his expression told her he knew her brother had already received his Army Air Corps wings.

"Sorry, Honey, I picked up Joe's letter at the mailbox yesterday." Ian grinned sheepishly at a gasp from his wife. "I couldn't wait to read it when I saw it was from Joe in Arizona. I meant to give it to you last night, and then Mollie came home, so I decided to wait until dinner today to make Joe's announcement a special surprise for the family reunion." He tossed it into her lap and turned to Mollie. "You knew didn't you, Mollie?"

She nodded. "He was ahead of the rest of the group because of his already having his license. He got his wings last week. I received a letter from him yesterday too." Mollie noted the widened eyes of her younger sister and brother searching her face.

Mike whistled, his eyes gleaming. "Oh boy! What kind of planes will he be flying, Mollie? Hope it's fighters."

A choking sob sent Lou McAllister to the bedroom and Ian followed. An hour passed before they returned.

Mollie noticed her mother's eyes were still red and swollen as she served the chocolate cake no one but Mike wanted.

"Dad, I think I should head back to St. Anne's when you go to town for the Civil Defense meeting. The service men will be trying to get back to their posts. Radio said all leaves are canceled."

"I was thinking the same thing, Mollie. You'd need to take the six o'clock ferry anyway, and I don't know how long the meeting will last."

~ * ~

Two hours later, Mollie, clutching a package of cake, climbed the ramp to the crowded ferry. Bremerton teemed with frantically hurrying sailors, some trying to sound cheerful, others silently staring straight ahead, looking shocked and numb. No wolf whistles echoed across the dock on this black Sunday.

After searching unsuccessfully for a seat Mollie stood leaning against a waste can for the hour trip. Conversation among the passengers was so muffled it reminded her of church or a funeral. A low voice interrupted her thoughts.

"Mind if I share your garbage can?"

"Be my guest," Mollie said, glancing around to face a tall man with expressive eyes and a smile to rival Clark Gable's. He wore a gold University of Washington Husky letter on his purple sweater. "You going back to the U.?"

"Yeah. Barely made the ferry. Where are you headed?"

"St. Anne's. I'm a student nurse there. Awful about Pearl Harbor, isn't it?"

"You said it," he said, his expression reflecting worry. "Hoped we'd stay out of the war until I finished school. The Japs may have changed that."

The ferry whistle drowned out the last of his words. Mollie hurried to the passenger exit stairs.

"Hey," he shouted, "didn't get your name. Mine's Ron."

"Mollie," she mouthed over the noisy debarking crowd. He disappeared in the rush of folks hurrying to the car deck. He couldn't have heard her name. Why should she care? But regret shadowed the back of her mind.

At seven, when she walked up to First Avenue from Coleman Dock, the usually busy streets were nearly deserted. No lines at the movie theater. Everyone must be home listening to the radio for the deadly details.

As she exited the bus half a block from the nursing residence, piercing sirens coming from everywhere brought a gasp of stark panic. A real air raid or just practice? How could you hear enemy planes over all that noise? She choked back a scream when something black darted from one of the bushes. A big cat. She ran across the street toward the shelter of the nursing residence. The street lights flickering to blackness sent her stumbling the rest of the block, disoriented and swallowing terror.

She rang the bell, surprised to find the door locked so early, and Sister Anne opened it a crack to let her in. The nun looked ashen in the dim light, worry clearly etched on her face.

"This is a practice blackout, Miss McAllister. We must not show any light until the 'all clear' sounds."

The only illuminations in the hall were dim green exit signs and the little light over the elevator. Mollie hurried up to her room and opened the door to find Dorrie and Carmen lying on the floor beside a desk lamp, smoking and listening to instructions on the radio. The windows were covered with the new shades.

"Ghosty isn't it? Just like Halloween," Carmen said.

Barbara slipped behind the other girls to push the edges of the blinds into the window frame. "We weren't supposed to go outside the building at all, but I sneaked down the fire escape to see if the shades worked. If we keep the lamp below the window they do, otherwise there is a tiny crack of light around the edges."

She settled down beside Mollie. "I don't know how Mother managed to get this throw rug in her suitcase and on the plane from California. She probably had to pay for extra weight."

"Is she flying back?" Mollie asked.

Barbara smiled. "She bought a round trip ticket, but some Army general bumped her from her seat and she'll take the train tomorrow if she can get on. We managed to find her a room at the Olympic for tonight."

Mollie knew Barbara's smile was because of her mother's attending the capping ceremony. She hadn't quite understood the problems that caused a divorce between her friend's parents. Clearly Barbara had been hurt and had just begun to discuss her step-parents without malice.

Dorrie was unusually solemn. "Have you heard the awful stories on the radio, Mollie? They say President Roosevelt will ask Congress to declare war tomorrow morning. Why do we have to do that when the Japanese already started it at Pearl Harbor?" A little choking sound garbled her voice. She reached for an already damp hanky and blew her nose.

"Guess even war has to have an official beginning." Mollie said. "Were you out with Jake when you heard the news?"

"Yes. We went to the matinee at the Music Box, but I didn't see any of it." Dorrie sniffed again into her handkerchief. "We were in the last row of the balcony and we kissed and kissed and I didn't care if his hands got to places they shouldn't have." She drew a ragged breath and continued.

"Jake suggested we go to a hotel for a couple of hours because it might be our last chance to really make love. I told him no. What if I got pregnant? Some do the first time. I'd be left alone." Dorrie began to cry."Just then, an M.P. came and tapped Jake's shoulder.

"He said, Come, Corporal. All military personnel must report to their stations immediately. I have a squad car outside."

Dorrie finished her story with a shuddering sigh and mopped away fresh tears. "I might never see Jake again...ever."

Mollie patted her shoulder. "Jake will probably stay here awhile, Dorrie. Didn't you say he barely made it into the army because of his poor eyesight? Someone has to man the quartermaster's office."

The windows rattled when sirens sounded again at nine to signal the "all clear." Mollie opened the shades to watch the lights blink on over the city. It would have been exciting but for the needle of fear inside her stomach. Was there really danger of air or sea attack as the radio reported?

She recalled the newspaper headlines from the past two years with sudden clarity. America faced the nightmare so long forecast by her dad. She'd watched the newsreels of the war in Europe, but it seemed worlds away. Hitler had subdued Poland, Czechoslovakia, Austria, Belgium, The Netherlands, France, and now marched toward Leningrad. Italy had declared war on England and France and the Luftwaffe's bombs were dropping everywhere.

She shivered. Would Seattle get her share of that horrible destruction from Japan? The whole world had gone completely mad and she realized life would never be quite the same for the McAllisters and millions of others. How long until they could wake up from this bad dream?

Quickly finishing her letter to Joe, she licked the three-cent stamp and patted it onto the envelope. Glancing through her script, she decided to add a paragraph about Taiko, the sweet Japanese girl who had the best grades at St. Anne's.

~ * ~

December 7, 1941

I am sure the whole world knows what happened the day after our capping ceremony. I went home with Dad, Mom, Sally and Mike. Everything went haywire after that pleasant evening. Like Mom, I kept hoping we'd stay out of the war.

Golly, Joe, I hope they don't cancel your leave. We all need to be together once before even Christmas changes for the duration of the war. Mom is planning the holidays like she hadn't even heard about Pearl Harbor. We had our first blackout tonight and were all just a tiny bit scared. All sorts of wild tales are circulating about sabotage and stuff.

We had a little Japanese-American student nurse at St. Anne's, and she didn't come back from a visit to her parents yesterday. Hope nothing is wrong because she is a senior who will graduate in June and is one of St. Annie's best nurses. Love, Mollie.

Four

Mollie watched her brother pull up and park in front of St. Anne's. Glancing behind her, she grinned. Half of her class was also waiting to meet Joe. She ran down the steps and hugged him.

"Golly, am I glad they let you keep your leave. Lots of guys didn't. Come on in and meet some of my new friends."

"Can't wait." Joe whistled through his teeth. "Two hundred girls all in one place!"

Dorrie managed to be the first to crowd up to them.

"Joe, this is Dorrie," Mollie nodded, "and another room mate, Carmen. Of course you know Barbara." She grinned at rustling sounds of starched uniforms behind her. "And here are Shirley, and Ginger." She steered her dark-haired brother around the girls and toward the door. "You probably won't remember all their names."

"Wrong, Mollie. Your written descriptions fit so well, I knew which was which without introductions." Joe turned from his sister to scan Carmen's curves, his mouth forming a silent whistle in the direction of the brown-eyed girl, "but like the song says, real live dolls are a lot more fun than paper ones."

Carmen fluttered mascara-coated eyelashes, displaying her dimples in practiced flirtation. "And it's keen to finally see the real live Joe Mollie uses so much paper and stamps on. Will you be bringing your sister back to the nursing residence after Christmas?"

"If you'll be here, Baby, you can bet on it." Joe spoke softly, glancing backward at Mollie.

Carmen just shrugged. "I work Christmas, but get the week end off."

"Joe!" Mollie called from the door, but Joe just grinned and leaned closer to Carmen.

"How about taking in a movie when I bring Mollie back the day after Christmas?"

"I'll think about that," Carmen said. "Second lieutenant's bars and with gold wings, wow!" She rolled her eyes like Eddie Cantor. "Okay, it's a date, Joe."

Mollie sighed, watching the girls gather around her brother to admire his uniform. "Come on, Joe. We'll miss the ferry."

Carmen tugged at Joe's arm. "I'll be at my folk's place near Tacoma for the weekend. Maybe you can call me there if I can't make it the twenty-sixth." She scribbled something on a slip of paper and tucked it into his pocket.

"Swell, Carmen. Thanks." Joe slowly backed away and turned to face Mollie.

"What was that all about, big brother?" Mollie opened the car door and spread her pleated skirt carefully over the seat. "Carmen got her claws into you already? You better believe me when I say she's a born flirt and loves having every man in town ogle her. Should'a tried out for the movies. Take it easy, Joe, she breaks a lot of hearts." Mollie smiled but felt a cold seriousness.

"Pull in your own claws, Mollie. Carmen's a real dish." Joe opened the car trunk, pushed Mollie's bags inside, and hurried to the driver's seat for the trip home. He looked back toward the door of the nurse's residence, blew a kiss at Carmen and several other girls gathered there, gave the horn a couple of toots, and drove away.

"Carmen has a long string of men trailing her. You may get trampled waiting in her line," Mollie muttered, wondering if she ought to mention Doctor Tolan, who had begun to see Carmen on the sly. All the girls swooned over handsome Doctor Tolan, a native of some Arab country. He could have had his pick of seniors who were twenty-one and could go to the bottle clubs where most of the older men took girls. St. Anne's nuns frowned on student nurses, especially the younger ones like nineteen-year-old Carmen, dating interns and residents.

"I'm gonna ask her to go to a dance at Fort Lewis Officers' Club this weekend. It's handy because she lives in Tacoma. I hope Dad can spare the car." Joe pulled up to the ticket window, fished into his wallet for the fare, and then eased the car down the slip to the waiting ferry.

"Army Air Force men work fast. I must make a note of that." Mollie still felt upset over the way Carmen had maneuvered Joe so quickly. She stole a glance at him as they mounted the stairs to the upper deck. Her gawky brother had gotten a lot better looking. The uniform helped.

Joe grinned when a tall Navy officer scanned Mollie's figure and four sailors at the coffee bar saluted her with loud whistles. "You don't do so badly yourself, Sis. Got the Navy wolves howling. Try to hold them off while I hit the head."

"They howl over anything in skirts," Mollie said, sliding across the chipped leather booth seat. "Still drink your coffee with cream? I'll get it while you're in the latrine."

Mollie took the tray from the bar and opened her purse to pay for the coffees.

A voice startled her, "Let me," the tall Marine said, smiling. "Where are you sitting?"

"I...thank you, but my brother just arrived and I'm dying to know what he's been up to the last six months."

He smiled. "Worth a try. Hope to meet you again sometime."

"Small world. Could be," Mollie replied. When he strolled away, she sighed. Sister Anne had lectured them about being too casual in allowing servicemen to pick them up. Yet, it would be neat to date a guy that good looking. Carmen would be envious, and probably try to snare him for herself.

Mollie remembered the nightly pillow gossip. Carmen and Dorrie were in the habit of reporting graphic accounts of their dates. If you could believe their tales, neither were virgins. They discussed diaphragms, douches and something mysterious called Sheiks; all sorts of weird stuff Mollie had never heard of. But she would not flaunt her innocence like Barbara and Ginger. Asking her mother about birth control methods would embarrass them both. Staring out the ferry window at the choppy gray water, she remembered a recent discussion.

"Aren't you two afraid you'll contract syphilis or gonorrhea?" Barbara had asked. "How do you know they didn't just finish doing it with some floozy full of the stuff?"

"That's why it's safer to have the guys use rubbers. You hafta insist they use them, I mean. They keep G.C., syph and babies from starting." Dorrie spoke with authority, dragging hard on the last bit of her Chesterfield before stuffing it into an overflowing ashtray.

Barbara, coughing for emphasis, opened a window and fanned away clouds of blue smoke. "Nicotine probably sterilizes your reproductive system, but it sure doesn't help my lungs."

Joe waved his hand before her face. "Come back to the world, Sis. You're letting your coffee get cold." He placed a jelly doughnut on each saucer.

After finishing their coffee and doughnuts, they went down to the car deck. When Joe drove off the ferry, Mollie gasped. "What are those big gray things hanging over the docks?"

"Barrage balloons. Dad says they installed them right after Pearl Harbor. They're supposed to prevent low flying bombers and strafing planes from attacking the Naval Ship Yards. Looks like there are hundreds of them around here."

One of the dirigible-shaped balloons floated over the back acre of the McAllister property and Lou had invited the six soldiers manning it for Christmas dinner.

The next day, the McAllisters' big oak table had all its extensions in place when they and their guests gathered around it for the festive meal.

After the dishes were washed and Lou McAllister hung up her apron, she went to the old upright piano to accompany Mollie and Joe in their traditional duet of *O Holy Night*. The soldiers joined the family in singing carols. Ian's deep bass voice brought tears to Mollie's eyes when they ended with *Silent Night*. Mollie tried to ignore a creeping chill of fear nudging her holiday.

She helped her mother and Sally stuff turkey sandwiches and mince pie into bread wrappers for those who were on duty. The servicemen grinned their appreciation and hurried out in order to be back to their balloon base by nine.

"Beat all of you in Monopoly?" Joe opened the board and the family gathered once more around the dining room table to play until, one by one they lost all the paper money to him.

"Next time, I'll hide Park Place in my pocket," Mollie said, yawning.

Mollie wondered why she didn't feel completely contented after such a good reunion with her family. She lay sleepless thinking about Gabriel Heater's nasal preacher voice on the ten o'clock news. He made the war sound downright scary. Was there truth to persistent rumors of submarines lurking off the Washington coast shelling shorelines and sinking ships? The papers had for three weeks speculated about imminent enemy invasion and warned of likely atrocities. Fear sent cold tingles and she drew her favorite patchwork quilt around her ears.

~ * ~

When Joe drove Mollie back to the nursing residence the day after Christmas, he took Carmen out to a movie matinee. Mollie was puzzled and a little miffed when Carmen came in afterward and went on duty without a word to anyone about her date. Usually she gave detailed accounts of the movie, newsreel, cartoon and her escort's necking. Was Joe's technique so bad Carmen felt embarrassed talking about it to his sister? But that was impossible. She'd double-dated with Joe and the girls usually fell in love with him.

Mollie fidgeted all week expecting and rather hoping Carmen would brag a little about dating Joe. She didn't. Nor did she mention any special weekend plans. She packed her bags and took the bus for Tacoma as if going home to see her folks. Period. Mollie slammed her book down hard on the bed causing Barbara to look up sharply. "She had better not trap my brother."

"What?"

"Don't act so innocent, Barb. Everyone in the building knows Joe is spending most of this weekend with Carmen," Mollie hissed, her hands clenched tightly.

"Well I didn't," Barbara said.

"Me neither," Dorrie mumbled. "Sounded to me like she had a date with an old boyfriend from Stadium High School."

That baffled Mollie more. Why had Carmen been secretive with Dorrie? She shrugged and opened a book, vowing to forget the whole thing. Why should she feel so possessive about Joe? He'd never asked for her approval of his dates and was unlikely to start.

Mollie had formed a habit of scanning the newspapers in the lounge while enjoying a cup of coffee after class. Yesterday, the war emphasis for citizens of the West Coast centered on the

Japanese invasion of the Aleutian Islands. She had looked for them on the map the nuns had installed on a wall. It would be a temperature shock after Arizona should Joe be sent there. He had revealed rather furtively to the family that his training was for a bomber squadron, and speculated whether the European theater or the South Pacific would likely be his overseas station. Joe's ten day leave had passed far too quickly and she hadn't had a real talk with him since Christmas. Today, he would fly back to Kingman to receive his orders.

~ * ~

Mollie hurried through the airport and found Joe waiting near a door marked "Ticketed Passengers Only." She hugged him tightly, pulled back to fumble with a shiny button on his freshly pressed uniform, then stretched to kiss his cheek. "Bye, Joe. Behave yourself and don't get too involved with those little cuties in Arizona."

Breathless, Carmen ran up to them. "He wouldn't dare!"

Joe lifted Carmen off her feet and attacked her lipsticked mouth far too long. "I thought you wouldn't make it, sweetheart. Here, I brought you something to remember me by." He pulled a small box from his jacket pocket. "Wear it over your heart while I'm gone."

Mollie felt like an uninvited guest when Carmen pulled out a locket on a long gold chain.

"Joe darling, it's beautiful. I'll wear it until I see you again." Sniffing and blotting her eyes carefully to keep from smearing her mascara, she said, "Write as soon as you get back to Kingman. I've gotta hurry. I have to be on duty in an hour."

"So do I," Mollie mumbled, watching Carmen run to a waiting cab. She squinted and thought she could see the shadow of another occupant inside...a man.

"That gal is absolutely beautiful and I think I'm already in love with her." Joe watched the yellow cab pull away, his expression of longing changing to a fleeting frown of suspicion. "Look after her while I'm gone, Sis."

"Carmen's a big girl, Joe; a rather self sufficient one I'd say." Mollie squeezed her eyes to force away tears she had resolved not to allow. "Bye again. My rank may be higher than yours if I get into the Nurse Cadet Corps."

"If you don't decide to quit nursing and marry Phil, or Wally, or one of the fifty other guys you write to. I'll try to send you some money now and then to help out." He reached for his wallet. "Here's a twenty. Buy yourself a nice pair of shoes before they start rationing them, or maybe you'd rather have a Jantzen sweater. I didn't get time for much Christmas shopping."

"I loved the bath powder and you might need this, Joe. I'm doing fine. You have to keep something to eat on."

"I get a GI box lunch on the plane and payday is next week." He smiled at her puzzled look. "Carmen was a cheap date. We went dancing at the officer's club at Fort Lewis and took a nice long drive to the beach."

Mollie wondered if that was all...

"Come on, Lieutenant. Say goodbye to your girl fast." An Air Force Captain in a dress hat, floppy after the removal of the stiffening to accommodate earphones, eyed Mollie's figure thoroughly, looking envious of Joe. "Sorry she can't come along. Real sorry."

"Captain Terrence Reed, meet my sister, Mollie, student nurse, friend of everyone, sometimes even her brother."

"Sorry I didn't interrupt sooner, McAllister. Hope I run into you again, Mollie. Goodbye now."

Mollie watched from the bus stop near the gate as he and Joe climbed into the waiting Air Force cargo plane. Then it taxied down the field and lifted off.

She raced from the bus up to her room and donned her uniform for duty, knowing she'd be late and hoping Sister Marie or the charge nurse wouldn't notice. Rounding the corner from the hospital elevator, she crept silently past Carmen and Dr. Tolan kissing in the shadows of an alcove. How had she gotten back so quickly? She clenched her fists angrily. Joe had barely left Boeing field and his girl was already two-timing him. But Carmen wasn't actually Joe's girl. He had gone out with her three times and maybe hadn't even scored. He had given her a locket though, a symbol of commitment. Concern for her brother twisted in her heart.

Mollie hurried to her station. Though not a very challenging, afternoon and evening shifts lent a new perspective to hospital routine. Because it was a holiday period without classes, student nurses' duty hours were increased to eight. Afternoon duty was much easier and she enjoyed the chance to know the patients better. There were back rubs, meal trays, temperature and blood pressure checks, with the scurry of an occasional emergency to keep things exciting.

Barbara was assigned to Orthopedics and Mollie to a medical a floor below. During dinner hour, Barbara hurried down to meet her.

"Come up and take a peek in Room five-o-one Mollie. There's the cutest guy in there. He broke his leg skiing." Barbara pulled Mollie by the arm to the rear stairs, little used on the upper floors except for personnel.

She smiled at a patient sitting in a wheelchair in the sun room, his heavily casted leg stretched toward the radiator. "Mollie this is Don Brooks. He's going home Monday." Barbara glanced toward the corridor and leaned to fluff his pillow in order to appear busy if the charge nurse looked in.

The older man in the chair next to Don's grinned and whistled through his teeth. "Don gets all the attention. How about fluffing my pillow," he squinted at Mollie's name tag, "McAllister?"

Mollie laughed, made an exaggerated fuss over his pillow, and then turned to Don. "Where's home, Don?"

"Spokane. I work at Boeing, but will be off for at least a month with this thing. I'm going to try to get a flight home. Barbara said she would go out to the airport and pick up my ticket." He grinned shyly at Barbara's blush.

"Right now, we'd better get our dinner before they close up the cafeteria," Mollie said, leading Barb to the stairs.

"Isn't he something else? Those eyes, that curly hair... He promised to write when he gets home."

Mollie laughed, feeling much better. "Well he's the right age, and breathes without wheezing. Everyone in our room has fallen in love except me. Come on, or they'll be out of Chicken ala!"

~ * ~

St. Anne's Nursing School
December 28, 1941
Dear Joe,
It was great having everyone at home for Christmas. I can't believe I also lucked out and got New Year's Eve off, though I do have to be on duty at seven the next morning.

Gloria, my rich classmate, invited a bunch of us to a big New Year's Eve party at the Canal Yacht Club. She's arranged blind dates for some of us.

All my roommates are out with boys tonight. Guess I'd better find one for myself. Maybe I'll get lucky at the New Year's party. Every guy I meet seems to go overseas the week after one date. Suppose I have BO or bad breath? Barbara's a little goofy about this Don, a former patient, but he's leaving for the service next week!

Here's some fudge we made last night. Had to make three batches from sugar we filched from the diet kitchen. The first two flopped and Dorrie made chocolate milk out of them. Hope this one isn't all melted when you get it. If it is, you won't be able to read this anyway. Love, Mollie.

Five

"This one fits and I love it, but costs twenty-five dollars," Barbara muttered as she caressed a dusky rose rayon taffeta evening dress. It had padded shoulders, small covered buttons down the front, and a ruffle reaching to the top of her shapely hips.

"Go ahead and buy it, Barb. It's perfect for you." Mollie chewed her lower lip over her own decision and fumbled in her purse for the money her dad had given her to buy a formal dress for the party, a special Christmas gift and for good grades, he said. After shopping all afternoon from the scant stock of formal wear in the department stores downtown she felt too exhausted to look further.

Barbara pulled the dress carefully over her high-piled pompadour curls. "I can't afford shoes if I get the formal, but who could see them anyway under the long skirt? I'll see if the shoe repair shop can fix the straps on my old sandals."

"I have just enough for this blue one, but I don't know...haven't worn that shade before. Did the sales clerk call it teal? It's more green than blue." Mollie removed the dress and hung it on the dressing room hook.

The gray-haired sales lady tapped on the door, and entered the crowded little room. "The gown would be lovely with your auburn hair, Miss, and I fear the choices of long evening wear are limited for the duration. These are reduced to half price because few people want to wear frivolous clothing since the war started."

There was an unmistakable air of snobbery or disapproval in the woman's tone. Her attitude annoyed Mollie. Frivolous? Evidently the fraternity hadn't been told because the dance invitations said 'formal.' The clerk acted like she was doing her and Barb a favor by showing the dresses at all.

The girls paid for their new gowns and carried the bulky boxes toward the elevator. "You might be able to wear my black sling pumps, Barb. I have trouble keeping them on when I dance because they are half a size too big."

"Still makes them only five and a half. Remember I wear sevens." Barbara led the way from the elevator when the operator called, "Bargain Floor, Hosiery and Shoe Repair, Books, Delicatessen."

"I have to stop at hosiery repair to see if the girl has mine done. Mom loaned me a pair of her silk ones and I got a run right away." Mollie turned toward the counter near the double doors of the Bon Marche'. She watched as a small woman, probably the most harried person in the store, squinted over a light bulb to mend ladders in silk stockings. Because silk and nylon were so superior to rayon, every woman who owned a pair of the hose had them mended until the runs were beyond salvaging. Several minutes passed before the woman found Mollie's.

She handed over fifty cents. "Boy, I wouldn't have your job for any amount of money. Aren't you afraid of going blind?"

"Without this, I would." The woman tapped a magnifying glass hanging around her neck. "Guess we are a little like watch repairmen. Some of these are as challenging as broken mainsprings.”

Barbara glanced at her watch. “Hurry! We’ll have to run for the bus. We’ve just forty-five minutes until we have to be on duty.” She handed a box of Cracker Jacks to Mollie and opened another for herself. “Not a very nutritious dinner. Hope they have good snacks in the lounge when we get off.”

“Good thing the stores are open later for the war workers or we’d never have made it.” Mollie munched the last peanut, pocketed the little prize, and stuffed the box into the refuse container at the bus stop.

They scurried to their duty floors barely in time. The seven to eleven P.M. shifts were a grind because they had to be in class at the college by seven thirty in the morning.

~ * ~

Mollie got off duty at three-thirty in the afternoon of New Year’s Eve and found all floors of the nursing residence buzzing with preparations for the party of the year. Only Dorrie, among the occupants of room 401, had decided not to go to the dance. Jake wasn’t invited. But Carmen would be there. Mollie frowned because she had seen Joe’s letter arrive Friday. She shrugged mentally reminding herself once more that she wasn’t her brother’s girlfriend’s guardian. She’d done her best to discourage his dating Carmen and certainly hadn’t planned for him to fall to her charms so heavily.

Taking the bobby pins from sausage-like coils of hair, Mollie brushed hard to coax it into a fashionably smooth page boy. Her hair kept crawling into loose curls. “I give up, Barb. It’ll just have to hang like it always does. Won’t stay in an upsweep without my cap to hold it, either.”

She always fussed about unruly hair, secretly knowing it was one of her most attractive points. It had a sheen of dark mahogany and lay in soft waves to the middle of her back when she allowed it to fall from the upswept style she wore under her nursing cap.

"I should have such a problem," Barbara said. "You could use a little more mascara and just a tiny bit of pencil. It will be so dark no one will think you're too made up."

After final glances in the lounge mirror, Mollie and her friends piled into several elegant cars waiting at the curb in front of the nursing residence.

Ginger, who had gotten into the car last, twisted around in the jump seat to peer through the glass divider toward the stony faced driver. "Bet this Lincoln has carried a lot of very rich people around Seattle."

Shirley rubbed the plush red mohair upholstery. "Gold Rush Days from its age. Sounds like a gasoline engine though, not steam power."

"The shiny black 'forty-one' Packard up there belongs to Gloria's folks. Good of her to hire cars for us. She sure has kept her family's money quiet, hasn't she?" Barbara said.

"It is almost as if Gloria wants us to think just the opposite. Wonder if she drinks to hide something she's ashamed of?" Mollie mumbled half to herself, shifting to tug at her garter belt that had crawled into an uncomfortable twist.

"Gloria's the only girl in our class who has a private room, which does make her a little bit different. Evidently even Sister Marie listens to the clink of gold," Ginger said.

Mollie had wondered about that, especially when the rest of the class were stuffed in four to a room. "It was nice of Gloria to invite us to such a fancy bash. Let's try to have a good time tonight to please her."

Barbara whistled as they entered the long drive to the beach-side club."Here we are. Not just ritzy elegant, I would say."

A valet helped them from the cars and ushered them to the door, and inside, a uniformed waiter took their coats and led them to the ballroom. Round tables covered in white linen surrounded the soft sheen of a maple floor. The waiter seated them in gilt chairs, taking invitation cards deftly from each girl.

Mollie picked up her place card. "You'll note the table is set for eight and we're separated carefully. Suppose our dates will join us soon. Hope they aren't a bunch of dopes."

"There's Dorothy Bennet with Gloria's brother. What a hunk of man! She met him at the U when she was in pre-nursing," Barbara said. "He plays quarterback on the Husky football team."

"Gosh, I wonder if she has another brother." Shirley sat and pushed her long legs under the table. "I'll probably get someone about five feet three."

Ginger's eyes widened. "Is that champagne the waiter is bringing? Surely they won't serve us alcoholic drinks. We aren't old enough!"

Barbara laughed. "Probably just ginger ale, Ginger."

"Wrong, Barb. They don't put corks like that in pop." Mollie giggled nervously, unsure if she could handle the bubbly essence herself, resolving to keep her wits no matter what everyone else did.

The waiter placed crystal glasses in front of each girl and towel in hand, popped the cork and poured the sparkling liquid. "Your escorts will join you in a moment, ladies." A twitch of a smile curved his mouth as if he could barely keep from laughing out loud.

"I don't like that guy's smirk," Shirley whispered. "He knows we're all too young to drink. Probably has a bet on who'll be the first to make a fool of herself. Pretend to sip this stuff and if they bring more, that palm behind us will get expensive alcoholic roots."

Ginger feigned sophistication by taking a small sip from the rim of the glass. "When I was sixteen, I drank a glass of white wine at my brother's wedding."

"Here comes Carmen with Doctor Tolan." Mollie watched the couple locate their chairs across the dance floor. She frowned as

Carmen rose and led the handsome resident over to visit their table.

Carmen smiled sweetly. "I'm sure you all know Doctor Dan Tolan."

Dr. Tolan bowed like one of those European noblemen in the movies. "My pleasure." He repeated each name as if trying to memorize them. "It is a treat to see you ladies in something other than white."

He's charming, thought Mollie. And that accent? What nationality? Lebanese I think Carmen said. A tinge of resentment surged. Why wasn't he in a medical service in one of the branches? She vowed to find the answer to the puzzle.

"My God! I should'a known." Shirley shrank as a roundish young man approached. She breathed an audible sigh of relief when he pulled out the chair beside Ginger.

He displayed his card. "I believe I'm to be your escort, Miss King. I'm George Rossi, sophomore in Business Administration, and R.O.T.C."

Three young men followed George. Mollie smiled. Gloria had carefully selected them to fit her friends' sizes and style.

A gangling red head, a good six feet six inches tall introduced himself to Shirley. "Larry Daniels, Physical Education, Husky Basketball team, also R.O.T.C."

Barbara's date, a slender man with meticulously styled finger waves in his blonde hair, leaned over her chair. "Bob Warner, Drama major, R.O.T.C."

"We're all in Reserve Officers Training Corps. I'm Ron Van Ness, Senior in Journalism." He smiled and whistled. "Wow! I owe Gloria a real favor." He slapped his forehead. "You're the gal I met on the Bremerton ferry Pearl Harbor night. Been trying ever since to figure out how to reach you at St. Anne's when I didn't catch your name. Thought it might seem rather odd if a nun answered the phone and I described your dimensions."

Mollie took a deep breath, feeling his sensuous eyes remove her clothing. *'Uh oh, thinks he is Clark Gable. Hafta remember how Scarlett handled him.*

"Ron's also Student Body President and editor of the *Husky News*," Bob Warner said.

"I know him too," Barbara whispered, while Ron accepted champagne from the waiter. "He's probably forgotten me, but I went to school with his sister when we lived on Queen Anne hill."

Ron turned just in time to see Barbara giggle and cover her mouth. "Don't I know you from somewhere?"

"Your sister was in my class in grade school. You were three grades ahead." Barbara blushed, revealing the awe she still nourished for him.

"Andrews, isn't it? You have a little brother named Alan. Yours is Bonnie or something like that." He scraped his chair between Barbara and Mollie.

"Close. It's Barbara. We moved to Bremerton three years ago. Mollie's my friend from high school and my roommate at St. Anne's." Barbara looked as though she regretted their dates were not reversed.

"Trade you roommates!" Ron's eyebrows rose for another close appraisal. "Come, Mollie. Let's not let *Elmer's Tune* go to waste." Ron took her arm and they floated smoothly into the swing number.

The eight young people were soon talking, dancing and sipping from the constantly refilled glasses. After a couple of the bubbly drinks, Ginger began to thaw from her school teacherish attitude. She giggled, swayed and surprised everyone with unsuspected wit. Mollie raised an eyebrow toward Shirley, who nodded at the signal.

Shirley leaned to mutter, "Better skip the next round, Ginger. This stuff is known to lower inhibitions and sometimes underwear."

A flicker of worry crossed Ginger's face, and she snuggled against George. She had removed her glasses long ago and squinted impishly at the figures around the table. The waiter refilled her glass.

Mollie watered the potted palm behind her chair with most of her drinks and fought Ron's roving hands under the table cloth. He managed to fondle a breast every time they danced a slow number, and to avoid wrestling with him, she sneaked to the powder room at the next set. She loved dancing with him, just didn't want to encourage him too much yet. He begged to drive her home and she could guess the struggle she would have keeping him in line if he decided to park somewhere.

"I see why you're majoring in Journalism. You must get straight "A's" in undercover reporting. Come on, let's get out of this dark corner and enjoy the party. You're in competition anyway. I have a boyfriend in the Marines stationed in Hawaii." Mollie sort of regretted that remark. It was a shame to discourage such a dream boat, but she could remember no other date as handsome or with such wandering hands. If only his mind would travel above her shoulders... To her surprise, Ron turned serious and said, "I promised my family I would attend graduation, after which I'll be going into active service with the Navy. I've already received my commission."

"Oh." A small stab of guilt crossed her mind. But she had not lied. Besides Phil in the Marines, she wrote to four friends away at college. Several more classmates, like her brother, had entered the armed forces. Somehow, she would feel better if Ron and these three young men were getting their training like Joe. He hadn't graduated before joining the Air Force. He'd earned his rank by a different route. Joe would soon be dodging bombs and anti-aircraft shells while guys like Ron drank expensive champagne and got fresh with his sister.

Ron tugged her arm.

"Come, Mollie. Let's take a walk during band intermission." After helping her into her wrap, he led her through the French doors and across the broad flagstone terrace to the lawns below.

Mollie saw couples in various stages of embrace on the benches among the trees. Never had she attended a party without visible chaperones and she tensed with insecurity. It was cold. Frost crunched beneath their feet and she pulled the short fox fur jacket borrowed from her mother closer over her shoulders. Ron took the hint and squeezed his arm around her tightly as they walked down a broad path toward the lake.

"Is this the usual kind of party fraternities hold? No chaperones, lots of booze?" She stifled a little cry as Ron pulled her to the right to avoid a couple lying atop a picnic table. From the movement, there was real action under the purple and gold stadium blanket covering them.

Ron chuckled. "Usually, our lover boys can wait until they get the girls in bedrooms or cars. That bubbly stuff does wondrous things for passion."

Mollie caught the glint of a red dress peeking from the blanket as she passed. She suspected it was Dorothy Bennet and Gloria's brother. Carmen said Dean was such a stud he could take on several girls in one night.

"Let's go back, Ron. I'm getting cold out here."

Ron caught her hand and led her on. "Just a little farther. I'll keep you warm, sweetheart." He cuddled her closer as they rounded a corner and faced a small tool shed near the boathouse. "This is my own little Shangri-la."

"Looks more like a storage shed to me." Mollie's mind raced. She considered running back to the club house, but Ron challenged her ingenuity. He was older and more suave than the boys she'd gone with before. Her plans were, like most other girls she knew, to enter marriage a virgin. That precious commodity must not be lost on a blind date with a near stranger. To honor such moral vows would take real stamina with a guy so tall and handsome.

Ron opened a door nearly hidden by a big rhododendron bush and led her into a small room, outlined from lights at the boathouse dimly through a dirty window. He pulled her down beside him on an old divan covered with a clean woolen blanket smelling of moth balls. He had planned well. The rest of the shed was filled with lawn mowers and stuff and under the blanket the old upholstery had a moldy odor.

She felt his hands pull her hair back from her face. His sensual smile in the dim light from the lake made her heart thud. Oh, but his kisses were dreamy...

"Mollie McAllister. Your name matches your image pretty, practical, and mmmm sexy." A longer harder probing kiss, then he pulled away and tilted her chin. "You're the most beautiful girl I ever dated, no kidding. I almost didn't, you know. I avoid blind dates like stinging nettles. Every other one turned out to be a real dud."

He moved slowly and smoothly, a lover rivaling Cary Grant. Mollie fought the urges he disturbed. His fingers moved to the bodice of her gown, unbuttoning it slowly, methodically, like something set to music. Testing her. She placed her hand over the deft hands and slid her mouth from his urgent probing tongue.

"So you are the protective kind, Mollie sweet. Want to know what you're doing to me?" He took her hand and slipped it into his pants, closing her fingers over the swollen pulsing organ inside his jockey shorts.

Mollie jerked her hand away and slapped him sharply on the face. She rose and turned to run out the door.

"His arm pulled her back."Sorry, Mollie. I thought since you were a friend of Gloria you would..." His mouth covered hers.

"Well I wouldn't. I'm sure Gloria has some friends who don't." Twisting away, she bolted, a tearing sound announcing a ripped sleeve.

Halfway to the terrace, Ron panted to her side, still buckling his belt.

Mollie was furious and tears stung her eyes as she hurried up the steps.

Ron caught up and took her hand. "Wait, Mollie. Please don't be mad at me. I'm really sort of glad you ruined my highest goal for the night." He moved in front of her. "And you'd better let me re-button your dress before you make your entrance, unless you want them to know my reputation is well earned."

"I'll handle the buttoning." She pulled her wrap around snugly and smiled, feeling better. "I've heard cold showers help your problem. Or you might try one of those polar swims in the lake!" She entered the ballroom. "Be back in a minute. The new year is only an hour away." She hurried to the powder room and searched her bag for a safety pin to fix the seam under her arm.

When she returned to their table, Gloria, her eyes glazed, swayed against it, jiggling the glasses. "There are rooms reserved upstairs for anyone who can stay." Her speech came slurred with the S's sounding like they were paired with H's.

Ron flashed a quizzical look at Mollie which she answered with a knowing squint. "Sorry, Gloria. The party has been fun, but I have to be on duty at seven."

"Just thought I'd see if anyone wanted to beat the late leave and stay over. I'm off tomorrow." Gloria steadied herself and concentrated on walking back across the floor to her date.

Ginger dozed on George's shoulder. She opened her eyes, stared fuzzily at Mollie and whispered, "I...don't feel so good."

"I'll take you to the powder room, Ginger." Mollie helped her stand on wobbly high heels.

"I think a walk in the cold air might be better, Ginger. I'll take you out to the terrace." George took her other arm and Ron followed them out to the veranda.

"She'll be okay, Mollie. Let's finish this dance." He grinned at Mollie's anxious glance in Ginger's direction. "Good old George won't harm her virtue. He's practically a priest."

Half an hour later, bells began to ring and balloons falling from the ceiling covered the dance floor. The band struck up *Auld Lang Syne.* Mollie allowed Ron's mouth to cover hers for a marathon time.

"I have a deep feeling this has been a fateful evening for you and me, sweetheart, and nineteen forty-two will see us beat the Japs and Nazis."

"Let's hope it's better. Things can't get much worse for the whole world." Mollie pulled his face down to hers and kissed him with more feeling than she intended. She'd enjoyed a wonderful evening in spite of Ron's attempted conquest and hoped to see more of him, a lot more.

He rubbed his forehead, the nights imbibing beginning to be obvious. "We had better get in line for the buffet. You're probably starved."

Shirley and her date, Barbara and hers, followed them.

"Oh, boy! Kippered salmon. What's this black stuff?" Shirley asked.

"You've never met caviar in Boise?" Larry smiled, still looking athletic and fresh-faced, probably the only one except Mollie who wasn't a little bit tipsy. Basketball players in perpetual training didn't drink.

"No, never had fancy food on the farm. Hello caviar! How about an itsy bitsy bite?" Shirley scooped a spoonful onto a cracker. "Not bad. A little too salty, but I think I could develop a taste for it."

Mollie filled a plate with deviled egg, salmon and cold chicken. She smiled at Ron, who took only a few crackers and some cheese.

He reached for a small glass of tomato juice and asked the waiter for beer. "Would you by chance have an aspirin in your purse, nurse? A certain episode in a tool shed sobered me up fast," he whispered.

Mollie fished around in her black grosgrain bag for a small cellophane package. "Take a couple of these. They're Anacin. Maybe you should skip the beer."

He swallowed the pills with a swig of tomato juice mixed with beer. "Right, but I find this unlikely combination usually helps." He leaned on an elbow to watch her eat. "The invitation to drive you home is still on. I'll be okay in half an hour."

Mollie watched George and Ginger move slowly past the buffet. Ginger walked like a zombie. "Didn't I hear George say he rode with you?"

Ron brightened. "I'll let him drive. He and Ginger can ride in the front. Rrrr" A low growl came from his throat and he grinned, looking suddenly quite healthy.

George had to stop twice to allow poor Ginger to throw up. She stood shakily to exit the car when they arrived at St. Anne's.

"We made it, Ginger. Good thing Sister Marie gave us until two." Mollie took one of her arms and George the other to get her up the steps.

They stood on the broad entry stoop where several girls and their dates, oblivious of others, were gathered in the alcove around the door. Mollie accepted a long goodnight kiss from Ron. She turned toward the door.

He called her back. "I'm not sure I can wait that long, but are you busy Friday? Maybe we could go ice skating."

"I don't have duty that night, but there's one problem. I can't skate."

"I'd love to teach you. I'll call you every night since I have your number now."

Mollie smiled as Larry buzzed Shirley good night with a short, rather brotherly brush on her lips.

"It's wonderful to find a girl who comes up past my belt buckle, Shirley. When can I see you again? Tomorrow, maybe?"

"Unless you kiss me better than that, no." Shirley pulled him to her lips and began a long passionate kiss that left them both gasping. "That was much better. Come over tomorrow, Larry. We need more practice."

A tiny bell tinkled inside, breaking the various embracing contortions of the lovers. Mollie hurried to help Ginger. Crowds would disguise her condition.

Shirley reached to open the door, then took her roommate's other arm. They steered her inside quietly and quickly to the elevator, glancing over their shoulders toward the strip of light under Sister Marie's office door.

"Better put on your glasses, Ginger. Sister is still up and if she sees you without them, she'll know you're drunk." Mollie steadied her while Ginger searched in her purse and put the spectacles a little askew over her nose.

In the elevator, Ginger's face paled and she searched wildly for somewhere to vomit. In desperation she opened her purse and spilled the scant contents of her stomach into it.

~ * ~

At noon, Mollie took time from lunch to check on Ginger. She opened the door to the room and raised the blinds to bright sunlight. "How do you feel?"

Ginger pulled the blankets over her head. "Oooo, Mollie. My head throbs. Make me a bromo, will you? There's some in the medicine cabinet." She rose to an elbow and tried to focus her eyes.

"Down it fast and it won't taste so bad." Mollie handed her the effervescent liquid.

"I promise never to touch a drop of alcohol again, Mollie. Why didn't you gals stop me?" She sank back into the pillows. "Ohhh, golly. I hope I didn't make a complete fool of myself. Did I?"

"You were a little funnier than usual, but cute and dignified and you weren't the only one who was beguiled by the bubbly stuff. Few made it to breakfast except those who had to be on duty. I knew I didn't dare drink much when seven in the morning came so soon after two." Mollie patted the mound under the covers. "Get up and get dressed, Ginger. George has called twice. He sounded worried. There's lots of coffee in the lounge." She suspected Sister Marie had made certain of that.

Shirley walked in with her wet hair wound turban-like in a towel. "Want to hear the latest?" She smiled as Ginger buried her head. "Sister Marie caught Carmen trying to enter through the auditorium door early this morning. She has a locksmith replacing the lock. Carmen's restricted for a good long term."

"What about Dorothy and the other girls who stayed all night?" Mollie asked.

"That's the loophole in their wonderful honor system. Unless the nuns do a bed check every night, they don't know who simply didn't sign out. You have to be a little honest," Shirley said. "I hope Sister Marie didn't watch me sign in last night or try to read my signature."

"I don't plan to disobey any rules for a long time," Ginger mumbled from under her pillow.

"As if you ever do," Shirley muttered.

~ * ~

St. Anne's Nursing School
January 77, 1942
Dear Joe,
It's been a month since the Japs bombed Pearl Harbor, a month full of changes for everyone. Mom has adopted several servicemen for Sunday dinners to make up for you and me being gone. Since you left the Monday before New Year's Eve, you haven't heard how my night at the Canal Yacht Club fancy ball turned out. The dance was hosted by Gloria's brother's fraternity. Remember Gloria Rollins, the rich girl in our class, the one who drank too much capping night and also at the dance?

And Joe, Am I glad you taught me how "not to drink" at that picnic on the canal last year. I thought I would die from that hangover and wanted to die of embarrassment over what

Wally and your girlfriend thought. Since then, I've learned to make one drink last a long time. I don't plan to go to another Frat party. Drunken orgies aren't for your little sister. I'll stick to Cokes with the lonely guys at the U.S.O. I did let Ron Van Ness, my blind date at the party, talk me into going ice skating. Says he'll teach me how. Hope I can learn without breaking something, like an arm or leg! Love, Mollie

Six

Mollie did a pirouette in front of the full length mirror in the lounge. She'd dreamed of spinning around gracefully on ice skates like Sonya Heinie since first seeing one of her movies. A tingle of apprehension warned her that Ron would soon learn how little she knew about the sport. Why had she agreed to such a nutty idea for their first real date? Glancing at her watch, she murmured. "You're ten minutes late, Ron."

Ginger and Shirley joined her near the door.

"Stop grumbling, Mollie. Mr. Van Ness didn't stand you up. He just parked his car at the curb," Ginger said.

Mollie noted that both girls carried ice skates. "Oh, no! You two aren't going to the rink!"

Shirley glanced in the mirror to fluff her hair. "We didn't plan to chaperone your evening, Mollie. Didn't you know we go to the arena every Friday night?"

"Then why do I get the feeling you're going tonight to watch me make a fool of myself? I've roller skated lots, but never tried ice before."

"Skating on ice is a lot more fun than on wheels," Ginger said.

"And really a lot easier too," added Shirley. "Think how much fun you will have with a handsome teacher like Ron."

Ron entered and greeted Mollie, then spoke to her friends. "Come along with us, gals. Lots of room."

At the rink, Mollie soon learned Shirley and Ginger were wrong about how easy it was to skate on ice, a fact she learned as soon as her ill-fitting rental skates touched the glistening surface.

Ron moved beside her."You won't get the hang of it if you keep clinging to the rail. Another thing—Don't lift your feet so high. Let the skates glide. They'll do most of the work for you. Watch."

Moving smoothly onto the ice, he performed several figures with a flourish. He grinned back at her still twisting and clutching the bar.

"Show off!" Mollie yelled. Clenching her teeth, she managed to wobble for a couple of yards before lurching for the rail. Still swaying to keep her balance, she scanned the rink. A pretty blonde girl she'd seen at the frat dance reached for Ron's arm as she swooped past.

"Okay for you, Mr. Campus King. If you don't want to help me learn, I'm going home!" Mollie muttered. Stiffening her back, she pushed out shakily, the skates in a pigeon-toed angle, her arms flailing wildly. She wobbled for about twenty feet before sprawling backward onto the wet rink floor. Skaters zipped by terrifyingly close, spraying icy water over her face. Slipping and wiggling, she got to a squatting position. "Eeee" her voice squeaked, as she whizzed across the floor with her skirt dragging the ice. A couple in the center of the rink where the fancy skaters practiced their figures, parted to let her through. Their laughter echoed in her ears.

Ron raced to scoop her upright and steered her, tottering like a skid row drunk, toward the coffee shop.

Mollie puffed out her cheeks and allowed the air to whistle through her teeth. "I told you I couldn't skate. I'll go back to the nurse's residence and leave you with 'Blondie'."

He tucked his arms snugly around her waist and helped her struggle onto the wood floor. "Let's have a cup of hot chocolate and I'll give you another lesson."

She hobbled to the counter, shivering when the sodden pleats of her blue plaid skirt plastered her underwear to her body. By leaning forward she managed to keep her damp sweater away from the chair back. Everything she wore felt cold and wet. She rubbed at a sore spot on her elbow. "I'll probably be as stiff as a morgue corpse tomorrow."

"I'm sorry I didn't stay with you, Mac. I forgot how hard it was to learn." He scanned the contours under her red sweater. "Even drenched in ice water, you look beautiful."

"I usually lop people who call me Mac off my list of favorites." Mollie looked across the rink toward the whizzing figures of her two friends skating a fancy dance number with two soldiers.

"Sorry again. Mac fits you somehow. Ready to give up skating for the night?"

"I'll watch awhile. Maybe I can learn something. Shirley and Ginger are having a good time with those two soldiers."

"Let me take you back to change and we'll pick them up when the rink closes at ten." Ron glanced at his watch.

Mollie didn't miss a little rise of his eyebrows.

"I don't know...Okay, it's already eight thirty. We'll have to hurry. Just let me tell them." Mollie motioned to Ginger, who whirled sharply to a stop at the gate to the snack bar, ice scattering from her skates.

Ron wobbled over to speak to Ginger, and after a few minutes, returned to Mollie. "Ginger and Shirley are having a great time. Their Army friends will see them home on the bus."

His grin made Mollie wonder if he had omitted part of the conversation. "Guess it will save you a little gas not having to make another trip."

"I have enough, but it has to do me the rest of the week."

Mollie untied her skate laces, a frown crinkling her brows when she saw her ankle. "A little puffy. Must have turned it when I fell?"

Ron moved his hands over the swelling tissue carefully, then up her leg to the thigh before she caught them firmly.

"I won't allow you to take me home unless you promise to behave better than that."

"Innocent, sweetheart. Just checking for broken bones." He nodded at Shirley and Ginger who were watching from the edge of the ice.

"Make the big bad wolf behave, Mollie, or we'll come along to chaperone" Ginger said, her expression stern and judgmental like Mother Superior's.

"You aren't her keeper, Ginger. You're barely a month older." Shirley smiled eagerly at the handsome soldier behind her and skated off. Ginger followed, casting a last apprehensive look toward Mollie.

At the car, Ron produced a plaid woolen stadium blanket from the rear seat and pulled it around Mollie."Warmer?"

"My teeth are no longer chattering." Mollie snuggled into the blanket. "Do you always come prepared for emergencies?"

"Boy Scout motto is 'Be Prepared'." He turned the car into the *Volunteer Park* entrance.

"I've never known Boy Scouts who drove Chryslers and maneuvered girls into dark parks!" She pointed a finger to tease, grinning at a thought Joe might have if he'd owned a Chrysler when he got his Eagle Scout badge.

"While you're getting warm, I thought you might enjoy the view of Seattle from here." He pulled Mollie closer, managing to feel her sweater and everything beneath it in one movement.

"My sweater is nearly dry, as you've discovered, campus snoop Van Ness!" Mollie forced her voice to drip sarcasm, but she couldn't help laughing to spoil the whole effect. "Come on let's talk about you before I have to chuck you into the pool with the fishes to cool you off. Mother would lecture me for dating someone I know so little about."

"Your mother still approves all your dates?" Ron teased, hugging her tighter and moving over the broad seat to be free of the wheel.

"She probably should. All I know about you is that the student body elected you Campus King at Homecoming last year. Several good authorities have warned me about controlling your charm in time to save mine. Gloria told me that you fraternity guys keep long lists of conquests."

Mollie felt heat in her face. She sounded just like the worldly girls in the senior class, who were jealous that she had a date with the infamous Ron. Why copy them for the benefit of this egotistical man? Suddenly she felt like her mother really was sitting in the back seat frowning at her daughter's slang. She chucked Ron under his appealing chin, meaning to taunt, but wanting to caress the dimples making deep lines in his cheeks.

"Pure propaganda. I will now tell you the truth. I was twenty-two last week. I have a sister named Dee, short for Dolores, and a mother. My father died of a heart attack two years ago, and I'm struggling to finish college before the small trust fund left to me is gone. I attended grade school and high school on Queen Anne Hill where my mother still lives in our family home. And I like action much better than all this talk." His mouth moved slowly over her neck to the top of her sweater.

Mollie shivered, but not from cold. Ron endangered her promise to herself to stay uncommitted to any man for the duration of the war. She must discourage him before her shaky vows tumbled completely. Keep him talking... "You didn't ask about me. That was supposed to be your next line."

"Sorry, you distract me from polite conversation. Living at the U. does little for good social grace. I know you're almost nineteen years old, have a brother in the Army Air Corps and a boyfriend in Hawaii. And I'm sure dozens of men besides me have wanted to unfasten your chastity belt!"

"They would have gotten a sharp blow to a tender spot if they'd tried."

Good thing it was dark because Mollie knew her face turned crimson at his last statement. "To continue the family background, I have a younger brother, Mike, who is eleven years old, a sister, Sally who is sixteen, a mother and a father. Our dog is named Casey, and our horse Patches." She leaned backward on his outstretched arm. "You're a trifle spoiled by always getting what you want. But I suspect beneath your romantic facade, you're a regular guy."

"And I'll bet you got an "A" in Psychiatry, Miss McAllister." He kissed her long and fervently, moving his tongue along her lips. "God, Mollie. I want all of you."

Mollie pulled away. "No, you don't. You only want to add another notch to your fraternity pin." She held his face in her hands, smiling. "You know, I haven't seen you in daylight, but they look green. Cool and limpid green eyes, like that song?"

Ron had flipped the radio on and Glen Miller's band was playing the current top of the Hit Parade.

Those cool and limpid green eyes are cooler in the soft light... Mollie sang, realizing she was leading him on and making it more difficult. Not that she really wanted to stop him... Not at all. But she must not fall for the first civilian guy who dated her, the only one around...with a car. "They're probably really greenish yellow to keep you in common with wolves. Eyes reveal character, they say, and I didn't mean to be nasty. Wolves probably have character as well as tenacity for gaining their prey."

Ron laughed and brushed the hair gently back from her neck. His soft kiss sent goose flesh over her arms. "God, I hope that shiver isn't because you're cold. Come, Sweetheart, give me a chance to live up to the vast reputation report." A hand covered her bra, the other settled on her inner thigh.

Mollie clutched the one on her thigh firmly. "What about my reputation for purity, honor, duty, all those things men really expect from *good* girls? Would you want your sister to lose her virtue on a second date, even with a great lover like you?" She kissed his cheek, like she would Joe's or Mike's. "I think it's time you took me home. It will look very funny if I arrive later than my friends."

"Believe me I wasn't thinking of you as a sister." He held his watch toward the dim park light by the pool. "We still have half an hour and suddenly I find the car too warm. Will you feel chilled if we climb the stairs to the observatory? The city looks beautiful from there." Ron opened the door. "Keep the blanket around you. No one else is out here tonight."

They circled the fish pond and climbed fifty steps to an observation tower where the empty mount from a telescope reminded Mollie of the war. Its scope had been removed to prevent unauthorized observation of the ships on the bay.

Mollie caught her breath sharply at the sea of sparkling lights, bright in spite of the recent restrictions on Neon advertizing. "Funny no one told me about this place, though I walk to the park from the nursing residence a lot. It's beautiful."

Ron pressed his body against her from behind, his arms encircling her waist. With that physique, he could not be spending too much time at his desk, Mollie mused. The firmness of his muscular thighs and his abdominal region emphasized the hardness between his legs.

"Yeah." He pulled her around, tilted her chin and lingered over her mouth sweetly this time, with deliberate restraint. "You're a different kind of girl, Mollie. You know what you want and stick to goals. I admire that in anyone." He stared silently at the lights for several minutes. "You challenge my selfish plans to score with you, and I promise to keep trying."

Mollie turned again to the lovely view of the dark patch of bay surrounded by lights. The outline of streets under the lamps and the bluish flashes of the electric trolleys could be seen clearly. The flashes proved to be a real problem in the recent blackouts. Unless the whole city transportation system was halted, they would be visible to aircraft attacking at night.

She squeezed his hand. "I like guys who have thoughts besides romantic conquests, and I sound as prudish as Ginger."

He laughed, and mumbled into her hair, "You don't know how hard I'm trying. Other things are hard when you're so close to me, honey. Ummm. You must bathe or shampoo in lemons."

"I do use lemon juice when I rinse my hair to cut the soap scum. At home we catch rain water for shampooing, but I decided it might look a little crazy to install a barrel on the nursing residence roof." Mollie took his hand and led the way to the stairs. "It's nearly curfew time."

"Another damn curb to romance. When can I see you again, Mollie?"

"I'm going home next weekend." Mollie slid into the car seat.

Ron closed her door and walked around to the driver's side. "What's your schedule tomorrow? We could pack a picnic lunch and go to Madison Park to watch the ducks parade." He glanced at the gas gauge.

"If you don't have enough gas," Mollie said leaning to see the needle. "We could walk from here."

"Plenty for that, but there's talk of rationing gas, oil and tires. This car drinks fuel so I may be walking a lot. If it rains tomorrow, we might need to have our picnic in the car."

"Okay, I'm off duty at eleven and back on at seven. Split shifts are definitely not my favorites. Want me to get some sandwich materials from the grocery?" Mollie stepped from the car and turned toward the nursing residence door.

"No. I'll bring everything. I still have kitchen privileges at home. I'll be here about noon, Okay?" Ron kissed her goodbye at the residence door. Several whistles echoed from the upper floor windows when he strolled back to the car.

~ * ~

St. Anne's Nursing School

February 5, 1942

Dear Joe,

I cried all through the Academy Award Winner, Mrs. Miniver, because I kept thinking you might be in that beautiful green country where bombs are falling. Or maybe you ended up in the biggest desert in the world. (They'll probably censor all of this)

I went ice skating tonight with Ron Van Ness, the guy I told you about in my last letter. I guess I'll never challenge Sonya Heinie. On ice, I never got beyond several ways to fall down and get wet. I think I'll stick to dancing with the guys at the U.S.O. There will be another this Friday. Some day this awful war will end and we can get back to normal.

Until then,

Love and XXX, Mollie

~ * ~

Mollie sealed the envelope and another to her friend, Phil in Hawaii, and dropped them into the mailbox in the lounge. No sense in telling Phil and the other guys about Ron. GIs had enough to worry over without thinking all the girls at home were out necking with 4-Fs and draft dodgers.

She shrugged. Why did she keep putting Ron in those categories? Why the little nudge of guilt when Ron was technically already in the service, just getting his college first? He had everything she liked in men, looks, brains, a gift for leadership, and a sense of humor. But something pricked the dreamy bubble she'd built around him. He was entirely too smooth, like one of those door-to-door encyclopedia salesmen. Well, she vowed with clenched jaws, he will not add me to one of his lists.

She sighed. Her mind needed to push hard to nudge Ron Van Ness from her heart, and if she kept dating him, it would be impossible.

Seven

"Hurry, Mollie. Ron's here, and woweee is he handsome in his Navy uniform!" Barbara jerked curlers from her hair. "I sneaked down a second for the mail and he caught me in these. I've never felt so embarrassed."

Mollie's Pharmacology book thudded to the floor. Hurrying to the mirror, she dabbed on a touch of fresh lipstick, rubbing her lips together to spread the bright red evenly, and then blotting them on a piece of toilet paper. She pulled a brush through the snarls in her hair, shook the strands over her shoulders, and fluffed it with her hands.

"Guess I'd better not keep Ensign Van Ness waiting. He has a train to catch." Mollie glanced at her watch smiling, a fluttery feeling in her chest, her usual practicality wavering. "Ron invited me to go to the station with his mother and sister to wish him good luck. He's early."

Barbara's brows rose a trifle. "Good luck? I'd wish him a lot more than that! Gollie, I'm envious. Too bad I have to be on duty, or I'd tag along for old time's sake." She ducked a pillow." Kidding."

Shirley joined Mollie at the elevator. "Ron is the handsomest man I ever saw in a Navy uniform, and sooo tall. Need any help getting him to the station, Mollie? I could drive so you two can sit in the back seat and neck." She whistled low through her teeth.

"Ensign Van Ness has to be well aware of his good looks with all you gals whistling at him." Mollie wondered if his attitude would change. According to Joe's last letter, flight training, especially in the Navy Air Corps, quickly lowered everyone to the same level, flat on their stomachs. At the moment, Mollie felt sorry she hadn't taken the driver's license test when her dad taught her to drive last year. "I suppose Dorrie and Carmen have joined his crowd of fans downstairs. Where's that elevator? Someone must have it blocked open," she called to Shirley who was turning the corner toward the showers.

"Don't know about Carmen, but Dorrie went to Volunteer Park with Jake." Shirley waved a "V" sign as Mollie entered the elevator and the door clanked shut.

Mollie checked her stocking seams before going into the lounge to greet Ron. He rose from a chair and her breath caught for a second. She felt like one of those swooning star-struck Errol Flynn fans.

She forced out a whistle. "Hello. No wonder you wowed Barbara. Navy blue does look mighty fetching on you." When he smiled like that she was reminded of the Navy recruiting poster. A strand of curly hair escaped at the edge of his forehead. The dark shadow of beard over the cleft in his chin looked like it might challenge the sharpest razor. The Navy officer's uniform appeared to extend his six-foot two frame, lean from four years on the Husky Crew, and emphasized his wide shoulders.

She sensed a thrill at his presence which she'd been trying unsuccessfully to subdue ever since the fraternity dance. The emotion threatened logical thought. This guy was entirely too handsome to get serious about, she told herself once more.

He leaned for a kiss, draped an arm tight around her waist, and led her out to the car. "Mother decided not to go to the station. She wanted to say goodbye at home...afraid she might cry or something, I guess." He opened the back door. "We have forty-five minutes before train time and Dee agreed to drive so we could spend it well."

"Less than that, Ronnie." His sister glanced at her watch and winked. "Better get busy and stop wasting time talking."

Mollie had met Dee when Mrs. Van Ness invited her and Barbara to dinner recently. Dee, tall and a little too skinny to be pretty, was a sophomore in Pharmacy at the University. Dee pulled away from the curb, grinding the gears and bringing a wince from her brother.

Ron quickly covered as much of Mollie as she allowed. When a roaming hand threatened her barriers, she gently slapped it.

"Damn it, Mollie," he grumbled. "I won't see you for months, maybe years. Give me something real to remember."

"In the back seat of a car with your sister two feet in front of us peeking in the rear view mirror isn't my idea of a romantic interlude." Mollie kissed the dimple in his left cheek. "And months and months is just the point. No doubt you'll soon be feeling half the girls in California. They're very easy conquests according to Joe."

"Maybe I should've gotten his address book!" He clutched her slapping hand. "Shut up and enjoy, Sweetheart."

Their mouths met and stayed in position until the car jerked to a stop at the station.

Dee turned around, laughing. "Are you two permanently attached or can you open the door by yourselves?"

Mollie pulled out her handkerchief to wipe the lipstick smears from Ron's mouth, and fluffed her hair, trying to act lighthearted. "Come on Ensign. Leave a little for the real farewell."

"There's Mother. I thought she wasn't coming." Ron hurried to a slender woman with short gray curls peeking from a smart veiled hat. "I'm glad you changed your mind." He gave her an affectionate peck on the cheek and coughed nervously when his mother pulled a lacy handkerchief from her handbag to catch the overflow of tears seeping under her glasses.

"I stayed home today to interview a couple of girls from Boeing. I decided to sublet yours and the guest room plus kitchen privileges to help alleviate the housing shortage. The rooms will just get musty while..." Mrs. Van Ness's voice trailed and she nudged her daughter. "Let's allow Ron and Mollie a few moments, Dee." She and Dee walked a short distance down the platform.

"I meant it when I said I would miss you more than anything, Sweetheart. I brought this little thing for you to remember me by." He fished in a coat pocket and pulled out a small box with a gold chain inside. "Nothing much, just a locket with my new uniform picture, but I mean it to be a promise that I won't forget you," His hands shook a little as he clasped it around her neck. "and I hope that feeling goes both ways."

"It's lovely, thank you." Mollie's voice cracked in spite of caution, and she cast her eyes toward her shoes. If she looked into his eyes, she'd cry and spoil the whole thing. She fought a fleeting memory of Joe and Carmen at the airport, vowing not to make any promises for either of them to break. "Here's the picture I promised. Its two years old— my senior one from high school. I'll have Dorrie take a new photo of me and send it to you."

"I want you to have this, too..." Ron leaned to fasten his fraternity pin on the lapel of her red plaid jacket. "Wear both of them and think of me a lot, Mollie. I plan to keep your picture under my pillow every night, but I won't need it to remind me how beautiful you look right now." He kissed her firmly, fiercely possessive, over and over until his mother's soft cough interrupted.

"I...I believe they are boarding, Ron," his mother said. "Perhaps you should move a trifle closer to the doors."

Steam hissed from the engine and a bell clanged continuously as the crowd moved toward the car steps. "Board!" yelled a conductor down the train.

Ron scooped Mollie, his mother and Dee into his arms, hugged and kissed them, then leapt onto the steps just as the train began to move. He waved until the curve of the track pulled him out of sight.

The three women joined hundreds of others walking dejectedly back through the milling crowds in the deafening pandemonium of the station. Many dabbed at tears. Others tried unsuccessfully to quiet their children's crying.

"God damn this war! There's scarcely an eligible man left at the U," complained Dee, kicking the steps as they climbed to street level.

"Your language has taken leave too, Dee," Mrs. Van Ness said absently, staring straight ahead. "I have the afternoon off. Can you join us for dinner, Mollie?"

"That would be nice, but I volunteered to go to a U.S.O dance tonight and I need to wash my hair." Having dinner with them might sooth the emptiness seeping into her heart, or being with Ron's relatives could deepen it. She needed a couple of hours alone to think, to try to sort out her feelings. A sudden irresponsible desire to follow Ron argued with duty to her family and finishing her training at St. Anne's. None of the other men she'd dated made her feel so completely reckless. Love? Couldn't be yet. Had to be infatuation. At nineteen, she had too much to accomplish before truly falling in love. But her mother had been married at nineteen.

~ * ~

That evening, Mollie joined fifty girls in party finery taking turns at the full-length mirror in the lounge for last minute primping.

"Are my seams straight, Mollie?" Shirley twisted around and extended a shapely left leg, trying to see the dark seams of her hosiery.

"Straight as these darn rayon things can be. How are mine?" Mollie walked a couple of steps in front of Shirley.

"The seams are fine, but the knees bag a little. Can you heist your garter belt up a smidgen?" Shirley's appraising eyes traveled enviously over Mollie's curvy figure and she thumped her own boyish chest."Thirty-two-A. Wish I could borrow a couple inches of Dorrie's boobs!"

Mollie giggled, the patter of her friends dimming slightly her troubling thoughts about Ron. "You could stuff these baggy things in the cups. I'd go without stockings if I had time to smear on leg makeup" She bent over to inch the reluctant stretchy rayon hosiery a little higher. It was impossible to keep them from bagging at the knees and ankles except for the first few minutes after they were donned. The girls tried everything. Some thought putting the hose on when slightly damp helped. Others added a little starch in the water when they laundered them. Even stretched over Dorrie's ample knees and ankles the things looked wrinkled and baggy after an hour.

"What you need is three more inches of leg, Mollie," Shirley said, stretching out a shapely one. "Guess we're never satisfied with what we got from our genes. I'll never quite forgive God for deciding I should look more like Dad than Mom."

"Sure would be nice to have a pair of silks or those new nylon stockings for special occasions. My mother still keeps two pairs sealed tightly in a mason jar and pulls them out only when it is a real special thing, like going out to dinner while Joe was home." Mollie frowned. There had been so little time to really talk to Joe.

He spent a lot of his last home leave with Carmen, and was headed overseas now.

"Are those new shoes, Mollie?" Shirley asked.

"Yes. I bought them right after Christmas. Real leather may be hard to find soon, according to Dad." She had bought the black toeless sling pumps with part of the money Joe had given her. There were rumors they'd be rationing a lot of things, including leather goods and gasoline.

Barbara approached to squint into the mirror. "Did you get them at Canby's?"

Mollie nodded. "They were a trifle expensive. Ten dollars, but I thought I might as well enjoy my special gift from my brother." Mollie raised her voice good and loud so Carmen, a few yards away, wouldn't miss that piece of news. Irritation with her roommate nagged her conscience. She had no right to monitor Joe's affairs or choose his girlfriends, but why hadn't he picked one who wouldn't cheat the minute he left her?

Two big Army trucks lumbered noisily up to the door of the Nursing Residence and Sister Anne peeked into the lounge. "The trucks are here girls. Don't forget you must be back in your rooms at twelve-thirty. The sergeant says he will be personally accountable for your safe return." The little nun smiled broadly at the soldier standing at her side ogling her fledgling nurses.

"Trucks!" Carmen turned as if ready to go back to her room. "We ride to the dances in trucks?"

"I suspect the Army has few available limousines, Miss Morales." Sister Anne led the troop of girls to the door. "See, they aren't so bad with ramps to walk up."

Two Army trucks, flanked by half a dozen soldiers in dress uniforms, were parked at the curb. Ramps covered in worn carpeting extended from the olive drab canvas-covered truck beds.

The girls, listing precariously on high heels, wobbled up the incline, their squeals and giggles piercing the night air. They were assisted, one at a time, by the soldiers. A tall corporal grinned broadly when Shirley's full skirt blew up in a gust of wind, revealing her long nicely turned legs to the brown tops of her hosiery.

"This has got to be the best duty I've drawn so far!" He whistled softly, turning Shirley's head. She winked, and blew him a kiss.

"Amen to that! Looks a little like Katherine Hepburn, don't she?" His partner glanced cautiously over his shoulder at the two nuns smiling from the door of the nursing residence.

The nurses settled onto hard benches under the canvas cover, hanging tightly to whatever they could for balance when the truck turned corners or stopped suddenly. Two soldiers sat on the end seats to keep their dancing hostesses from sliding out into the street.

Mollie laughed, relishing the adventure. "It's a lot like our Rainbow Girls hay-rides, Barb. Isn't this a lot more fun than riding the city busses to the U.S.O. dances?"

Barbara was too busy keeping her carefully dressed hair intact to share Mollie's enthusiasm for riding in the truck. Like most of the girls, she quickly fished into her bag for a scarf to protect her blonde hair from the breezy ride. "Wagons don't do thirty-five and suffocate you with dirty exhaust fumes," she grumbled.

At the base, the girls exited the trucks the same way they entered, listing on high heels. Mollie pulled off her shoes and skipped down, then replaced them at the bottom. Soon, others followed her example.

She waited for Dorrie to descend, gasping when the ramp thudded to the pavement. Two soldiers rushed over to lift her, Barbara and the last two girls out.

Dorrie laughed. "Wouldn't you know the sight of me would break something? Thanks, guys."

The husky red-faced private puffed when Dorrie's feet reached the ground. "Could you by any chance be Dorrie?" He looked about to see who might hear. "We aren't supposed to know your names or talk with you until you're inside. Jake said to tell you he's waiting at the Coke bar."

~ * ~

Dorrie met Jake inside. "How did you know I would be here tonight? I could've been on the truck that went to Fort Lawton. Isn't this Boeing Field?"

"You forget I work for Colonel Clark. I see everything that goes across his desk. I just made sure the truck you were in got here." He pulled her behind a screen hiding boxes of equipment and covered her mouth with a lingering kiss. "I wasn't so sure Sister Marie would let you out after last weekend."

"She hasn't caught me sneaking in through the auditorium yet, but the nuns did catch Carmen once. One of the seniors found a way to jam it again so dozens of girls still use it to get into the nursing residence after curfew."

When the music started, Mollie and a skinny, bowlegged private spun dizzily around the crowded floor. When she returned to Dorrie and Jake's table he pulled out a chair.

"My gosh, Mollie, you can really swing," Jake said.

"Wish I could, but I can't seem to make my feet do that little shuffle," Dorrie said. "I'm more the waltzy type, but we Polish kids learned to polka as soon as we could walk. That's fast."

"Hmm. Stay right here, Dorrie, sweet. I'll be right back." Jake went to the bandstand and spoke with the leader.

At eleven, the sergeant acting as announcer took the microphone and called for silence."The men of the H.Q. staff collected prize money for the best Jitterbugging. The contest will be decided by our C. O.s. He pointed toward two officers seated at a table in the corner. "And their decision will be greatly affected by the applause each couple gets. Find your partners, guys."

~ * ~

Mollie grimaced when she spotted the soldier who had spun her under his legs in the last fling at boogie coming her way. She darted toward the restroom to avoid him. Someone grabbed her hand. "Jake!"

"Come on, Mollie. You can't lose with a Jersey boy." He waved at Dorrie sipping a tall Coke at a table with his best buddy. She smiled back and made a "V" sign.

She kicked off her shoes and threw them to Dorrie. Jake took her to the center of the floor to join a dozen other couples urged on by the Army band's version of Tommy Dorsey's *Boogie Woogie*.

"Eeee!" Mollie squealed as Jake pulled her out, then under his arm expertly. "I knew I should've worn tights!"

Their feet moved through the double steps in perfect rhythm. Jake proved to be Fred Astaire in army clothes. The whole room broke into wild cheering and clapping after he pulled her through his legs and whirled her around without missing a beat. Mollie felt her face grow hot, but Jake wasn't even breathing hard. The judges eliminated everyone except them and one other couple.

The band switched to Glen Miller's, *In The Mood,* and they danced on, Mollie whirling like a ballerina. When the music was nearly over, even Jake puffed as he pulled her first under one arm, then the other. They finished their session by sliding under arms like an unwinding knot, ending precisely with the last beat of the drum.

Whistles and squeals filled the huge armory when the judges pointed to Jake and Mollie. After going up to the bandstand to accept the prize, Mollie fussed with her hair, which she had worn long over her shoulders in a shiny page boy. Now, it lay in chestnut tangles, and perspiration glistened on her face. Jake hurried toward Dorrie.

Before he got to their table, she bolted for the restroom, tears streaking her face. She nearly collided with Mollie headed the same way.

"What's the matter, Dorrie? My gosh, you aren't jealous of me?" Mollie put an arm over Dorrie's shaking shoulders.

Mascara and tears mingled with smeared lipstick when she faced Mollie. "N...not jealous, just envious. I'm so damned homely and dumb and about as shapely as a pumpkin. How could I expect anyone as smart as Jake to fall for me? I can't even dance very well and you can match him."

Mollie shook her gently. "Stop it, Dorrie, Jake picked you from all ninety of us. Why don't you get him to teach you to dance? Jake is as good as those expensive instructors, one of the best dancing partners I have ever had, maybe the very best." Mollie hurried into the toilet, flushed it, and moved to the mirror to repair her makeup, smiling when Dorrie washed her face and got out her mascara.

"I told Jake I would get you to come over to our table. You remember his friend from Brooklyn. Just a second and I'll be ready." Dorrie ran a brush through her curls and outlined her attractive mouth with a new fuchsia shade of lipstick.

Mollie watched, thinking Dorrie would be truly pretty if she lost about forty pounds. Hair she cursed because it was too curly was the envy of half the girls in the class and Dorrie's skin never broke out in pimples. Too bad she felt so insecure about Jake. It was obvious he liked her a lot. *Didn't make a pass at me, just wanted to dance. Guess I'll have to be careful and not give her any more cause for envy or jealousy.*

The two girls joined Jake and the dark-haired sergeant who had been the announcer. There were four Cokes on the table. Jake rose and pulled chairs out for Dorrie and Mollie.

"Mollie, this is Gene Fulton from Brooklyn," Jake said, smiling. "They're playing a nice foxtrot. May I, Dorrie?" He reached for Dorrie's hand and she smiled, eyes glistening as they glided smoothly over the floor.

"I'm not real sure you did Jake and me a favor arranging that contest, Gene. Still feels like ninety degrees in here." But Mollie accepted Gene's invitation for the slower dance and found he was also good at rhythm. "You dance well."

"Not Boogie, though. I grew up in a strict Baptist family who didn't believe in dancing, and my sister's secret efforts to teach me stopped short of anything lively. One day I'll learn boogie because the beat gets to me. How did you get so good at it, Mollie?"

"The school dances you didn't attend. The alumni organization donated a battered Nickelodeon, and we danced every lunch hour in the gym with socks over our shoes to keep them from scratching the floor."

Her thoughts returned to high school. So much had happened in a year. A year ago, the United States was not fighting a frightening war in several places around the world. Now, the Japanese controlled the Philippines and most of the South Pacific islands. Enemy planes were bombing Singapore, and their armies marching into most of Asia. Her dad had told her last week that the aircraft carrier *Lexington* had been sunk. She wondered if he should talk about things like that even to his family. *Loose lips sink ship* the posters said.

Sergeant Fulton wrote the nursing residence phone number on a paper napkin and tucked it into his pocket. "Would you like to take in a movie with me next Friday, Mollie?"

Mollie accepted his arm to help her into the truck. "Sure, Gene, I'd like that. It'll have to be early though. I have to be in by eleven." Sister Marie had given them the privilege of later nights on weekends now that they were through their first year of classroom instruction.

She caught her breath as the trucks passed by the Boeing Airplane Company with its little camouflage village on top. There were streets with names, real little houses, everything to make it look authentic to aircraft flying above. Crossing her fingers, she said a silent prayer the ruse would never need to be tested.

Another thought needled as she rode on through the streets, which were dim since the restrictions on neon lights. The Japanese-American student had passed her state board examinations for Registered Nurse, and then was ordered to report to a Relocation Camp in Idaho. Mollie had watched sadly as Taeko left St. Anne's with shoulders stiffly erect, tears streaming from her eyes. Taeko Fuji and her mother and father were born in the United States. Didn't that make her even more American than Dorrie, whose father was born in Poland? News reports said the Japanese were sent to the camps for their own safety, but somehow that didn't seem right. How could you tell if an Oriental person was Japanese or Chinese?

~ * ~

St. Anne's Nursing School
May 10, 1942
Dear Joe,
Thanks for the money order. It helps me squeeze by for another term. I thought I might have to drop out and go to work at Boeing for the duration. Dad slips me what he can spare.
It's past lights out, but my roommates are chattering up a storm and the blackout curtains serve another purpose. They keep Sister Marie from guessing we are up after hours. We stuff a rug in the crack under the door. The U.S.O dance was loads of fun. I won ten dollars in a Jitterbug contest with Jake Swartz. Remember he's Dorrie's boyfriend. I gave her half of it!
Here are some hugs ooo and kisses, xxx, love, Mollie

Eight

"Room five-twenty-two has his light on again, Mollie. Didn't you give him his morphine at twelve?"

"Yes, Mrs. Patterson. And Doctor Moore ordered a fourth instead of a sixth. I can't imagine why it didn't knock him out."

"Because he has a belly full of cancer, Mollie," Mrs. Patterson sighed. "I'll fix him a placebo and see if psychology will perform like narcotics."

The charge nurse looked exhausted. Seven months pregnant and her husband somewhere in the South Pacific, she worked to relieve both the nursing shortage and her financial situation. There were several pregnant nurses working at St. Anne's, all of them serving on night duty. Mother Superior didn't like the image they presented. Expectant mothers were supposed to stay home and await their babies regardless of a nursing shortage, poverty, or absent husbands. In spite of her biased view, it looked as if maternity shapes in white uniforms would be around for the duration because the government urged all nurses to work.

Mrs. Patterson tucked a stray bleached blonde hair into the chignon poking from her pleated black-banded cap, unlocked the narcotic cabinet and filled a hypodermic. "Cross your fingers. If Mr. Anderson is exhausted enough, this might work."

Mollie took the syringe, her forehead crinkling her puzzlement. Why had Mrs. Patterson unlocked the narcotics cupboard? The pink bicarb tablets were in plain view on the table below, along with the alcohol, swabs, disinfectant, and other innocuous stuff. "He'll know it's not morphine, Mrs. Patterson. He says he can tell because saline makes the needle sting."

Tucking a small flashlight into her pocket to diffuse its glow, Mollie hurried to the flashing light. Pushing the door open with her foot, she silently entered the dark room.

"I'm sorry to be such a baby, Miss McAllister, but I can't get comfortable any way at all. Could I have another shot? It's been two and a half hours," the man whispered.

Dim light from Mollie's flashlight revealed a gaunt face twisting in pain. She readied the syringe, and nearly dropped it at a loud throat clearing from the patient in the next bed.

The husky man grunted noisily and rolled over to face her. "Give him a real snort this time, Babe. I can't sleep with all that thrashing."

Mollie ignored the guy, thinking he'd be the biggest whiner in the hospital if he had real pain. She pinched Mr. Anderson's bony arm. The loose skin on it felt dry and tough as leather. "I'll give you this one in the hip, Mr. Anderson. Your arm is beginning to look like it has measles."

Mr. Anderson rolled slowly onto his side biting his lips from the pain. Mollie's breath caught when she saw a dark smear on the sheet. Tarry, black stool seeped from his rectum... Blood. It wouldn't be long until the poor emaciated man's misery was over. She pulled the needle out, expecting him to complain about the stinging of the saline, but he just sighed and closed his eyes.

89

On Mr. Anderson's chart, Mollie reported a placebo shot at two-thirty a.m. also noting the spot of bloody stool she had seen on the sheet. Replacing the metal folder as quietly as possible, she turned to whisper to the charge nurse.

"I didn't change his draw sheet, Mrs. Patterson. Should I have? I just thought it might make him more uncomfortable, and the spot could only have been from a couple of centimeters."

"That's fine, Mollie. As usual, we're short of linen." Mrs. Patterson, looking even wearier, raised her swollen white-clad legs onto a chair. "I think there is still coffee in the pot, Mollie. Pour me a cup, please."

Mollie took the cups from hooks in the linen closet, noting the scant stacks of much mended sheets, towels and pillow cases. There was never enough clean linen. Retired nuns from a convent close by spent most of their time mending linen and gowns for the patients.

Mollie filled two coffee cups, set them down on the charge desk and pulled a chair closer.

"Funny, Mr. Anderson didn't complain about the placebo. He just relaxed. I'm sure he knew because it wasn't time for another quarter of morphine." Mollie sipped the brew, smiling over Mrs. Patterson's head at Ginger coming down the hall, arms laden with soiled linen after cleaning up a messy bed.

The charge nurse stared into her cup. "Sometimes placebos work nearly as well as the real stuff," she muttered. "Join us in a cup of coffee, Ginger?"

"Mrs. Allen made a real mess of her bed with her thrashing around. I changed the draw sheet, then she spilled her bedpan over it and I had to redo the whole thing again. I rubbed her back. She's complaining of pain." Ginger took the cup eagerly and sipped the hot liquid. "Swears she didn't get her shot."

Mrs. Patterson rose with a grunt of effort and went to the cupboard to count the narcotics and other medicine for her morning report. "There's Allen's light again. Take her this empirin and codeine, Mollie. She had a morphine shot at midnight and isn't due for another until six." She handed Mollie a little cup with a pill in it.

Mrs. Allen scowled. "Where's my pain shot? The nurse never gave it to me at midnight and it's three in the morning. She must have forgotten and I hurt awful."

"I'm sure you had it. People often forget things like that after surgery. I brought you something for your pain though. Just lean on your side so you can take a sip of water to wash it down." Mollie angled the glass straw to Mrs. Allen's mouth. "Just take a little sip. Too much will bring your nausea back."

Mrs. Allen coughed slightly and swallowed the pill. "Thanks."

Mollie fluffed the patient's pillows, stuffed a small one between her ample knees, and tucked the blankets around her shoulders like Mrs. Allen was a child. Why had Ginger needed to use a whole new bed of clean linen, when a clean bottom sheet would have been enough? But that was Ginger, Miss Perfectionist. Mollie slipped out of the room and back down to the charge desk to finish her charting.

Mollie turned the chart around for the charge nurse to see."Mrs. Patterson, there isn't any reference to a morphine shot for Mrs. Allen at midnight. Maybe she's right. We did forget her."

"My fault. I forgot to chart it. When I gave midnight medications that whiny woman in five-twelve was making so much noise, I was afraid she would wake the whole floor. Leave space and I'll take care of it." Mrs. Patterson's attractive face wore a mask of innocence and she straightened to shift the baby to a more comfortable position. It was two hours until she could give her report and go home to rest her strained body.

Mollie stared at Mrs. Allen's chart and drew in her breath, realizing the charge nurse had found a way to ease the torment of a dying man with another patient's morphine. Her drug count would be in order and no one would guess. The patient's suffering from yesterday's hysterectomy paled beside that of Mr.

Anderson's terminal cancer. She would survive without her pain killer, maybe uncomfortably, but survive. Might be better off without it...could even be allergic or become addicted to morphine, Mollie rationalized. She had learned another valuable lesson not found in *Principles and Practices of Nursing*. At St. Anne's, there were many judgments about human suffering no book of procedures could possibly cover.

The following night proved to be tediously quiet: no new surgeries, no fussy patients. Mrs. Allen slept like Rip Van Winkle, her snoring echoing clear to the charge desk. Mollie yawned, envying the sleeping forms under their white coverlets.

Ginger had contracted stomach flu, and because of Friday night late leaves, there had been no one available to replace her. That meant just the two of them to cover the floor. Sister Agnes, in charge of the whole hospital, checked every couple of hours to see how Five South fared.

"I'll be in the linen closet if you need me, Mollie." Mrs. Patterson slipped into the small room and a chair scraped as she pulled it up to receive her tired feet.

Mollie nodded. If lucky, she might catch a little nap. Besides being tired and uncomfortable, Mrs. Patterson hadn't heard from her husband in six weeks. Fear of receiving the dreaded telegram about him showed in little worry lines forming in her forehead and bluish shadows under her eyes.

A frantic male voice from the direction of room 522 broke the peace of the darkened hospital corridor.

"Hurry someone! In the sun room, he's gonna jump!"

Mollie ran to the solarium with Mrs. Patterson huffing behind, her cap askew.

"Judas!" Mollie gasped. The tall French-style windows were wide open and Mr. Anderson teetered precariously on the ledge, his open-backed hospital gown flapping over yellowish, skeletal buttocks. He shivered from the cold, his bony legs knocking together.

"Come down now, Mr. Anderson." Mrs. Patterson's voice came quiet and authoritative from the doorway. She crept slowly forward until only an arm's length from the blowing draperies at the window.

"No. It's better this way. I can't stand the pain any longer." Mr. Anderson stared down at the cement service entrance five floors below. He wobbled, nearly toppling toward it, but grasped the window frame just in time.

Mollie knuckled her mouth to keep from screaming and she saw Mrs. Patterson swallow hard, then clear her throat to regain composure. She moved a trifle nearer, glancing sideways at Mollie. They were both a bare yard away from the patient.

"Your wife and children will be the ones who are hurt if you go this way." The charge nurse kept talking in calm firm tones. "Your family will blame themselves. Do you realize that? They'll be filled with guilt if they're denied the right to do some last thing for you. Suicide is not brave. It's selfish!"

Mollie inched closer hoping to clutch the patient's gown. She dared not startle him by grabbing his ankles or he might pull her out the window after him. Mr. Anderson teetered again and she lunged to catch the ends of his gown with her right hand. He wasn't a big man anymore, but the advantage was his if he really intended to jump. Holding onto the flimsy gown wouldn't stop him.

Mrs. Patterson's voice grew louder and she began to sound like Mr. District Attorney on the radio. "What about your insurance, Mr. Anderson? Can your wife get along without it? Many policies don't pay if you take your own life."

Mr. Anderson wavered, shaking so hard the casement he grasped tightly moved and banged against the brick wall outside, shattering the glass. A shard cut his arm and blood spurted over his side.

"Let us help you down, Mr. Anderson. We're all freezing. I'll fix you a hypo, and tuck you into nice warm blankets with hot water bottles for your feet." Mrs. Patterson jerked her head toward Mollie.

Mollie took her hands from his gown and quickly grasped the patient's ankles. She held them tightly while Mr. Anderson rocked unsteadily, fell hard onto the ledge, and then slithered backward onto the tile floor of the solarium, grunting with the impact.

Mollie's hand covered her mouth when she saw his half-healed incision gaping open. The seeping from that and the blood from the cuts on his arm spattered her uniform. Mercifully, Mr. Anderson slipped into unconsciousness.

Hastening footsteps echoed down the corridor. Sister Agnes and two orderlies rushed into the solarium.

"Get him to surgery, Stat!" Sister Agnes commanded. "Call his doctor, Mrs. Patterson!" She knelt to feel the poor man's pulse while the orderlies hurried for a gurney.

"Miss McAllister, please run and bring Father Patrick. He's having coffee in the cafeteria."

~ * ~

Mollie brought the priest and he followed the squeaky gurney down the hall. At the door to surgery, Father Patrick administered last rites while waiting for Doctor Nason, the resident on duty, to scrub.

An hour and a half later, Mr. Anderson, reeking with anesthetic, was wheeled back to his room, an oxygen tank hissing into a mask on his face. Mollie assisted the orderlies in setting up their apparatus. When Dr. Nason searched for a vein, finally resorting to one in the top of the patient's foot, she noticed the faint red outlines of her fingers where she had grasped his ankles so desperately two hours ago.

At the chart desk, Mrs. Patterson turned to Mollie. "This night turned out to be rather exciting after all. I wonder if we did him a favor. We know the poor man is tired of suffering. He just wanted to die quickly."

"You were right about his wife. You said some very wise things to him." Mollie brushed a tear from her face. "He began to have doubts when you mentioned the insurance."

"The hard part, Mollie, is that Mr. Anderson's wife doesn't know he has terminal cancer. His doctor chose not to tell her that her husband won't live more than a week or so at most. It's damn cruel to withhold information affecting the lives of that poor man's family."

"She must suspect something."

"They always do. Men are such dumb protective asses, and lots of doctors think women can't bear things like that." The nurse reached for Mollie's hand and smiled wanly. "You really saved him, Mollie, but you nearly scared me into premature labor. I was sure you were going to join him on that pavement five floors below."

Neither heard Sister Agnes creep up behind them. "You were both very brave, but God saved him." The nun smiled. "He evidently isn't quite ready for Mr. Anderson. Perhaps there is something left to be done."

The following two weeks felt like a lifetime to Mollie. Mr. Anderson's struggle made her own life at St. Anne's scarier. Adding to her concern was that Joe had been sent overseas. She decided to write him a long letter to tell him about her night duty scare. Maybe it would help pry her mind from worry about his flying missions over enemy territory. She also feared the accusations from Dr. Moore, Mr. Anderson's doctor. Furious that someone had told the family the man was dying of cancer, the doctor threatened to have her expelled from St. Anne's.

~ * ~

St. Anne's Nursing School
September 6, 1942
Dear Joe,
Great to be in contact again. You've joined the other A.P.O.s Sister Anne teases me about. You'd think I was the only girl here

who writes to servicemen! Since Ron left, letters are about the closest I get to men! I thought it was bad a year ago, but now every male in Seattle is either 4-F, too young to shave, Father Time, or on their way overseas.

I am on night duty this week and have the typewriter in the wash room writing this before I go on at eleven. My dear roomies are doing a rare stint of studying. Dorrie, especially, needs to put more time in on her books. Ever since she met Jake Swartz, her head is in the moonbeams. Graveyard shift (11 pm–7 am) is both challenging and spooky because just one Registered Nurse and two students care for a floor full of patients.

~ * ~

She told him the suicide story in two pages dotted with smears from tears that still fell when she recalled that poor man.

Mr. Anderson suffered on another week, but someone wrote his wife a note telling her in plain terms about her husband's cancerous intestines. The family had a few days to get things of life and death in order. Mrs. Anderson wrote us all a lovely note and sent a box of chocolates to the charge desk.

His doctor wasn't as charitable. He threatened to have Mrs. Patterson fired and tried to get me suspended from training. Doctor Moore took his complaints before the medical staff and got downright nasty, and even used profanity. Sister Agnes testified in our behalf while Mrs. Patterson and I chewed our fingernails. The nun got very angry with Dr. Moore for his treatment of us and for not telling Mrs. Anderson about the gravity of her husband's illness. I suspect Sister Agnes wrote the letter!

But Sister Agnes didn't see Dr. Moore catch me by the sleeve as he walked out. He snarled, "I'll be watching you, McAllister. Don't try that again!"

He gives me the shakes and I dread taking care of any of his patients.

Mrs. Patterson had some false labor pains yesterday. She still hasn't heard from her husband, an officer in the Marines somewhere in the South Pacific. Got to hurry and write a letter to Phil and to Gene Fulton, an army sergeant I met at the U.S.O. He is a nice guy, and I like him a lot, but we only had three dates before he went overseas. Take care, big brother, and send me some pictures of the scenery over there, including English girls. I'm sure you must have found at least one by now. Love, Mollie.

Nine

The knock at the door of room 401 woke Mollie and three other sleepy roommates stirred in their beds.

Sister Marie opened the door a crack and called softly, "Miss McAllister, your father is on the phone."

"My father?" Mollie pulled on her red chenille robe, tied the sash snugly, slipped into fuzzy slippers and followed Sister Marie into the shadowy hallway.

Sister Marie had blocked the elevator door open. "It's some sort of emergency, Miss McAllister. We must hurry."

Mollie's heart thudded anxiously. Joe? Dear God I hope he's okay. In Sister Marie's office, she picked up the receiver.

"Dad," she gasped into the phone, "what happened?"

"It's Mike. They think he may have polio." A long pause, then a muffled cough." I-I just put your mother on the ferry. She and Doctor Matthews are riding with Mike in the ambulance. They're taking him to Children's Hospital." His voice broke completely and trailed away.

Mollie caught the phone receiver tightly to keep her hand from shaking. She swallowed to clear her voice. "Dad? You okay?"

"Can you meet them at the hospital, Mollie? I'll be coming on the next ferry and will have to hurry to make it." He blew his nose hard. "I had to go back home to get Sally squared away or I'd be with your mother and Mike."

"I'll ask Sister Marie."

The serious-faced nun nodded vigorously.

"I'll be there, Dad."

Mollie stood in stiff silence for a minute, unable to speak her concern to the little nun holding her hand.

"They think Mike has poliomyelitis, Sister." Mollie swallowed the sudden thickness in her throat. "I was home for his birthday party just this afternoon. He was running and playing ball with the other kids, but he did complain of a headache after eating his birthday cake."

Sister Marie's hand fell to her rosary. "Hurry and dress, child. I will wake Sister Anne and have her drive you to Children's. It would not be wise to go by bus this late.

Sister Anne drove quickly through the empty streets with the street lights dimmed or shut off entirely because of the chance of air raids. The nun pulled into the emergency entrance drive and Mollie climbed from the car. "God go with you my child," the nun said.

"Thank you, Sister," Mollie called over her shoulder as she ran toward an ambulance just squealing up to the emergency door. She gnawed her knuckles, fear clutching at her chest, as she watched her mother climb from the vehicle, and the driver and doctor pull a stretcher out the rear door. Mike, with an oxygen mask over his face and a portable tank hissing at his side, lay swaddled in blankets. Doctor Matthews ran panting beside the stretcher, struggling to keep the tank level.

Mollie took her mother's hand and they hurried to keep up with the gurney as it was pushed through the entrance.

In the elevator, Mollie reached under the blankets for Mike's hand. "Here I am, Mike. I'll stay until you're better." She shot a glance at white-haired Doctor Matthews' worn face. No encouragement in his expression, only concern for his patient.

"I'm glad you came, Mollie," the doctor puffed, his face glistening with sweat. "We'll get him into a respirator quickly, and then have a talk."

Mollie and her mother watched through the hallway windows of the large room where three monstrous looking iron things made huffing sounds. Medical personnel rushed about hooking up a tangle of wires and tubes in a vacant machine and lifted Mike into it. He looked like a small frightened puppy, dark eyes searching over the various dials, his face still covered with a mask until the lung began to breathe for him. Mollie blew him a kiss.

Doctor Matthews came into the white tiled corridor after the nurses and interns got Mike hooked up to the machine everyone called an "Iron Lung."

"It isn't very good news, I fear. Mike has contracted the type of polio affecting the diaphragm, which often progresses very rapidly as you can see." The doctor lit a pipe and puffed furiously until the tobacco glowed and foul smoke spewed from it. "Have you had any training with iron lungs, Mollie?"

"No. I'm due for polio training at Harborview next month." She paused, noting a fleeting look of hopelessness on the old doctor's face. "We don't have the machines at St. Anne's."

"I know. Well, you'll get your training a month early, it seems." He leaned to a sand-filled ashtray to dump his pipe and packed another load into it.

Lou McAllister, looking pale and strained, kept her attention on watching Mike through the corridor windows.

Mollie could think of nothing positive to say and she fought fright and despair herself. Doctor Matthew's expression reminded her of physicians she had seen at St. Anne's when they faced a worried family. The doctor hadn't mentioned further paralysis and she remembered reading that it was usually evident within twenty-four hours. But the lungs and thorax were the worst place. It must be horrible to be unable to breathe without help. Tears seeped from her clenched eyelids. Dr. Matthews obviously skirted revealing Mike might...No...He wouldn't die. Not dear freckled-faced little Mike. She had pinned diapers on and treated him like a real live doll when he was a baby.

She felt Doctor Matthew's fatherly arm around her shoulders. "Come, you two. I'll get you a cup of coffee. We will just be in the way until they get blood and urine tests done and Kenney apparatus set up. While we rode over on the ferry, I started the hot packs on his legs to keep the muscles warm." His thin smile didn't fool Mollie at all.

They had barely finished their coffee when a stir at the door brought them both to their feet.

"Your son is asking for you, Mrs. McAllister," A roundish motherly looking nurse said. She nodded at Mollie. "You may come too."

After donning sterile gowns and masks, Mollie and her mother crept gingerly around the big iron lung covering Mike. His twelve-year-old body looked pathetically small through the little window in the side, and a mass of curly red hair emphasized the whiteness of the face poking from the collared opening at one end. Even Mike's freckles looked faded.

"Hi again, Mike." Mollie bent low over his head, ignoring the warning about infecting herself. She kissed him through a mask the hospital had insisted she wear in the room. He didn't wince like he ordinarily did.

"My head... hurts... awful...Mollie." Mike's voice came in funny jerks from the mechanical expiration of his breath at a trial setting of twenty-five times a minute. He squinted in the dim light.

Mollie took the cloth from his head and replaced it with an ice pack an intern handed her. "That feel better?"

"Little." Mike clenched his eyelids tight, but a large tear rolled slowly down the side of his face. "This is... an iron lung...isn't it...Mollie...I have polio...don't I? They...only...use them for polio."

Lou McAllister gasped and Mollie cast a questioning glance toward Doctor Matthews.

His calm voice answered. "Yes, Mike. You do have polio, but this machine will breathe for you so you can rest your whole body and get over it. Isn't it already easier?" He touched a small plate on the lung labeling it *Drinker-Collins*.

Mike's eyes looked less frantic and he forced words with the rhythm of the machine.

"It feels...kind'a funny... like in Scouts...when we practiced artificial...respiration...on each other."

"For awhile I guess you'll have to pretend you're Buck Rogers sleeping in a space ship. You'll get well, Mike. I promise you that." Mollie pushed the last sentence out, feeling Mike needed a shred of hope, but knowing she must hurry from the room or transfer her fright to her little brother.

A shadow darkened the doorway. Lou McAllister ran to meet Ian, whose red eyes peered over the top of a white mask. He walked softly around to Mike's head, bringing a flicker of a smile to the small freckled expanse.

"I have polio...but I'll be...okay, Dad. Mollie's...here to take...care...of me." Mike yawned from the effects of the mild sedative given after the lung began its work.

Lou McAllister smoothed his warm forehead with her hand. We'll be right outside the door if you need us, Mike."

Dr. Matthews and a resident doctor led them into a lounge area at the end of the corridor.

"He is at the most infectious stage, which is why I insisted you wear the masks and gowns," the young resident said. "Mike is a very sick boy. The next twenty-four hours will be the worst, then we should know more about the damage. We have called in our polio specialist, Doctor Millan."

Ian coughed and forced out the feared word. "Paralysis?"

"He will almost certainly have some, and we have started Kenney Packs."

"You mean the treatment Sister Elizabeth Kenney discovered. Do these packs really help?"

The resident lit a cigarette and inhaled deeply. "Yes, we believe they do. Mike could barely breathe on his own even with oxygen, but the respirator is beginning to work well for him now. Your son is in our latest model. Do you have a place to stay while you are in Seattle?"

"No," Ian said. "We will just rest here on the couches in the lounge until we see how it goes with Mike. Our daughter Mollie here, is a student nurse at St. Anne's"

"Do you know of a room we could rent for a while so Mother can stay nearby?" Mollie asked.

The doctor frowned. "I'll check, but I can't be very encouraging. Everything available is full of war workers arriving to work at Boeing." He turned to Dr. Matthews. "You can take my bed for the rest of the night, Doctor Matthews. Come and I'll direct you."

"Thanks, I need to be on the Five o'clock ferry so I can open my office on schedule." Dr. Matthews said.

Mollie and her parents settled onto wicker couches in the lounge and turned off the lamp to try to sleep. She heard her dad fidgeting on the hard cretonne-covered cushions and her mother's muffled sniffles on the couch next to his. Mollie tried to relax, knowing tomorrow would be a long day full of worry.

The odor of a freshly lit cigarette woke her at three and she heard her father's long strides echo down the hallway. Her mother sat up and stretched.

"Would you like to go with me to the chapel, Mother? I think Dad might be headed that way." She reached for her mother's hand and they moved silently in stockinged feet to the end of the corridor and through the arched door of a tiny darkened chapel. They sank to their knees beside Ian and prayed silently, hand in hand, with only the early morning noises from carts penetrating the stillness. Rising, still without speaking, the three walked into the light, blinking their eyes, then moved down the long corridor past dozens of partly opened doors. Sick children slept fitfully, or cried with pain and fear as they passed. Some lay too quiet, staring at the ceiling.

They stopped at the end of the corridor outside the glass windows of the lung room for a minute, and then crept slowly and silently past, each stealing a look at the shadowy figures working around the three respirators. Mike lay in the right corner where two masked nurses were changing his packs through the sleeved windows.

"We should try to sleep a little, or at least rest. Mike will need us to be fresh." Mollie took her mother's hand and her father followed them back to the uncomfortable couches in the sun room. Settling under the blankets the staff provided, Mollie relaxed when she heard her father's familiar and welcome snore.

A vivid dream about Joe woke her and she muffled a cry. Why Joe? Mike was the one in a desperate fight for his life, but she had clearly seen Joe walking away from a huge bonfire of some kind, and holding his arm like it was burned. Not both brothers, dear Lord. Her parents stirred.

"I hear the bedpans coming down the hall. Guess night's over," Ian said.

"Wish I had thought to bring a toothbrush," Lou said, fumbling for her purse.

"I didn't bring one either but there's a small store downstairs where you can buy them, Mom. Come to the lavatory. We can at least wash our faces. I'll go back to St. Anne's this afternoon to get some things if Mike gets better." She remembered something else. Quarter finals were today.

A slightly built gray-haired man in a spotless white hospital coat entered the sun room shortly after they returned from their quick toilet. He cleared his throat and settled into a chair.

"Your son is holding his own," he said. "His temperature is still quite elevated and he has some paralysis in his right leg, but his headache is much better and he's mentally alert. The lung is doing an adequate job with his breathing." The doctor spoke rapidly as if he didn't expect to be interrupted.

This must be the polio specialist, Mollie thought. *He has that air of assurance that usually means arrogance as well.*

"When can we see him?" Ian asked.

"As soon as the spinal tap is finished. They are doing it now." He stood. "I'm sorry, I forgot to introduce myself. I'm Doctor Walter Millan."

"What is Mike's prognosis, Doctor?" Mollie asked.

The doctor's pause lasted far too long. "Guarded is the best word. I think by tomorrow, if he continues to hold his own, I could say hopeful." He rubbed his chin as if wondering whether to say more. "Are you the student nurse?"

"Yes. I'm in the middle of my second year at St. Anne's," Mollie answered.

The three McAllisters donned sterile clothing and followed the doctor into the lung room. Mollie felt certain the pounding of her heart must be audible. Mike's freckles looked a little darker, more splotchy, but his jaws were clenched, she guessed from the remembered pain of the spinal tap needle. It was a hopeful sign that he could feel anything.

"Hi, Mike," Ian said, moving closer to the small face at the opening of the machine.

Mike tried to turn his head, but they had immobilized it tightly with the collar. "Hi, Dad."

Three pairs of eyes filled.

"Does your head still ache, dear?" Lou asked.

"A little...but not as...bad today." Tears streaked Mike's face. "Mom...I can't...feel my legs."

Lou McAllister swallowed with a little choking sound, pressing her shaking hands flat against her hips. "It's probably because they have them so tightly covered with those Kenney packs, Mike." She bent to brush her mask to his cheek, tears glistening in her eyes, and turned quickly to give Mollie her place.

"You're going to be all right, Mike, and soon be playing first base." Mollie's voice grew higher, unreliable. "They have given me permission to stay with you today. Can you tell me when the packs get cool?"

"I think so...Mollie. Maybe they... feel a little...warm now." He swallowed when the air was expelled from his lungs, waited until the next time and continued. "Sometimes... they feel...sort of... cold."

Then he did have sensation in the legs, just couldn't move them. Mollie remembered something about sensitivity to heat and cold being hopeful. She would grasp at every tiny glimmer. She must, to keep Mike's spirits up as well as her own.

Mollie surveyed the white tile. "You're getting very good at talking, but will get awfully bored looking at the ceiling. We'll have to put something interesting up there."

"I'll bring his Seattle Rainiers poster from home. Anything else you want, son?" asked Ian.

"I don't know...Dad." Mike blinked his eyes.

"I'm going home for a little while today to find someone to take care of the livestock and to stay with Sally so she can go to school. But I'll be back tonight, and your mother and Mollie will stay here with you until we know you are lots better." Ian rubbed his son's forehead gently with a work-creased hand, and then strode softly out, his expression frozen to keep from breaking down.

"Dad?" Mike called after him. "Could you...find that picture... of Casey and...bring it....when you come?"

Sure thing, son," Ian answered hoarsely.

~ * ~

Two days later, Mollie kissed Mike through the mask and he grimaced. She giggled and rumpled his hair. "You're better, Mike. You scowled when I kissed you, like always."

She read his chart and found that his temperature had dropped to normal and vital signs were stable. Doctor Millan had sounded hopeful this morning. It might be a long time, but Mike would probably breathe on his own, he said. Walking might be another matter. They were working on his legs, but it was very hard to tell about the extent of the damage. A lot depended on the will of the patient to go through the trial of learning to use the limbs.

Mollie moved from the nursing residence to a closet-like room at Children's, barely large enough for her cot. She planned to remain there until special nursing duties with Mike were over.

Her mother and father had gone home briefly to take care of immediate concerns. Several of the soldiers at the barrage balloon base, who had been raised on farms, had eagerly taken over chores of milking the cow and caring for the horse and chickens. Sally was staying with neighbors so she could continue to go to highschool. Ian and Lou came every morning and took the seven p.m. ferry home. They were showing increasing signs of strain.

Mollie fed Mike his lunch, pleased he'd learned so quickly to swallow with the rhythm of the iron lung bellows. They'd seldom needed to use the aspirator to clear his nose and throat. She gathered up his tray and entered the corridor just in time to collide with Barbara. Books slid from Barbara's arms and a glass drinking straw from Mike's tray tinkled to the tile floor.

They knelt in unison to scoop up the broken glass.

"Sister Marie sent me over with your books so you won't get too far behind, Mollie." She plunked the stack down on a table in the sunroom. "Sister said you can take the finals whenever you're ready. It's cleared with the college."

Mollie sighed. She'd feared she might need to give up nurse's training to devote full time to Mike's recovery. Doctor Millan had brought several books on polio for her to study. Her stay at Children's looked like a long term thing. "Did you happen to bring writing paper and stamps? I forgot them when I ran in to get the changes of clothing I needed."

"Right here. Couldn't carry the typewriter, though. Ron's sister offered to bring it in a couple of days. She says he's upset you haven't written him about Mike." Barbara stretched her legs out from the chair, kicked off her shoes, and wiggled her toes. "I just got off eight hours' duty and it always does bad things to my feet."

"I've been too busy to write to anyone and he has a lot of nerve talking about not writing. I've had just one letter from him since Christmas!" Mollie paced nervously, trying to think of everything she needed to tell Barbara. Life seemed so hard lately. She had too much on her mind, and was too tired to think beyond the life and death struggles in the lung room. "I should have remembered Ron's folks live nearby."

"How is Mike?" Barbara asked. "Sister acted vague about that"

"Not good, not bad. He would be...dead if it wasn't for the iron lung doing his breathing. One leg is paralyzed and his diaphragm is still not working. Several cervical vertebrae are involved. He is in a neck brace."

"Poor little kid. How is he taking the whole thing?"

"Mike's a fighter. If a secondary infection doesn't hit him, I have a feeling he'll make it." Mollie wasn't quite as sure as she sounded. Mike had a long hard battle ahead.

When her parents arrived, Mollie left them visiting with Mike and walked to her tiny room. For the duration of his critical period, she'd have to be content with a packing box desk, a metal chair and hooks in the wall for clothing. Showers were taken in the doctors' lounge and the toilets were half a block away. The only good thing was privacy something lacking at St. Anne's.

She pulled out a sheet of the writing paper Barbara had brought, and opened her fountain pen to write a post script to the letter she had started a week ago.

~ * ~

St. Anne's Nursing School

February 12, 1943

Dear Joe,

The war news is more encouraging in the two areas we hear about lately, Stalingrad and Toubruk. President Roosevelt sounded hopeful in his speech last night. You keep mentioning things the censors don't like. It's a challenge to read letters that look like checkerboards with every other word blacked out.

We are fine at home, but Mike had a slight temperature and a headache after his birthday party today. Probably just ate too much cake and ice cream that Mom saved coupons for months to provide.

I never got this letter finished, Joe. Have to write the rest with a fountain pen. By now you should have got the cable about Mike. He is better and beginning to eat well by mouth. In fact, I can hardly feed him fast enough to suit him. Eating is not easy when you have to wait for air to expel then swallow. Just try talking or swallowing on the intake of your breath and see what he had to master. With your engineering background, you probably understand better than I do how the airtight chamber works to lower air pressure and expand the lungs, then atmospheric pressure allows the lungs to release the air. The breathing rhythm is set for each individual.

Mike has his baseball posters and yours and Casey's picture on the ceiling above the iron lung. As soon as his temperature is down for twenty-four hours, I will get him a book frame so he can read. I'll also bring your radio over here.

Perhaps I tie both my brothers together, but I had the oddest dream about you the night Mike got so sick. There was some kind of fire. Love, Mollie

~ * ~.

She took out another sheet of paper to answer Ron's letter, glancing over the one page note she'd just gotten from him.

~ * ~

Dearest Mac, I'm being assigned to a carrier in the Pacific theater and will write when I know my APO address. When I tried to call you long distance today, Sister Marie told me the sad news about Mike. I wish you had found a minute to let me know because you and your family grow more important to me every day. I love you, Mac. See you someday. Wish it was tonight.

The hated nickname had become welcome.

Ten

The charge nurse tapped on the open door and called, "Mollie! Doctor Millan wants to speak with you in his office on Two South."

Mollie shoved aside the letter she was writing and followed her to the floor below.

Doctor Millan looked up from a chart where he was scrawling out orders with a gold fountain pen. "Mike has contracted a kidney infection; a rather common complication in patients who have little mobility. He's a very sick boy. I just tried to call your parents and got no answer."

Mollie's heart stopped a second. She glanced at her watch. Nine. Her mother and father were probably on their way to catch the ferry. They wouldn't be here for an hour and a half. "I'm sure they're on their way over, Doctor Millan. What can be done for the kidney infection?"

"We have Mike on massive doses of Sulfa and if he isn't allergic to the drug, he should respond rather quickly." He fumbled with a sheaf of papers on his desk. "I have also put in an emergency request for the new antibiotic, Penicillin, but there is little chance we'll get it."

"Is there something special you want me to do for Mike, Dr. Millan?"

The doctor's long pause before answering proved he searched for a positive reply.

"Keeping his spirits up is vital, and see that he drinks the quantities of fluid he must have. A glucose IV is running." Doctor Millan removed his glasses and smiled. "How are you doing with your own polio research, Mollie?"

"I've been reading all of Sister Elizabeth Kenney's, and the rest of the material you gave me. Sister Marie also sent some books from the college."

Nothing Mollie read sounded good. Poliomyelitis was not a hopeful disease at any age and especially discouraging for an active boy of twelve. She had grown accustomed to the idea Mike would probably be crippled but prayed a miracle would keep him from spending the remainder of his days on a respirator and in a wheelchair. She'd heard Polio patients say they didn't want to live under such conditions, making it plain death was a more merciful prognosis. But many did recover the use of paralyzed limbs and others like President Roosevelt, were able to stand and even walk with the aid of heavy braces.

Mollie straightened her back and turned to leave, fighting to shed her dark thoughts before she confronted Mike. She must try to find faith that he would recover from the infection now threatening his life or she couldn't make him believe it.

"One day we will find a cure for this thing, Mollie." Doctor Millan walked around his desk and draped his arm over her shoulders. "When the war is over, it will be medicine's first priority. Come. Let's go visit our favorite patient. He was asking for you when I left." He took her arm and led the way to the Iron Lung ward.

An ice pack rested on Mike's head once more. Mollie had to step around the IV apparatus at the side of the lung, dodging tubes running through pressure holes into a thin arm. She ran a finger over his cheek. It felt dry and hot.

"Mike?"

Fever glazed eyes cracked open. "Hullo...Mollie." Mike managed a weak smile. "My arm...feels wet. Can...you see...if the IV is...leaking out?"

"Aren't you getting medically wise?" Mollie patted his cheek. "Right. It is leaking. I'll call the IV nurse."

Mike frowned. "You said...you've done...IV's. Why can't...you fix it?"

Her little brother thought she could do anything better than the stern-faced IV nurse. The needle had probably hurt him worse this time. She shrugged. Spoiling him was a privilege.

"I haven't tried doing them inside the lung yet, Mike. It's tricky working through the sleeves."

"No time like the present to learn, Mollie." Doctor Millan crossed the room from one of the other lungs. "Come around here and I'll demonstrate." He reached inside and removed the tube and needle from Mike's arm. "I think we'll put this one in your ankle, Mike. The tissue in your arms is a little saturated." He opened a fresh IV pack and watched Mollie pull on rubber gloves.

Mollie fought nervousness, trying to remember each step of the procedure so recently learned. She had done several I.V.s, but none in the leg veins. Feeling for the vein in the top of Mike's ankle, she tested it with the needle. When blood appeared, she sighed with relief and quickly inserted the needle. Pulling her hands from the openings, she reached to adjust the tubing valve to start the I.V.

"Fine, Mollie. Why don't you take over all the duties of special nurse for Mike until he is better?" Doctor Millan's hand squeezed her arm when she turned to blot sweat from her face and tears from her eyes. The busy doctor hurried out.

Mollie felt a surge of pride that the prominent polio physician trusted a student nurse. He'd punctured one of her notions about specialists. Doctor Millan was not cold and arrogant like Doctor Moore. She reached back through the sleeves to move Mike's ankle to a better position. She gently tapped his shin bone. He didn't react. Was the left leg paralyzed too? "You didn't complain about the needle, Mike. Did I do such a good job you didn't feel it?"

"I felt it...but you were...a lot better...than Miss Morgan." Two big tears rolled from his dark eyes and glistened on his cheek.

Mollie sighed, relieved. Now, dear God, she prayed silently, please let him get over this infection. She pulled the thermometer from his mouth...104! The sulfa hadn't begun its work yet.

She turned away to avoid Mike's watchful expression reflected in the mirror. It had been installed over his head to enlarge the restricted views of his world from the lung with a glimpse of his roommates.

"Mollie...am I gonna...die?"

His question startled her. Mike spoke aloud the fear in her own mind. Why were children always so candid? For more than two weeks, his question had lurked in everyone's mind. One of the lung patients had died yesterday and she felt certain Mike knew. She soothed his forehead with her palm, standing behind his head so he could watch in the mirror as she spoke.

She knew her pause had been too long. "We must all die some day, but when is for God to decide. I'm only your big sister, but you know I won't let anything bad happen to you without a big fight. You've developed a bad infection in your kidneys and there is an army of white corpuscles battling it, thousands and thousands of the little things you can only see with a microscope. They will surround the enemy, those germs, and kill them if you get lots of rest, drink plenty of water, and are very patient with the needles."

Her childish way of explaining his illness was far beneath Mike's intellect and he started to protest before the lung took his voice for an instant. It reminded her of the stories she told him when he was a little boy.

He accepted her babying with a faint smile."Like the... allies...fighting the ...Japs and...Germans."

"Yep. We'll root hard for the corpuscles until they eliminate every one of those bad germ...ans!" Mollie forced a laugh with the silly pun. "But you can help by doing everything Dr. Millan and the nurses order."

Mike sighed. "Guess I...better have ...a sip of...water now."

Mollie hurried to bring the glass straw to his hot mouth, then replaced the ice pack and pulled her chair closer. Mike closed his eyes and dozed.

Lou and Ian McAllister crept softly into the room, their expressions grave and eyes red from recent tears. They nodded at the patients in the other two lungs, one a teenage girl, the other a pale boy near Mike's age.

Mike's eyes fluttered reluctantly open when Lou bent to kiss his cheek. "Hi, Mom...Guess I have...an infection...but Mollie... says my...corps pussles...will fight it...like Joe...is fighting...the Germans." He yawned. "I gotta get...back to sleep...so they can...win."

Ian gulped audibly and hurried through the door. Mollie caught up with him in the sun room where he sat, head between his hands, crying. She moved to the cretonne-covered settee and put her arms around her father's shaking shoulders.

"Mike's trying Dad, and that's hopeful. He's getting sulfa drugs and lots of fluids. Doctor Millan has put in a requisition to the government for that new drug, Penicillin. They release some for special civilian cases, he says."

Ian pulled out a large white handkerchief and blew his nose. He squared his shoulders and took several deep breaths. "Sorry, Mollie. I just couldn't take seeing that poor little guy pale and feverish again. Do they have to use a catheter on him?"

"It's the way we measure intake and output of fluids and check the urine for sediment rates and other things." Mollie patted his shoulder. "Yes, it is necessary and Mike didn't complain at all about that. What he hates are the intravenous needles."

"A terrible way to start his thirteenth year." Ian coughed, reached in his shirt pocket for a cigarette and lit it with shaking hands, drawing deeply. "Doctor Millan admitted to us that Mike is sicker than he was the day he came down with polio, that this is a bad complication. Dadgummit! We just can't lose him." His head bowed, smoke curled from a cigarette between the fingers of his right hand. He pounded angrily on the couch arm with the other one.

"I know. Oh golly, Dad." She had repressed breaking down in front of her parents and Mike for over a week. Now, fountains of tears came. When her breath stopped coming in sobbing jerks, she cuddled into her father's arms.

Ian rocked her like he had when she was a child. "I feel much better now. How about you?"

Mollie blew into the big handkerchief he offered. "Thanks, Dad. Guess I needed a good cry. Things look awful, but we must keep hoping. We owe it to Sally and Joe and Mom, most of all to Mike."

A tall shadow covered the doorway. "Can I volunteer a car, dinner, a shoulder?"

"Ron!" Mollie's voice rose to a high squeak. "I thought you were being sent overseas." Mollie hurried over to kiss him. "Dad, I'd like you to meet Ron Van Ness."

Ian shook his hand. "Good to meet you, Ensign."

"Glad to know you, Mr. McAllister." Ron turned to Mollie. "Didn't Dee tell you I called?" He paused, scratching at a spot behind his ear.

"I didn't see her when she brought the typewriter. I was with Mike in the lung room." Mollie dabbed at her eyes, wondering if Ron could guess they had been much wetter moments before. "Mike has suffered a serious setback, a kidney infection."

Ron's expression reflected genuine concern. "I'm sorry, Mollie." He stared out a window for a moment as if unsure what else he could say.

"You are on leave?"

"No, en route to my ship in Bremerton."

Mollie had forgotten her dad until she heard him clear his throat. She turned toward him. "I met Ron at that New Year's dance last year. He was in the R.O.T.C. then and went into the Navy Air Corps in June." She felt like she had at sixteen when explaining a late arrival home from a date. Why did she think it necessary to explain? She glanced at her dad, who looked approving. Ron's usually flirtatious eyes were stone serious, his jaw tight. He looked different, older. Changed somehow.

"I'm afraid you haven't caught us at our best, Ron. It's been quite a shock, Mike's polio." Ian smiled weakly and rose to greet Lou at the doorway.

Mollie hurried to introduce Ron to her mother.

"They chased me out while they did some kind of tests," Lou said. "We're very worried about our youngest son. I hope you'll excuse our apparent lack of enthusiasm about other things today, Ron."

"I stopped by, Mrs. McAllister, to extend an invitation from my mother. One of her boarders got married and moved out so she has a spare room if you would like to make use of it while Mike is so sick."

Lou smiled brightly at the suggestion. "Why, that's most thoughtful. I believe I might consider staying a few days. Ian really needs to go home to be with our other daughter as soon as we know Mike is better."

"I've missed a lot of days at the Navy yard, but until Mike gets through this crisis, I'll miss more," Ian said.

"Does your mother live nearby?" Lou asked.

"My family home is about four blocks away walking distance, Mrs. McAllister. My sister managed to save me a tank of gas and I'll be happy to drive you there when you're ready to leave."

A buzzing alarm startled them all, and Mollie leapt into the corridor to join two nurses and an orderly running toward the lung room. At the door, she clapped her hand over her mouth to stifle a scream. Clouds of black smoke rose from the motor on Mike's respirator. The bellows were not working. The orderly stooped to unhook the hand crank and the nurses wheeled in an oxygen tank, quickly clamping a mask over Mike's face.

Mollie forced her feet forward, unsure what to do. She moved to Mike. His eyes froze her. They loomed round and terrified over the oxygen mask. She placed her hand on his red curls and spoke into the mirror, trying to sound calm in spite of her racing heart. "It's okay, Mike. We're pumping the bellows by hand just like the motor does. That's why they installed a hand crank."

Dr. Millan hurried into the room and fiddled with the dials on the lung, then spoke to Mike. "We're going to slow your breathing, Mike. With the extra oxygen, you'll be fine. Don't talk. Just try to relax. An electrician is on his way with a new motor."

Mike understood and didn't struggle. He closed his eyes, and then blinked them open. There were tears at their corners.

Mollie couldn't relax until two hours later when the new motor returned the lung to normal and Mike slept. His temperature had dropped by two points. The sulfa had been working even when the lung hadn't.

She came from the ward laden with a tray, and almost tripped over Ron, leaning against the wall.

"I'm still waiting to take your mother to my house. I couldn't leave until I heard how things turned out. Is Mike okay? The doctor's in there talking to your parents." He nodded toward the sunroom. "They look pretty shook up."

"Mike raised my blood pressure, but his temperature has dropped. I have a better feeling about him." Mollie set the tray down on a cart in a small dressing room and motioned Ron to follow. Her eyes prickled. "I didn't get a chance to tell you how good it is to see you."

His lips covered hers.

"I have so much to say and so little time, Mac." He grinned. "Sorry. It slipped out. Guess Mac is the name I give you in my dreams."

"Sounds more like a truck than anything dreamy." Mollie leaned against his chest listening to his heart thump. "But I'll forgive you this time."

"I've learned something special since I've been away. I love you. Hadn't realized how much you meant until..." He released her when footsteps approached the door of the dressing room. "Can you break away when I take your mother to my house? I'll drop you back here when I drive your dad with me to the ferry."

~ * ~

After driving Lou McAllister to his mother's house, Ron returned Mollie to the hospital and parked at the curb. He stole a glance toward the dashboard clock. "Just half an hour and I need days to tell you how much I want you to be waiting when I return. Promise me you won't marry anyone until I get back, and then it'll be me."

None of his egotistical college hero attitude was evident in this serious request. She pulled out the locket he'd given her. "I've never felt like this about any other man. I'm sure I love you, but with so much war ahead of us I don't think we ought to make binding promises."

"I've spent nine months thinking about binding promises and they don't bother me at all." He stared at the steering wheel. "I've fought falling in love with you by going out with other women, lots of them, to prove you were just another girl. I ripped around acting like a horny fool, drinking too much, anything to keep me from thinking about things I was afraid I'd never see again. Things like home and you, Mac." He reached in his pocket, pulled out a pack of cigarettes and offered one to her. "Still don't smoke? Good. I started after …Might as well tell you the rest.

"Three months ago, I watched my best buddy die. We'd been together for a night on the town. Sneaked out when we knew we had a dawn training mission to practice a new flight approach to the carrier." He paused to shake ash from his cigarette. "My head felt like a hot balloon when I got into my plane. Jeff just laughed. He never got hangovers. He took off first, circled to land, missed the carrier and dived right into the ocean." An audible swallow took his voice for an instant. "I stayed up there circling until my fuel gauge pushed empty. My commander screamed into my earphones. "You can go to hell, Van Ness, but bring the friggin' plane in first!" Trying to push aside panic and remember instructions I knew perfectly the day before, I closed my eyes. All I could see was your face. It flashed like some kind of beckoning angel. I'm sure I wouldn't have made it to that ship without that image. Know the landing was marginal. I nearly lost my wings."

Mollie felt his pain so deeply, she couldn't force out words. She patted his hand like she would Mike's. Tears blurred his face when he kissed her. She slipped quickly from the car and ran up the steps to tell her dad Ron was waiting.

His tires spit gravel as the car spun into the street.

After checking on Mike, Mollie entered her own room, emotionally drained. She couldn't sleep. Pushing the covers aside, she went to her desk to finish Joe's letter.

~ * ~

St. Anne's Nursing School
March 2, 1943
Dear Joe,

The dream I had the night Mike got polio must have been some kind of eerie premonition. In it you were walking away from a fire so real I could almost feel the heat. It had to be near the time you crashed in Cornwall, probably the same day considering the time difference. Thank God you survived with only a broken arm! Take care of that Air Corps Uniform. Please don't burn any more holes in it! Mike is getting physical therapy, still has the packs, and had a slight temperature today. Probably just coming down with a cold or something.

Later, much later.

Joe— This past week had to be the worst of my life. We almost lost Mike again, but sulfa brought the infection under control. Good thing, because government bureaucrats rejected the request for penicillin. Guess they need it for the war.

Then, the motor on Mike's iron lung burned out and we had to hand pump the bellows while another one was installed. It is downright scary when machines must breathe for someone so very special. I wanted to breathe for him myself.

Love, Mollie

Eleven

Mollie returned to St. Anne's after six weeks of special nursing Mike at Children's, and found herself immediately back in St. Anne's routine.

After working the evening shift, Mollie hadn't gotten to bed until twelve, and had stuffed her pillow over her head in order to sleep through her roommates' preparations for duty. She overheard snatches of the conversation between Carmen and Barbara.

Carmen spoke. "Dorrie didn't come in last night. She's on nights the rest of the week and doesn't have duty until eleven."

"Bet she stayed out with Jake in that cheap hotel on Third Avenue," Barbara said. Half asleep, Mollie hadn't heard the girls leave. The door opened with its usual squeak and she mumbled, "Dorrie said she'd be back. Something about Jake having to be at the base by twelve. And she's got to do her case study today."

"You're right, Mollie. Jake took the bus at eleven-thirty," Dorrie said as she closed the door. "Seems awful damn cold in here. Must'a turned down the heat again to save oil. Brrr."

Mollie squinted down from her bunk. Dorrie's clothes and hair were dripping wet. "Small wonder. Why'd you take a shower in all your clothes?"

"I spent the night cuddled in that goddamn auditorium alcove. Might be June, but I haven't been so cold and wet since my mother's water broke to deliver a fat baby girl!"

"You're shaking. Better get into a hot bath right away." Mollie climbed from the upper bunk. "I'm not on duty until three. Let me help." She pulled Dorrie's sodden blouse from her back and hung it over a chair, then reached for a pink robe and bundled it around the shivering girl.

After her bath, Dorrie lay against her pillows balancing a thick book on her chest. "I'm too tired to concentrate on pediatric procedures. I have until tomorrow afternoon to finish the case study." She snuggled under the covers until a violent sneeze brought her upright to search for a handkerchief. "I'll probably have a snorty cold."

The following morning, Mollie heard Dorrie come in after night duty and fill a hot water bottle from the lavatory in the corner of their room. The springs of the bed below squeaked when she settled into it.

Dorrie's restless turning interspersed with coughing kept Mollie awake. Yawning and stretching, she climbed down from her bunk. Dorrie's plump body beneath the blanket, her winter coat, and her robe shook with her violent chills. Concerned, Mollie placed her hand on her forehead.

"You're scorching. I'm going down and ask Sister Marie to have one of the residents come and look at you."

"No! Don't do that, Mollie. I just caught a cold with a touch of croup like I always got when I was a kid," Dorrie protested through a fit of wheezy hoarse coughing.

Mollie slipped into her robe and slippers, hurried out to the elevator and pushed the button before Dorrie could finish her argument. She found Sister Marie at her office desk and quickly told her about Dorrie's symptoms.

The nun sat frowning and tapping her pencil before speaking. "Sister Anne and I took our stroll a bit later than usual night before last, near eleven. We caught a glimpse of Miss Koski and her young soldier in the auditorium alcove. Instead of sending her into the nursing residence, we decided to give her a few minutes with her young man. In these awful times, one never knows when a serviceman might be sent overseas to be maimed or to die on some bloody battlefield."

"Yes, Sister." Mollie felt tears sting her eyelids. She'd long suspected the nuns knew about the girls jamming the auditorium door.

"I ought to have checked to see if Miss Koski got back into the building. All doors to the hospital except the ambulance entry are locked at eleven-thirty. "Oh Dear. The auditorium. The new locks. Poor child but we cannot allow students to continue flaunting curfew." Sister Marie picked up the phone receiver and dialed a number. "Dr. Sandstrom, please come to the nursing residence to look at a student with a temperature. I fear the girl might be developing influenza."

Mollie waited, wondering if the nun had other plans for her.

"Go back upstairs, Miss McAllister, and prepare your roommate for the doctor's examination. He will be here in a few moments."

Mollie hurried to the elevator. She could guess what was meant by preparation. Dorrie was to be wearing a nightie, preferably a clean one!

Ten minutes later, Sister Marie tapped on the door of 401. Mollie opened it to admit the nun and the young resident who accompanied her. While the doctor examined Dorrie, she sat quietly at her desk in the corner.

Sister Marie stood watching as Dr. Sandstrom listened intently, moving the cold stethoscope over Dorrie's plump back causing her to shiver. He stopped at one spot several times. "Cough, Miss Koski. Ummm. Now breathe as deeply as you can."

Dorrie coughed violently before he finished, and reached for her handkerchief.

"You have a temperature of one hundred four." Doctor Sandstrom tapped several places and listened again. He rose and strode toward the door. "May I have a word with you, Sister Marie?"

They talked quietly, but their voices drifted from the silent corridor through the open door. "She has symptoms of pneumonia, Sister. There is fluid in the left lung and some questionable rales in the right one."

"Then she can't stay here, Doctor. I'll check to see if there's an empty bed on Two North and see to the arrangements." Sister Marie followed Doctor Sandstrom to the elevator.

Fidgeting anxiously, Mollie dressed and made her bed.

Half an hour later, Sister Marie returned, pushing a wheelchair for Dorrie.

"We must take you over to the hospital for a few days, Miss Koski." The solemn nun turned toward Mollie. "Come along with us, Miss McAllister. I am taking her to Six North."

"Your...the nuns' quarters?" Mollie asked.

"We have a small ward there for our needs when we have minor illnesses. All the hospital beds are full and Miss Koski must have quiet and constant care." She motioned Mollie to help Dorrie into the chair. "Please tell the other girls the circumstances of her illness and why Miss Koski cannot have visitors."

Mollie followed Sister Marie's swishing black habit to the sixth floor of the hospital, feeling strange pushing the wheelchair past surgery and the long term care unit to the nuns' quarters. A doctor scrubbing turned to stare. Doctor Moore! The vision of Mr. Anderson's frail body returned to haunt. She shivered, hoping the haughty doctor hadn't recognized her, and hurried through the double door leading to the north end of the floor.

Twenty nuns occupied rooms in this section. Mollie wheeled Dorrie behind Sister Marie, past a small chapel, and a solarium furnished with wicker chairs, plants, and two sewing machines. Several nuns worked at the machines mending hospital linen.

She pushed the wheelchair into a room partitioned into four small cubicles. Sister Marie pulled back the white covers on the bed nearest to the door, and motioned for Mollie to help Dorrie from the chair.

Dorrie crawled onto the hard mattress, shuddering violently when her skin touched the cold sheets. She hadn't said a word since Doctor Sandstrom finished his examination. A tight dry cough shook her body. She stared at her surroundings trance-like.

Sister Marie opened a closet door, took several hot water bottles from a shelf, and began to fill them at a lavatory in the corner of the room.

Mollie pulled a worn woolen blanket from the foot of the bed and draped it over the radiator under the window. "We'll soon have you nice and cozy, Dorrie."

Like a fussing mother, Sister Marie piled hot water bottles around Dorrie and tucked the blankets under her neck. "Please stay awhile if you don't have to be in classes, Miss McAllister. I must get back to my office."

After the nun's jingling rosary echoed down the hall, Dorrie turned to Mollie with fear-widened eyes. "What's wrong with me, Mollie? Is it pneumonia? It must be or they wouldn't send me up here."

"They haven't done your blood work yet, or taken X-rays. If you do have pneumonia you're in a good place for prayers, Dorrie." Mollie patted the shivering figure under the covers. "Are you getting a little warmer?"

"I feel like I might by tomorrow. It must be like a furnace under these blankets." Dorrie rolled over and tried to sit up, then sank back to her pillow. "Jeepers. Why did they have to put me up here? Jake won't be able to visit me!"

Mollie smiled. "It's the only vacant place in the hospital except the sunroom on the men's chronic disease floor and you wouldn't get much rest or warmth there. You'd have to listen to Mr. Sturgess wheeze with asthma and that old skid row burn victim beg for booze." She thought about the crowded maternity floor where two new mothers' beds were in a corridor. The ten solariums had been in use as patients' rooms for a year. "Anyway, do you want to expose Jake to your germs?"

"He could wear a mask," Dorrie mumbled, pulling the blanket tightly to her chin.

Steps and another clicking rosary echoed in the corridor and Sister Ruth appeared in the doorway. She carried a lab tray."I will need to take blood and urine samples, Miss Koski. Please bring a bed pan, Miss McAllister." The super efficient nun in charge of the laboratories and surgery tied a rubber tourniquet around Dorrie's right arm and tapped a raised vein.

Dorrie grimaced when the needle penetrated, and shivered when the bedpan met her ample buttocks. "Do you have to have a catheterized specimen, Sister Ruth?"

Raising an eyebrow, Sister Ruth replied crisply. "As you should know, Miss Koski, we need a sample clear of vaginal secretions."

Sister Ruth's icy blue eyes under the starched white head band made Dorrie turn a shade paler. After placing the specimens on her tray, Sister Ruth rustled out, her starched white habit crackling down the hall.

Dorrie coughed to clear her throat. "Old rigid Ruthie came to save me. Damn, why didn't they send one of the nurses?"

"'Cause you're up here in their quarters, and they **are** nurses, practically every nun at St. Anne's is a registered nurse. Sister

Ruth's okay if you're careful to follow procedures to the letter...her own style of procedures."

Mollie grimaced, wondering why the nun needed to sound so cold and superior. All the girls and most of the interns were in awe and not a little fear of Sister Ruth. The needle of tension triggered her memory of Doctor Moore's animosity. She always felt like wincing when she saw the man. Sister Ruth had the same effect on the students.

Dorrie forced a little grin. "She didn't need the catheter. She could'a scared the shit out of me!"

Mollie laughed. "Sister Ruth's not a fire-breathing dragon. She's a good-looking woman beneath that cap."

"God, you couldn't prove it by the way she acts. You ought'a know, I guess. Didn't you have her for a patient?"

Mollie nodded. Her encounter with Sister Ruth had been three months ago when the nun was a patient on the surgical floor after an emergency appendectomy. After being assigned Sister Ruth's care, she had entered the nun's room quaking with fear. Her first shock had been to find that Sister Ruth's short curly hair, the color of fresh scrubbed carrots, was not covered by her cap. On the nun's bedside stand were creams and lotions advertized in magazines for soft and youthful skin. Evidently the nun feared aging just like other women nearing thirty-five. When she bathed Sister Ruth's slender curvy figure, she couldn't help thinking the nun would bring whistles from the guys if she wore street clothes.

Mollie also discovered that Sister Ruth's surgical incision had looked just like every patient's and needed the same care. She recalled that the nun had watched every nursing detail as if grading an exam, as arrogantly aloof without her stiffly starched habit as she appeared just now in formal surgery white. The nun had spoken only when necessary and Mollie couldn't remember a thank you or a smile. Mollie still puzzled why she, not one of the Catholic girls, had drawn her for a patient.

Sister Ruth returned with a wheelchair to take Dorrie to X-ray. She and Mollie bundled the feverish girl in blankets for the draughty trip. By the time they returned, Dorrie was exhausted from the effort and they had a struggle to get her back into the bed.

Mollie stayed past the lunch hour and her stomach rumbled noisily because she had also missed breakfast. Sister Marie appeared with Doctor Sandstrom at one-fifteen.

"The X-rays show double pneumonia, Dorrie." Doctor Sandstrom said soberly, leaning over the mound in the bed to be sure she heard. "We're going to place you in an oxygen tent to give your lungs as much rest as possible," He nodded toward Sister Ruth entering the room wheeling an intravenous standard and carrying a bottle of glucose. "And get you on IV's and sulfa.

"I have called your parents, Miss Koski," Sister Marie said."They'll be over to see you tonight."

Dorrie's eyes widened. "You'll allow them to come up here, Sister?"

Sister Marie nodded, "Of course, dear."

A tear made its way down Dorrie's cheek. She turned to the doctor. "I could die of pneumonia, Doctor Sandstrom. and I'm only twenty years old!"

"I think we caught it in time, Dorrie. I don't want you worrying about anything but getting well quickly. You'll have lots of rest, no distractions, no smoking." Doctor Sandstrom's expression was not as encouraging as his words.

Sister Marie turned to Mollie. "Miss McAllister, I have arranged for you to stay and special Miss Koski for a few days. You may sleep in the bed next to hers tonight. I suggest you eat lunch. I ordered a tray for you."

That evening, after Dorrie drifted into sleep, Mollie hurried over to the nursing residence to tell the other girls about Dorrie's illness. She quickly packed the things needed for her night in the cloistered surroundings of Six North.

During the two weeks Mollie worked as a special duty nurse, she saw Dorrie close to death several times. In addition to pneumonia, she developed an allergy to the sulfa drugs, then a kidney infection reminiscent of Mike's. The nuns, especially the intimidating Sister Ruth, whose room was right next door to Dorrie's, assisted in her care. They and Mollie watched their patient twenty-four hours a day.

Dorrie's illness reached a point of crisis. Mollie took the half hour while her patient went to surgery for a lung tap, to go to the hospital chapel. Somehow, she felt more comfortable there than in the one in the nuns' quarters. She gasped when a figure knelt beside her. "Jake?"

He turned to face her. "The very one. I just heard about Dorrie. Is there any way I could see her?"

"I don't know, but follow me and I'll ask." She led the corporal to the nursing residence and tapped on Sister Marie's door.

Sister Marie glanced up from the clutter of papers on her desk to face them. "Yes?"

"This is Corporal Jacob Swartz, Sister. He wonders if he might see Dorrie."

Jake twisted his cap and spoke haltingly, "I-I just heard Dorrie...Miss Koski might not... I didn't know about her being sick because orders sent me away for two weeks. I hurried to the hospital as soon as I could."

"You are her very special friend, aren't you?" Sister Marie rose from her chair and smiled. "Miss Koski has just returned from surgery where her left lung was drained. She is gravely ill. We are praying for her recovery, Corporal Swartz."

"If God sets any priority to Jewish prayers, Sister, mine are at the top of the list," Jake said, his Adam's apple jerking hard, a weak smile struggling to curve his mouth.

Mollie stood silent as Sister Marie scanned Jake, who was nervously shifting his feet. His rather plain face showed no impudence. Like everyone at St. Anne's who knew Dorrie well, he wore a look of deep concern.

Sister Marie spoke at last. "She has been asking for you, Corporal Swartz, and hoping you would come. One moment please."

The nun dialed a number and spoke a few words, then came around her desk and took both of Jake's hands for a moment. "Come, son, I will take you to see Miss Koski, but only for a few minutes. She is in an oxygen tent and won't be able to do much talking."

Mollie followed Jake and Sister Marie, her black habit swishing along the corridor. Jake's eyes were set straight ahead, ignoring the surroundings and the stares from the scrub nurses near surgery. He blinked when she unlocked the doors to Six North, but remained silent as the nun led him into the little clinic.

He drew in his breath sharply when he saw the hissing dark green oxygen tank. He and Sister Marie squeezed past it to Dorrie's bedside. Dorrie appeared to be sleeping, eyes closed and skin deathly pale. A rattle echoed after each anguished breath.

Sister Marie took one of Dorrie's hands. "Someone special is here to see you, Miss Koski."

"I'm dreaming again." She blinked. "Is it really you, Jake?" she whispered, closing her eyes and turning her head away. "You can't be here. I must have died."

"You aren't dreaming, baby, and your good St. Peter hasn't opened the gates to Heaven yet. I was sent away on maneuvers, but I came as soon as I found out." He took her hands and kissed them, his voice coming through in a hoarse croak. "I love you so much, Dorrie. You just have to get well."

Dorrie took a short quick breath, the only kind she could, and cleared her voice with a shallow cough. "I love you too, Jake. You must know that by now. I fell hard for you that first date... In a week, I'll be out of here, Jake." She squinted through the oxygen tent at the black figure of Sister Marie, who smiled without showing surprise, and moved to the end of the bed.

Jake and Dorrie stared at each other, oblivious of Mollie and Sister Marie standing silently. After a few minutes, the little nun reached out and pulled gently on the soldier's sleeve. "We must not tax her, Corporal. It is time to leave."

Jake squeezed Dorrie's hands, blinking back tears. "I'll be back tomorrow, Dorrie. I'll tell the Colonel it is a hardship or something."

This statement brought a bright smile from Dorrie. "I won't be going anywhere. Bye, Jake." She lifted a hand to wave as the door closed.

~ * ~

A week later, though relieved that Dorrie was recovering, Mollie felt unhappy over her own feelings. She needed to force her pen to write cheerful things to Joe. She realized her depression was because Ron had been gone three months and she had received just one short note. The postcard picture showed palm trees lining a sandy beach in Hawaii. The postmark was APO San Francisco. So far, there had been no answers to her letters.

She opened her typewriter to write to Joe. At least she heard from him regularly.

~ * ~

St. Anne's Nursing School
June 15, 1943
Dear Joe,
Defeating the Germans in Tunisia is good news, and according to Dad, we're getting the Aleutians mopped up. He listens every spare minute to the radio and reads two daily newspapers, so I rely on his assessment of how the war is going. I'm afraid their phone bill gets high because of our talks, but Dad and Mom usually do the calling.

Remember me telling you about some of the gals sneaking in through the auditorium and Carmen getting caught? Well, Dorrie and Jake figured out a new way to jam that door, until two weeks ago when Sister had the locks changed again. Dorrie got shut out and spent the whole night in the rain and caught double pneumonia. She nearly died and I'm sure Jake's visit saved her life. Dorrie improved steadily from that day until she was able to leave the hospital. Funny, but she didn't go home for her recuperation. I don't think things are too happy there. The only blessing of the episode is Dorrie lost fifty pounds. You would be the first to say she's a real knock out! I always suspected there was a beautiful girl hidden under all that fat. But Dorrie has no idea she's attractive. She has eyes only for Corporal Jacob Swartz. I do think it is time she bought some new clothes. She keeps borrowing mine.

Love, Mollie

Twelve

Four months had passed since Mike's polio complication from kidney infection. Mollie visited him as often as possible. Today, she caught a bus to Children's, and took the elevator to the Iron Lung room. The Lone Ranger's *Hi Ho Silver* filled the ward. Mike had the radio volume turned far too loud. She reached to twist the little knob.

"Stop it, Mollie. Peggy and Lyle are listening too." Mike turned his head to face her. "Wait a second. When they play that music, it's almost over."

Mollie sighed noisily, feeling like a big sister again seeing Mike so much better that he could argue about the radio. He moved his head, a very good sign, and healthy skin color darkened his freckles. She touched his forehead. Cool. No fever, thank God. A remnant of Mike's old mischievous grin crossed his face.

She chucked him under the chin and he winced. She had him at a disadvantage. He couldn't duck or squirm away with his arms inside the lung.

"Okay, little brother, out with It. You're ready to burst."

"I made Doctor Millan let me tell you. They got me out of the lung and hooked me to one of the new portable respirators. It felt good to sit in a chair." Mike's eyes brimmed with moisture. He twisted his head from Mollie's kiss.

"That's keen, Mike. I guess I've been expecting something like this because they've been turning the lung off for short periods like right now."

"Yeah. Longer the last few days."

Miss Morgan rattled in with the thermometers and turned on the lung again. "He's getting awfully ornery with his new privileges. If he keeps it up, we may just have to expel him from this glorious institution."

Mollie grinned. "If he keeps getting better, Miss Morgan, they might even make him go back to school."

Mike laughed, unable to hide his excitement. "I can wait... a long time ...for school." But his eagerness showed. "Gotta learn...to walk again first... and to breathe...on my own...without Gertie...Doctor Millan says."

"Gertie?"

He pointed to the apparatus on a table in the corner."That's...what everyone calls...the respirator...Gaspy Gerty."

Mollie said a silent prayer of thanks that the first step, learning to breathe, was becoming a reality. Walking might take years, not months. She followed Miss Morgan out of the room. "How were his muscle responses?"

The nurse smiled. "I would say encouraging. Mike tries so hard. I don't believe I've ever seen a kid work like that on physical therapy. He's an inspiration for the other kids in the lung room."

Mollie knew better than to think about a time for Mike's release. This was his first day out of the lung. He would need a lot more strength, and many therapy sessions before they dared hope for that goal.

Shrugging her shoulders, she forced herself to relax. Couldn't allow anything to dampen Mike's happy mood. She kissed him goodbye and walked to the bus stop, feeling torn by mixed emotions. Mike's improvement and Ron. Since their brief encounter in March she'd received only a postcard with palm trees on the front and a brief written message. He'd acted so changed, so serious when he asked her to wait for him. War robbed carefree attitudes from a lot of guys. Was Ron angry because she hadn't exactly said yes?

She slipped a token in the box and sat staring out the dirty bus window. No letters had arrived from Phil for a couple of months either. She knew there was a difference in the way she felt about the two men. For Phil there was deep concern she shared for all the GIs serving in the war. Nothing, even tears, dislodged an ache beneath her ribs when she thought of Ron.

She pushed her own despair aside and worked at cheering the servicemen at the USO dance. Later, when she and the other girls entered the nurses' residence, they crowded into the elevator, chattering noisily about alliances made at the dance. The ancient lift sometimes balked when too heavily loaded, and the nursing students considered it part of the institution and didn't worry about its safety. At the third floor, Mollie and Barbara pushed toward the front of the elevator. The chattering doors squeaked open, followed by a thudding sound.

"Eeee," Barbara squealed as she stumbled over Gloria's prone shape.

"She's really knocked out," Mollie said, bending over her and holding the elevator door open with a foot. "Help me move her to the john."

Mollie, Barbara, Shirley and Ginger struggled to carry Gloria's limp body down the hall and into the shower. Mollie removed the girl's clothes while Barbara turned on the water.

Gloria made gurgling choking sounds as the cool water cascaded over her head, soaking her slightly askew salon hairdo. "God damn shit asses!" she spat, struggling to free herself from the arms holding her tightly.

"At least it can speak. If you can call that speech," Barbara grumbled, her own hair wet and tangled and her jacket sleeves soaked.

"Stop it, Gloria!" Mollie shook the struggling girl hard. "We have to sober you up. Do you want Sister tripping over you when she makes her rounds tonight to see if we are all tucked into our little beds?" Mollie, standing half inside the shower, removed her own sodden sweater.

The four girls concentrated on getting Gloria to her room without waking the rest of the floor. They removed the rest of her clothing. She fumed, threatened, and got sick all over the bed. Shirley and Ginger, shielding their noses from the odor, headed for their room next door.

"Let's get this icky mess cleaned up, Barb." Mollie mopped the floor and mattress with wet towels. "Wish we could get her a clean sheet.

"Get out! Just leave me alone, dammit!" Gloria mumbled.

"Talk about appreciation!" Barbara, grimacing her disgust, bundled the smelly towels to carry to the laundry chute.

When Gloria began to snore, the girls crept out crossing fingers that St. Anne's richest student nurse would stay there.

"She'll sleep it off by morning. I don't know why, but she never seems to have a hangover," Mollie whispered.

"Yeah, and I hope Sister Marie doesn't decide to inspect her room tonight," Barbara mumbled, turning the knob on their door.

"Gloria's going to kill herself if she doesn't stop drinking that stuff, Barb. Can you imagine how much alcohol she must have guzzled to pass out like that?" Mollie lay back on her pillow, unable to fall asleep.

"I haven't the slightest notion. It takes only a tiny bit to make me feel awful woozy." Barbara rose on an elbow. "What can we do to help her, Mollie? Gloria's a nice girl when she isn't drunk. She's not stuck up or anything even though she has reason to be."

"I know. And smart too. As much as she drinks, she keeps her grades passing and manages to do her floor work," Mollie paused a long minute. "She really likes nursing."

"I didn't want to believe it, but there's a rumor Gloria takes Seconal sometimes," Barbara said. "I wonder if she took some along with the liquor tonight."

"I hear they're checking on altered drug counts. We have to squeal on her, Barb, while there's still time."

"Tell who? Sister Marie?"

"Yes, tell her. She'll know who else should be told and who can help. If Gloria keeps taking those little red sleeping pills along with her liquor, she'll end up in the morgue. I hope it isn't already too late to help her." Mollie turned on the light and reached for her pharmacology book to look up the effects of such a combination. "It says Barbiturates can be deadly combined with alcohol and continued use of Seconal is addictive."

"Then we'd better go to Sister Marie first thing tomorrow morning," Barbara mumbled from her pillow.

"Not just you and me though, we'll get all the gals who know about this, anyone who isn't on duty. Numbers of us may help." Mollie closed the book and turned off the light, but didn't sleep very well.

After breakfast, Mollie, Barbara, Shirley and Ginger, and another close friend of Gloria's, Pinky Olson, crowded into Sister Marie's office.

The nursing director wore her usual tranquil mask when they told her about Gloria, but Mollie knew the petite nun much better since Dorrie's pneumonia episode and noted a slight narrowing of her eyes when she heard their story.

Sister Marie silently tapped a pencil on a green felt desk pad before speaking. "Thank you for your concern about Miss Rollins, girls. You are right. It is a very serious matter and something must be done immediately. Please go back to your own duties. I will see to it."

~ * ~

After the girls left the room, Sister Marie returned to her desk. She sat fingering her rosary several minutes before picking up the phone to call first, Father Patrick, then Gloria and her parents. Her office grew crowded when they all arrived two hours later.

Alton Rollins, Gloria's father, fidgeted until Sister Marie placed an ashtray on her desk in front of him so he could smoke. He mumbled a thank you.

Father Patrick cleared his throat to speak. "We called you together to discuss a serious problem, something I fear we have all been ignoring. Gloria is unable to control her use of alcohol. She has admitted that to herself and to me and has agreed to attend meetings of others with the problem."

Gloria's mother sniffled into a handkerchief. "Why, baby? Why did you drink more than you could handle?"

Her chin rising as if supported by a puppet string, Gloria obviously fought for control. Her head and hands shook and tears oozed from clenched eyelids."I don't know, Mother."

Mrs. Rollins continued, "Father Patrick, you can't mean that group of derelicts who meet to get dried out!"

"That isn't the term I would call these men and women, Mrs. Rollins. Many are business people, doctors, nurses and a few are of the clergy." Father Patrick reddened slightly and glanced at Sister Marie. "I am aware of several priests and nuns."

"Isn't there some other alternative? A private hospital, a sanitarium for people with this problem, Father Patrick?" Alton Rollins leaned forward, his voice, usually full of authority, wavered slightly.

"There are several such places. Yes, an excellent one in Tacoma, I believe," Father Patrick said." But they also rely on group therapy meetings as a follow up. Research indicates that alcoholism may be permanent, perhaps incurable, Mr. Rollins."

"How could this happen to our little girl?" Mrs. Rollins asked. "Gloria has everything, beautiful clothes, car of her own, anything she wants."

Sister Marie fought to keep her face from revealing her thoughts, wondering if Father Patrick knew she and Alton Rollins were cousins. Alton had inherited their grandfather Rollins' lumber business. He had met and married Angela Charter, from a prominent eastern family right after graduating from Harvard. The couple had been caught up in a constant social whirl and practiced a liberal attitude toward child rearing. The Rollins trust provided generous financial support to St. Anne's. Since entering the Sisters of Charity, Sister Marie had contributed her own income from the trust to St. Anne's scholarship fund.

Sister Marie had watched Gloria and her brother grow up where alcohol was readily available and parents weren't. Alton and Angela meant well and loved their children, but she suspected they were too busy with golf, bridge clubs, and business to really talk to Gloria. The girl had many good characteristics. Always friendly, she never acted snobbish or arrogant. Praise God the girls in her class were concerned enough to report the seriousness of her condition this morning. She decided not to tell Alton about the Seconal right now.

Alton and Angela Rollins faced each other, their expressions reflecting shock that their daughter was so deeply troubled. Alton shrugged and raised pleading eyes toward his cousin.

Sister Marie pulled a folder from a drawer. "Some people cannot drink alcohol without becoming addicted. Gloria happens to fall into that category. I've gathered brochures about a small, but very successful Catholic sanitarium. I fear it may be rather expensive."

Angela Rollins turned toward her daughter. "Rainbow. That sounds rather nice, doesn't it, Gloria?"

Gloria ran her tongue over her lips and swallowed audibly. "Guess so, Mother. It's fine with me."

~ * ~

An hour later, Mollie heard Gloria's and her mother's high heels click down the corridor to the elevator. She and Barbara moved to the window to watch Mr. and Mrs. Rollins load the weeping girl and her baggage into the Packard and drive away.

Mollie shook her head. Tears stung her eyes. "Poor Gloria. I hope she'll forgive us one day, but I'm sure we did Gloria a favor even if she doesn't."

"I wonder if Sister Marie knows Gloria got her liquor right here at St. Anne's. Or suspects it's that pure stuff? Did you see her wince when we told her about the Seconal?" Barbara said, opening the window to the warmth of July.

"Know what, Barb? Sister Marie, Sister Anne and Sister Ruth find out about everything that goes on at St. Annie's." During Dorrie's illness, Mollie had gained a new respect for the Order. Being a Protestant, she had not appreciated or understood the sacrifices of this dedicated group of women, many of them quite young. Most were registered nurses, some with degrees in both education and nursing. She sighed, thinking Mother Superior, the hospital director, had a Master's in Business and Nursing, yet was the one nun besides Sister Ruth, who acted cold and unapproachable to the student nurses. Even Sister Anne and Sister Marie walked stiffly in her presence, yet Mother Superior practiced the same selfless attention to human suffering as the rest of the nuns when she dealt directly with patients.

Mollie remembered a rare look of tenderness on Mother Superior's stern face when she visited Dorrie during her pneumonia crisis. It seemed doubtful Dorrie would have been as well treated had she been a student housed in a regular college dormitory. And poor Gloria would probably have been expelled, or worse; allowed to continue her drinking and self-destructive actions until it was too late until she died.

~ * ~

St. Anne's Nursing School
July 6, 1943
Dear Joe,

Being an upper classman has benefits. I now live on the third floor with just Barbara for a roommate. Gloria Rollins' room is next door and she has been drinking heavily and we talked to Sister Marie. Her parents sent her to a sanitarium in Tacoma. We got a letter from Gloria today, she says she is doing fine, getting counseling from a battery of psychiatrists and hoping to return to St. Annie's by September. The Sisters dried up the supply of alcohol, and placed strict regulations on the pharmacy reports. Besides that, a certain resident got kicked out of St. Annie's. The last I heard he had joined the Army Medical Corps. Hope they watch for signs of alcohol abuse and that he never has an occasion to treat anyone I know.

It is late and I am under my blankets with a flashlight finishing this, so excuse the scribbling. The best news is Mike. He is acting like our little brother again, spoiled and ornery. I cried when I saw him sitting up in a chair by himself with that puffing bellowed thing he must wear. Now he can read his comic books and grumble about the lessons his teacher sent over.

My first twenty-dollar stipend from the Cadet Nurse funds granted by Congress came today. The program provides tuition, books, and twenty dollars a month. A real life saver for me! Sister Marie says we'll get dress uniforms as well as new St. Anne's whites. After two years, mine are wearing out. I used a good part of the first check to buy new white shoes and stockings, the ugly things.

Love, Mollie.3

Thirteen

The Cadets

Mike grinned. "Gosh, Mollie, you look like a general or something, like that French one De ...whatever his name is. You know, that tall guy who's always in the papers."

"I hope my nose isn't as long as General de Gaulle's, Mike!" Mollie leaned to rumple his hair. Mike had been moved from the iron lung and into a ward next door. Today, he sat in a wheelchair, now able to breathe pretty well on his own, but the portable respirator was still strapped to his chest. A physical therapist helped him with daily exercises and reported improvement. "How are you doing this week, Mike?"

"Fine. I want to go home, but Doctor Millan says I'll have to wait until I can get along without this thing." He tapped the respirator.

Mollie noticed a set of crutches near the door and decided to wait for Mike to tell her about them. "And how long can you breathe without Gaspy Gerty?"

Mike shrugged. "I think I could be without Gerty if they would only let me try. I go outside every day now, and I'm trying to learn to walk with crutches."

Mollie brought them over to his wheelchair. "That's wonderful. Can you demonstrate for me?"

"I guess it'll be okay. The nurses make me leave Gerty on while I work with them. They're afraid I won't get enough air or something." Mike turned on the respirator, pushed the wheelchair footrest aside, and with shaking hands, grasped the crutches and wobbled to an upright position.

Mollie watched, her eyes filling, while he took a couple of halting steps, dragging his right foot and struggling to keep his slipper on. She bent to replace it.

"The crutches are a little tall for you, Mike. Let me fix them." She unscrewed two little nuts and lowered the arm rest half an inch. "That better?"

"I think so. I'll get the hang of it pretty soon." Mike struggled back to the chair and sat down hard, looking more exhausted than he pretended to be.

"I have to leave you now, Mike. I'm going home for the weekend. It's the first time since you got sick. Anything you want me to bring back?"

When tears formed in his eyes, Mollie turned away, almost wishing she hadn't told him.

Mike made a funny face, wrinkling his nose like there was a bad smell in the room. "I really miss Casey and dogs aren't allowed in hospitals." He nodded toward the iron lung room. "There's a new kid in my old Iron Lung. He's only eight. Heard them say he's real sick."

Mollie had noticed. The blonde boy was a lot smaller than Mike, and probably with a slimmer chance of recovery. She squared her shoulders in an effort to dispel the gloom settling over her previous high spirits. Poliomyelitis gave her a feeling of total helplessness. It was such an awful disease, a crippling, maiming thing. So many lives were lost and ruined forever by a germ of some kind, elusive even under the most powerful microscopes.

As Mollie hurried to catch a ferry home, she decided on a specialty. Discouraging as sick children were for medical staffs, she'd be a children's nurse when the war was over. She caught a glimpse of her figure in the ferry terminal window, and straightened her shoulders. She'd get used to the new uniform, or at least be less self-conscious about wearing it. Sailors on the dock aimed a chorus of whistles toward her when she boarded the streamlined ferry *"Kalakala."*

She felt her face flush as two marines in the coffee shop stood at attention and saluted. She grinned. "Relax guys. I'm not an officer...yet."

"That's a relief. Then what are you? What uniform is that?" The tall one asked. "We thought you might be one of those Limey girls from the *Warspite* or something."

"I didn't know there were girls serving on the ships of the British Navy," Mollie said.

"We heard there are. Wow! Whatever you're in must really be important," the other Marine said.

"I'm a member of the Cadet Nurse Corps in training at St. Anne's Nursing School. Next June, if I don't flunk out, I'll be a registered nurse and an officer in either the Army or the Navy Nurse Corps. This is my first whole weekend home in more than six months." She grinned. "Join me for a cup of coffee and a doughnut to celebrate?"

"You bet and it's our treat." One scrambled to open the door, another to secure a table where they could watch the skyline of Seattle as the ferry pulled away.

Mollie needed to use all her wiles to keep from accepting dates with the marines, or inviting them home. She wanted to be alone with her family this weekend. A sense that something unsettling was about to happen gnawed inside, like the time she dreamed about Joe when he was in the B-17 crash.

While waiting for her father to pick her up at the terminal in Bremerton, she bought a paper. Rome had fallen to the Germans, yet the Italian Navy had surrendered to the Allies, a little puzzling. Bitter fighting raged all over Sicily. She felt thankful Joe was in England. A mixture of fear and curiosity made her scan the obituary column. "Oh, no!" Tears nearly obscured the black heading. *Sergeant Philip Edgar Jackson killed in South Pacific action.* She'd call Phil's folks when she got home. It would be hard.

Her mother met her with a hug. "I fear you won't see much of Sally. She has a serious boyfriend. You probably remember Dave, the Army Sergeant from the Barrage Balloon group stationed here last spring."

"He won't be a non-com very long. Dave's going to Officer's Candidate School next week," her father said. He poured a cup of coffee and sipped it with relish. Now strictly rationed, it was the commodity he missed most except for an occasional shortage of his favorite brand of cigarettes.

Mollie handed him the paper she had turned to Phil's memorial notice. "Guess that's why I haven't heard from him. Golly, Dad," she leaned to kiss him, "it's awful to read about Phil's death. But my first thought when I saw the notice was thanking God it wasn't Joe."

"Mine too, Mollie. I suppose that's selfish. Phil was their only son," he said with a break in his voice.

~ * ~

Sunday evening, Mollie's heart leapt when she found a letter from Ron waiting in her postal box. Hurrying to her room, she flipped on her desk lamp and opened the V-mail letter, sadness and anxiety fading as she read the two closely written photographed pages. It eased a little the bad news about their classmate, Phil Jackson she'd have to report to Barbara.

Barbara burst into the room, her eyes red from crying. She fished in her purse to pull out a crumpled telegram.

Mollie guessed its message before reading it. Barbara's brother had been killed in action in Sicily. She moved to enfold her friend in her arms and they shared tears.

Barbara blew her nose and tried to speak in a hoarse tone.

"Alan had just turned nineteen. Dad tried everything to keep him from joining after he graduated from high school but he wouldn't listen. Alan didn't have to go overseas, being an only son, they say."

"Like Phil Jackson... "Mollie reached in her purse and pulled out Phil's death notice, her mouth trembling at Barbara's gasp. She stepped to the window to stare thoughtfully at the city lights.

"They'd have us think they don't send only sons overseas." Barbara's voice grew bitter. "If I had a son, I'd cut off his trigger finger or something!"

"No, you wouldn't. You'd be proud he served his country. Most of Alan's class joined. Sally said a lot of the boys talked to recruiters and went into various branches of the service before they graduated this June. And they're taking men who are nearly forty and have wives and children."

For over a month Mollie had felt unsettled. Strange perceptions that haunted and worried her came unbidden, mysterious premonitions of dreadful things. If the feelings forecasted good news like the end of the war, she wouldn't mind. Were good ones less intense? That must be the difference. She'd need to concentrate on thinking positive thoughts and in these times that grew difficult.

"I must have taken the ferry right after you did tonight. Sister Marie sent me home right after Dad called. He's taking it awfully hard," Barbara shrugged, "and Mother cried so much I couldn't make any sense of the conversation when I finally got through to her in California."

"Alan died in Sicily?" Mollie knew he served under General Patton, one of the toughest and most disciplined divisions in the army. Some feared the General, and he was nicknamed *Old Blood and Guts.*

"Yes. Near a place called Messina. I told you about him being a tank gunner. Mother and Dad will probably get a personal note from General Patton commending Alan for heroism, the notice said. That made us feel a little better. You know it's really something for a great important general to take time to write to an ordinary family." Barbara buried her face in her hands, the reminder renewing her tears.

Mollie felt guilty for her happiness in receiving Ron's letter. She pulled it from her desk drawer and glanced over it once more. It was full of love and vows he'd write every day from now on. The envelope had an APO stamp. So now she would face daily worry about two men close to her heart.

Her face heated when she reread the letter. He made love to her in detail on paper, leaving little to her imagination. She smiled, wondering what the censors thought about that. Anything of secret nature would be edited out like it was in Joe's. Remembering the weekend's sad news, she stuffed the letter back into the drawer.

Barbara managed a weak smile. "Ron must have written another of his *Banned in Boston* ones huh?"

Mollie nodded. "This one would be banned almost anywhere!"

If two people could fall in love by mail, she and Ron had. None of the other men she'd dated, or any of the current guys she met at the USO, came close to her growing passion for the handsome ensign. She worked to push the emotion away, still trying to deny being selfish enough to love in these terrible times. Like she had told him when he was home, it was better to wait out the duration to make serious commitments. There were too many chances for heartbreak, too many killed and maimed young men to make families like Phil's and Barbara's grieve.

"In nine months, we'll be in the service ourselves, maybe overseas in a year," Mollie said. "I'm going to take a shower, then write Joe a note. I haven't heard from him in more than a month. Neither have Mom and Dad. We're a little worried."

"It's the bad news that comes fast, Mollie." Barbara moved to the closet and hung up her clothing. "Wait a second and I'll join you. I want to be with someone tonight, even in the shower room."

"I forgot to tell you, Gloria's back. She looks wonderful."

~ * ~

St. Anne's Nursing School

September 15, 1943

Dear Joe,

Tonight I write bad news. Barb's brother, Alan was killed in Sicily.(Censors may cut this out, but see the end of my letter.)

I think Cadet Nurses have the best looking uniforms of all the women's services. For winter they are gray wool with red epaulets (had to look that word up!) on the shoulders. The hat is a perky wool felt beret, with a nice stiff shape, not floppy like General Montgomery's. The silver pin, designed around the caduceus of the medical profession, looks snazzy nestled into the left fold of the beret. For summer the uniforms are gray and white striped seersucker and the hat is felt with a brim. Barb is taking pictures and I'll send one when they're developed.

It's not mandatory that we wear our Cadet uniforms all the time, but we are requested to be dressed in them at official functions (whatever that means) so we will look like members of the armed forces. I surprised Mike by wearing mine when I visited him yesterday.

Poor Barb. Alan is gone so soon and so young. I hope Barbara is right about you, Joe. No news is good news. Maybe your letters got lost at sea. A nice long weekend turned sad...
Love, Mollie

~ * ~

She blotted a smudge from the paper. Couldn't seem to make her pen write Joe the other sad news about his old pal, Phil Jackson.

Fourteen

Mollie, her ears stuffed with cotton, sat at her desk trying to concentrate on writing a case study. She found it hard to ignore Carmen's hurried packing, still surprised that she was leaving. She took out the plugs in time to hear Carmen's announcement, and turned in disbelief.

"You're married? When?"

Carmen kept shoving things into her suitcase carelessly, stuffing hosiery and underwear into the corners. "Saturday night. We went to Portland for the weekend. They don't make you wait three days down there." She knelt on the bulging bag and pushed until she could fasten the latch, then scooped piles of books and uniforms into several cardboard boxes.

Mollie watched with mounting fury. "Of course you neglected to tell my brother about Doctor Tolan. And Joe thought you were so special."

"Uh... I haven't had a chance. Dan didn't expect his notice until December," Carmen stammered, turning away from Mollie's flaming stare.

"You were two-timing Joe from the day you met him and had no intention of making anything of his crush on you. And at the same time you were cheating on Dr. Tolan." Mollie clenched her hands, and realizing it, flattened her palms against her uniform. It took effort to keep from slapping Carmen's pretty face.

"Your brother's a real dreamboat, but Dan was here and I fell in love with him is all." Carmen puffed to reach the top book shelf, looked for space in the boxes on the floor and shrugged. She turned to Dorrie. "Tell Sister Marie to give these books to anyone who needs them, Dorrie. I haven't room for them."

Mollie took a deep breath or two to keep from exploding. "You could have told Joe. For two years he's been writing faithfully. Don't tell me you didn't have chances. If you hadn't answered some of his letters he wouldn't have kept writing."

"I tried," Carmen's voice dropped. "I really did. Just couldn't think of any good way to let him down. You see, Joe got too serious too fast and I hated to hurt him after he was sent overseas."

For a moment, Carmen looked genuinely sorry, but Mollie knew she could put on a convincing act about anything. "How do you think he'll feel when he comes home thinking you're waiting for him and finds you married and with a house full of kids?"

Carmen turned around sharply after pushing her bags into the corridor. "What I choose to do with my life is neither yours nor your brother's business. We weren't engaged or anything. What's done is over. I have to hurry. Dan's waiting in the car."

"For Dr. Tolan's sake, I hope he's the father!" Mollie threw a pillow into the wastebasket toppling it and a letter in Joe's handwriting, addressed to Carmen, slid out. It hadn't even been opened. She turned it over in her hand, and then tore it to shreds as Carmen closed the door.

The door banged shut as Mollie walked out of the room. "She sleeps with every man able to walk, then up and marries a doctor; a good-looking one at that!" While waiting for the elevator, she felt Dorrie's hand touch her arm. Dorrie had been silent during the whole scene with Carmen and hadn't even said goodbye to her long time roommate.

"Let's go over to Guys and I'll treat you to a chocolate sundae, Mollie." Dorrie had pulled on a red sweater and brought Mollie's blue one to her. She led the way to the corner drug store, a favorite gathering place for the student nurses.

"Chocolate ice cream with gobs of chocolate sauce over it and plenty of nuts," Mollie told the waitress.

Dorrie grinned. "I'll just have a small lemon coke. Can't get fat again, ever."

"I'm so mad I could eat two chocolate sundaes, maybe three!" Mollie scooped up a delicious spoonful and relished the velvety texture on her tongue.

Dorrie frowned. "I promised to pay for only one." She spread coins on the table. "Just have Fifty cents."

"It'll be awful writing to Joe to tell him the whole sad story. That's what really bothers me. I thought Carmen might be honest enough to do that." Mollie held the ice cream in her mouth until it melted. She always got a headache if she ate it too fast. "How can I tell him the girl he thought loved him, married the only man around in the right age bracket?" She swallowed. "And all the soldiers, sailors, and Marines she rolled around with don't count!"

Barbara came into the drug store and slid onto the red leather seat beside Mollie. "Well, I think Carmen's lucky. Didn't all the girls fall a little bit in love with Doctor Tolan?" She sighed. "Such a he-man type and those beautiful black eyes. Wow!"

"He's all right. Nowadays any warm breathing man close by looks pretty special, Barb." Mollie felt a shadow of depression settle when Ron entered her thoughts. She ached for the sight of his handsome face. "I have known better looking men than Doctor Tolan. There's Cary Grant, Clark Gable and Tyrone Power."

Dorrie grinned. "And Ron?"

"Ron's in the category and knows it better than anyone." Mollie's hand fumbled absently with the locket around her neck, hidden under her uniform. They were not allowed to wear visible jewelry on duty.

"Are you wearing his ring around your neck?" Dorrie teased. "Rumors, you know."

"Not a ring, just a locket with his picture. See." Mollie pulled the chain out and opened the heart-shaped little picture box. "I made no promises for either of us to break." But she hadn't found anyone to challenge a potential break of a promise to Ron, not that she hadn't tried. When his letters didn't come for weeks, she'd tried to forget by going out with other men. Soldiers whose names she couldn't even remember. GIs bound overseas who begged for one last night of love from a stateside girl.

Dorrie turned to Barbara, "And Barbara wears a certain curly haired lieutenant's bars on her charm bracelet, a former patient named Don, I believe."

Barbara's face flushed.

Don had gone into the Army shortly after his leg healed, and directly to Fort Benning, Georgia, to become a "ninety-day wonder" or "shavetail" as the GIs called the fledgling officers trained so quickly. According to Joe, the label was not meant to be flattering.

"So I, brag, brag, am the only one with a guy tied down." Dorrie held up her left hand and twisted the small diamond on her finger to catch the light. "I can't think of any other way to handle a man if you love him. Get his ring on your third finger, left hand!" She pulled a handkerchief from her sweater pocket and dabbed at tears. "He's leaving, you know."

"Jake? I thought his eyesight was too poor for combat," Barbara said.

"The whole headquarters is leaving." Dorrie glanced around to see whose unauthorized ears might lose lives like the posters said. She whispered, "From the clothing issue, Jake thinks to the South Pacific."

"We're St. Annie's hermits. There are thousands of men, all on their way to thousands of miles away." Mollie straightened her shoulders, feeling better.

Dorrie slurped the last of her Coke. "She's pregnant."

"Carmen is?" Barbara pulled out coins to pay for the vanilla sundae she had ordered.

Mollie lowered her voice when three new girls arrived after college classes and settled into the booth behind them. "I'm not surprised. She got so mad when I hinted about it. Probably trapped poor Doctor Tolan. Carmen knows about all the precautions, even had a diaphragm fitted."

"Meow! You sound catty, Mollie. Not much like St. Annie's class of forty-four's Girl Scout to say such nasty things. I'm sure it's Doctor Tolan's kid. Carmen hasn't gone with anyone else for several months and they've been spending weekends at a certain resort." Dorrie's face reddened.

"Sorry, gals. Mother would lecture me just like you did for judging Carmen like that no matter how good the reason." Mollie scraped the last of the chocolate from the little tulip-shaped dish and began to tap her toes to the juke box rendition of *Boogie Woogie Bugle Boy Of Company G,* her usually good disposition returning. She sipped water to wash away the sweet taste. Barbara slid out of the booth and pulled her jacket over her white uniform. "So Doctor Tolan is now Lieutenant J.G. Tolan. I thought he wasn't a citizen."

"If you're a refugee, it doesn't matter, especially for a medical doctor. Besides, Lebanon is probably one of our allies." Mollie waited while Dorrie fished in her purse for the fifty cents. "I buy the next one, girls, after our stipends come."

"Doctor and Mrs. Dan Tolan are just leaving." Dorrie waved at the couple in the '36 Chevy rounding the corner."They're driving down. Don't know how they managed that. He must know someone important to get new tires and gas. Takes a lot of coupons to drive down to San Diego."

"The government gives them out in special cases. Navy is short of doctors. At least I can tell Joe that Doctor Tolan isn't 4-F or fifth column." Mollie skipped across the street dodging water-filled holes in the pavement. These days, street maintenance overtaxed repair crews, many of them women. "Are you going to stay in four-o-one Dorrie?"

Dorrie grinned, with a mischievous glint in her eyes as if she was bursting with news. "No. Sister Marie has been waiting for a room on the third floor to become vacant so she can get four-o-one ready for the next class. I'm moving into three-eleven across the hall from you. Pinky Olson's my new roommate."

~ * ~

Mollie whistled as she hurried down the hall. It was like old times having Dorrie, Pinky, Shirley and Ginger close to her and Barbara. The six seniors walked in and out of each other's rooms as if doors were missing. The floor echoed with laughter when the good friends were together sharing secrets, sorrows, triumphs, and popcorn.

Pinky fit in well. A tiny girl, she'd stretched to reach the required height for nurse's training, five feet two, and drank cream to get her weight to one hundred pounds. Her real name was Inga, which she tried to forget, and her hair was not pink but cottony white. Cute, not pretty, fit Pinky's looks and her personality sparkled, making her stand out. Bubbly described it best. Pinky had one real problem; a weak bladder.

Mollie joined the five other girls lounging on pillows scattered on the floor in hers and Barbara's room munching on popcorn and sipping cokes.

"Jake told me a good Kilroy joke yesterday." Dorrie glanced at Pinky. "Better go down to the john first, Pinky. This one will run you over."

"I'm fine, Dorrie. Go on."

"You see, this sailor got so horny he went to a whorehouse and the girl he drew had '*Kilroy was here*' tattooed on her Port of Entry!" Dorrie continued.

Pinky giggled. "Oh my gosh!" Her hands covered her mouth and she ran from the room and down the hall trailing dribbles behind her.

"She should see someone about that," Mollie said. "In fact, I wonder how she passed the physical."

"Didn't tell them," Dorrie answered. "I told her she ought'a get her bladder suspended while she's in training and can get the surgery done free. She won't pass the Army physical for sure if they find out about it."

Ginger laughed. "Suspendered, Dorrie? That's a good example of what they do though. It is probably uterine displacement, causing a cystocele."

"Maybe we should talk her into it. We only have, let's see..." Shirley squinted at the calendar over Mollie's desk. "Seven months left."

Pinky came back wearing her robe."Okay, so I didn't quite make it. My mother taught me it was impolite to stare."

"We didn't mean to make fun of you, Pinky. But we were talking about you while you were gone. We voted to encourage you to see a urologist or a gynecologist, or maybe both." Mollie nodded at Ginger to show she also knew some long medical terms. "Your condition is probably curable with surgery."

Pinky looked uncommonly serious "I know. It's silly, but the very thought gives me the shakes."

"I'm going to be doing my stint on Six South starting November first. I'd be glad to hold your hand." Dorrie smiled, but her tone had lost humor. "We could hold each other's. Surgical Procedures scares the shit out of me, if you'll excuse the pun, Pinky. I spent all that time on the other end of Six when I had pneumonia, but I have to take Operating Room now or I won't graduate."

"I'm glad I got mine over early," Ginger said, glancing nervously at Mollie.

Mollie understood the signal. She'd been with Ginger their first day in the operating room. It was a nightmare of embarrassment for Ginger when she fainted the minute the surgeon's scalpel cut through the skin on that lady's throat during the thyroidectomy. Mollie had felt nearly as light-headed. She never told a soul about Ginger, even Barbara, though gossip about the student who passed out in surgery echoed through the nursing residence.

A frown creased Mollie's brow. She recalled poor Ginger lying on the cold tile of the operating room with Dr. Moore shouting, "Get that silly girl out and don't let her near O.R. again!" Thank God Ginger hadn't heard him complaining or she would have dropped out of nursing. Mollie remembered her own quaking fear that Doctor Moore would recognize her beneath the surgical scrub gown and mask. Sister Ruth, bless her, had reddened the haughty doctor's ears with a lecture about abusing a student nurse.

Mollie had liked O.R. after that initial incision; the excitement, the challenges, but she had decided her specialty would be the children's wards. Ginger would probably end up teaching her craft. She knew nursing procedures perfectly, yet feared many of them. As a college teacher, Ginger would be following her father's profession, which would make both happy.

"I loved every minute in surgery. After I get my R.N., I am going back for more surgical training, or maybe anesthesiology and hide behind a mask the rest of my career." Shirley stood and stretched her five-foot ten frame. "Guess I had better start by getting to bed so I can get up for class."

"Not surgery for me, I'm going for O.B." Barbara smothered a yawn. "Good practice for when I need it myself."

~ * ~

Pinky was scheduled for a corrective bladder surgery the week after Christmas when there were fewer patients at St. Anne's. She had chosen the time in order not to be away from assigned floor duty too long, and to escape the knowing stares of her fellow classmates. She hadn't counted on Dorrie, Mollie and Barbara taking a day away from their annual leaves to see that she got the ultimate in nursing care. They arrived when she was being prepared for surgery.

"I've changed my mind!" Pinky grabbed a robe and jumped from the bed.

"No, you haven't. You're already shaved. It'll stick like hell when it grows back and you won't want to do it again." Dorrie pushed her back and the prep girl sighed in relief.

"Get out of here, then, and let me go in peace! My God, I don't need an audience. I've already lost half my dignity to that awful pessary they tried last month and my pelvic anatomy's no different than every other female's. I'm maybe a little more blonde is all."

Dorrie laughed and laughed until tears ran from her eyes. "Did you think we had any interest in your crack, Pinky? We said we would hold your hand and we aim to keep our promise."

Mollie giggled. "We can't get into the surgery anyway. You are in one of the small rooms, not the amphitheater. We'll have to be content to stay in your room and watch you recover from the anesthetic."

"That's what I'm afraid you'll do. Out! Go home!"

Pinky grimaced when the anesthetist nurse in wrinkled green surgery clothing rustled in and swiftly injected a sedative into her diminutive behind. "Dammit. If you won't go home, then go have a Coke at Guys. I won't be back down until at least eleven."

The three girls crept out when the gurney arrived, then followed it to the elevator. Pinky, glassy-eyed from the sedative, clenched her mouth tightly as she passed.

Mollie stifled a gasp. Something about Pinky's face told her the truth. She and Barbara shook their heads after the elevator doors closed.

"Her mouth. Did you notice her mouth?" Barbara said.

Dorrie grabbed a hand from Barbara and Mollie. "Yes. Pinky wears false teeth. That's why she didn't want us to see her. Pact. We won't ever let a peep out about this. Promise?"

"Right. Poor Pinky. Wonder why she lost them so early? She's only twenty-one," Barbara whispered, already fearful of someone hearing.

"I know a girl who had hers pulled when she was sixteen and dentures were an improvement over the rotten crooked teeth she had," Mollie said.

~ * ~

Pinky soon recovered, looking better than Mollie had dreamed she could. She gained ten well-distributed pounds and there were no more leaks when she laughed or coughed. Doctor Leeton said it was a good thing Pinky had the repair surgery because her bladder was pinched behind her pelvic bone. A congenital thing. It might have been dangerous to have children if she hadn't had it done. Now, she was in good urological and gynecological shape, but her first words after surgery were:

"That is one hell of a way to lose your virginity!"

Two weeks later, Mollie read her brother's response to her "dear Joe" letter. It was full of blue invectives and despair over Carmen's lack of fidelity, but he enclosed a picture of a pretty girl named Penelope Arden.

His reply awoke a growing concern in her conscience. All through the war she'd written to men scattered over the globe. Like Carmen, did she encourage them to believe she waited especially for each one? A sharp pang settled when she thought of Phil, whose letters had spoken of his love and a future together when he came home. She had collected a large box of Phil's letters.

Ron worried her most of all. She enjoyed the other men's letters but cherished Ron's far too much. Lately, they came infrequently and she fought jealousy. No promises, she had said. Was her reluctance because she suspected he could not quickly change the habits formed in college? Girls the world over would fall for a guy like him.

The boys from high school were dim memories. Three years had passed since she dated any of them. And those from the USO? Impossible to even remember their faces, yet they kept writing and sending pictures to remind her of one night of dancing, or one movie. The sergeant in Italy had sent flowers from New York before he left for overseas, and she still got a weekly letter from him.

To her, they were like a bunch of brothers. She simply couldn't stop writing to them, encouraging the belief girls back home weren't waiting. Mollie McAllister waited very impatiently for Ron and Joe.

~ * ~

St. Anne's Nursing School
October 10, 1943
Dear Joe,
My fingernails suffered until I got your letter. Couldn't you find a post office when you were on leave in Scotland? I hope the Penny who took you on such a nice tour of St. Andrews is a new romantic interest, because I have bad news about another one.

Carmen married Doctor Tolan and left for California where he's stationed in the Navy Medical Corps. Carmen got pregnant and Doctor Tolan had to marry her. Of course, that's the end of her nurse's training at St. Annie's. I guess it's snippy of me to wonder if she'll be true to Dr. Dan while he is overseas. Carmen isn't worth wasting your time mooning over. I have a dozen other friends with whom she can't compare. If you haven't fallen too hard for that little English girl, I'll introduce you to them, but I'll decide which ones!

Love, Mollie.

P.S. Thanks for the pictures. Penny is cute. She looks like a natural blonde.

Fifteen

Mollie wiped her itching reddened hands on a towel. "I feel like an ad for Jergens lotion. Wonder what they'd do without student nurses for all this drudgery?" She mumbled to Barbara waiting to accompany her to their room after finishing duty at three.

"We're a tradition, Mollie and we come cheap. Won't be long until we're RNs and it's our turn to delegate the scrubbing to the students."

Mollie shrugged. "There's a guy down in admitting waiting for this bed." Beds stayed empty only minutes since war mobilization had swollen the population of Seattle beyond its hospital facilities. After dumping the disinfectant solution into the big sink in the supply room at the end of the corridor, she followed Barbara back to the nursing residence. A dozen girls were gathered in the lounge chattering and eating.

Barbara sniffed. "Smells like chicken soup. I'm starved. Hope there's good sandwiches to go with it. I didn't have time for lunch."

Mollie filled a cup with coffee and reached for a doughnut. She heard her name called.

"Miss McAllister, your father is on the phone in Sister Marie's office," Sister Anne spoke with a strained tilt to her voice.

Mollie's heart raced. It must be Joe this time. Oh God please let it not be Joe or Ron. No it wouldn't be Ron. She wasn't a wife or even a fiancée and Dad wouldn't call about Ron.

"Dad?" She held the receiver slightly away from her head as if it might burn her ear. Her father's voice sounded just like it had when he called about Mike's polio. "Missing over Germany? That means they don't know, Dad. Joe might have been captured or he might be hiding somewhere in France like Ed Lucas did when he was reported missing. All we can do is pray a lot. Guess we've joined thousands of other families. How's Mom taking it?"

Her father's words crackled over a rather noisy line explaining her mother's stoicism, and the blessing of having Mike at home after a year.

That should help a lot, Mollie thought. "Dad, I just this minute decided to enlist in the Army Nurse Corps and will ask to be attached to an Air Wing. I might have a chance to be sent to England. That way, if Joe manages to escape, I would be close by to greet him. Keep everyone's chin up at home. I'm on duty from seven until three tomorrow, then I'm off for the weekend. I'll catch the five o'clock ferry to Bremerton. See you then."

Barbara, waiting outside the open door, took her hands. "I overheard. Joe's missing. I'm sorry, Mollie."

In the lounge, half a dozen girls took turns hugging her. No one spoke because they knew only the most dreadful news came over the phone in Sister Marie's office. All other calls went directly from the switchboard to the phones in the dormitory hallways.

"Thanks, gals." Mollie wanted to be alone a little while and they understood. No one followed when she walked slowly through light drizzly Pacific Northwest rain toward the park.

She forced away the thought of her brother being wounded or dead. "Joe's alive," She muttered. "I just know he is." Her usual tinge of negative clairvoyance was missing. Maybe the nagging gift had gone for good, or maybe it had changed to a strong feeling that her brother had walked away from another crash. Was this because she needed to believe he was safe?

It helped to think positively, like the song. *Accentuate the Positive. Eliminate the Negative. Latch on to the Affirmative. Don't mess with Mr. In Between.* Humming the tune fit her mood perfectly until her voice grew too numb to sing it. Aimlessly, she walked down the mossy woodland path with branches of fuzzy wet pussy willows brushing her sleeves.

A small shaft of sunlight penetrated the grayness of the day and Mollie squinted up toward it. "Thanks," she said aloud, "for the cheer." Her eyes caught a glimpse of a slumping figure sitting on one of the park benches near the path. "Dorrie?"

Dorrie raised a tear-stained face and smiled weakly, moving her hand to blot the rain dripping from her saturated curly hair. "Jake just left. He's on his way to the South Pacific." She buried her face in her hands.

Mollie explained her own bad news and they sat in total silence for a long time in the misty drizzle before returning to the nursing residence. The girls in the lobby nodded, but no one tried to force conversation with either of them. Sorrow had become common among the young nurses.

Mollie and Dorrie stopped in the lounge where a memorial plaque had been installed for one of their own alumni, a nurse who had lost her life in Corregidor early in the war. Beside the plaque was a world map dotted by colored stick pins to show approximate areas other former students were stationed. Beneath the map, the nuns had placed a box and a notepad for prayer requests. Mollie and Dorrie silently reached for a pen to fill out petitions.

Mollie's heart ached for Barbara and the other hospital personnel who had lost brothers, sons or husbands. Mrs. Patterson had borne her baby boy alone. He would be one of many children who would never know a biological father because of this terrible war. The dreaded telegram arrived to her hospital room the day after the stoic nurse had her baby.

By April, the girls worked full shifts and assumed the duties of Registered Nurses. Their classroom work completed, they spent most of their off hours cramming for State Board exams. Many of the Cadets were assigned to work at one of the nearby military hospitals during the remaining two months until graduation.

This evening's shift would be Mollie, Shirley, and Barbara's last for awhile. Beginning tomorrow, they were assigned to Madigan Hospital near Fort Lewis. Ginger, who was joining the Navy Nurse Corps, had left yesterday to serve at the Naval Hospital in Bremerton.

After her duty hours, Mollie hurried back to her room to pack. She slammed her suitcase lid just as Pinky, clad only in a towel, burst through the door.

"Hurry, Mollie. Something's happened to Dorrie. She's fainted on the floor in the shower room. I was in another shower stall when I heard a thud and hurried out."

Pinky, breathless, tugged at her arm and they ran down the hall.

Mollie wiped Dorrie's forehead while Pinky patted her ashen face until she opened her eyes, blinking in confusion.

"Think I should get Sister Marie?" Pinky asked.

Dorrie struggled to her feet and reached shakily for her robe. "No! I-I'm fine. I just got a little dizzy from the hot shower." She had a funny expression.

"I think it is time we had a little talk, Dorrie. Just you, me and Pinky." Mollie closed the door to Dorrie's room and flopped onto a chair.

Dorrie sighed, and then laughed. "You guessed. And you're right. I'm pregnant. Stop staring like I'm some fallen woman. It's all very legal. Jake and I got married the last week end of January." She leaned to squint at a calendar. "It must have happened the very day Jake left. February Tenth."

Mollie grinned. "The same day I ran into you at the park? Where did you two hide from the public long enough?"

"Didn't. We stayed overnight at a sleazy old hotel downtown. Must have been the only vacant room in Seattle. I met Jake right after I got off at eleven." Dorrie began to rock on her behind, making the bed squeak. "What a wonderful last night we had together. We went at it again and again until we were both exhausted. The M.P. was in on getting Jake back to the base on time, but he had to pound on the door hard to wake us up at six in the morning." Dorrie's face crumpled, and she searched for a hankie.

Pinky hugged her. "That's wonderful news, Dorrie, and I'm so happy for you and Jake."

Mollie rose to leave for duty. "But, we can't let this good news get to Sister Marie. You'll have to be mighty careful or you won't graduate, Dorrie."

"I know. Better stop swooning. I've finagled schedules so I can work evenings until I get over morning sickness. I'm sure Mrs. Patterson knew I didn't have stomach flu when I held my hand over my mouth and raced for the john yesterday."

"Mrs. Patterson, of all people, will cover for you," Mollie said. "You haven't started to show yet. Maybe Sister Marie and Sister Anne will think you're just putting on your old figure again when you do."

"They'll be sure I'm either pregnant or awfully hungry if they spot me sneaking soda crackers from the diet kitchen to get me through the mornings. Thank God it has only been mornings." Dorrie fumbled under her pillow and pulled out a packet of crumbly saltines.

Pinky frowned. "Shouldn't you see a doctor, Dorrie? I don't think Doctor Leeton would report you."

"Pinky's right, Dorrie. You must. You might have a tendency for toxemia or something. Is this the first time you've fainted?" Mollie pulled a sphygmomanometer from the pocket of her uniform, glad she had forgotten to leave it in the dressing room when she left the floor for dinner. "Come on, might as well check your blood pressure."

"I could'a told you I'm a very healthy one-twenty over seventy. No, I haven't fainted before, but I haven't decided to take a hot shower lately either." Dorrie sat up, grinning. "I feel fine now. I think I will go over to the little store and get me one of those huge dill pickles."

On their next day off together, Pinky and Mollie escorted Dorrie downtown to see Doctor Harvey Leeton in the Medical Dental building. Pinky had made the appointment with the gynecologist who operated on her bladder, insisting that he promise to keep her friend's visit secret.

After a thorough physical examination, the doctor smiled as he went over the report with Dorrie and her friends.

"You're fine, Mrs. Swartz. You should deliver about Thanksgiving, maybe a little before." He peeked over the top of his glasses. "We'll keep your records in your married name. Your professional one will not be entered. Nurses make especially good mothers and vice versa."

Dorrie had several close calls in the next month, when she made running jaunts to lavatories, but she worked it off well, blaming the old standby, Chicken Ala Trots.

By mid-May, Dorrie got over the morning sickness, but her uniforms were becoming a problem. She'd let her belts out to the last notch and the stiffly starched white cotton began to ride up on her hips.

Mollie thought their secret was out when she and Dorrie were having cocoa and cookies in the lounge and Sister Marie swept in and came directly to them.

The nun surveyed Dorrie. "Are you gaining your old weight back, Miss Koski? I hoped you would remain slender for your health's sake." She paused, a slight frown creasing her brow. "I think we have a couple of uniforms left behind by a plump student who is no longer with us. Perhaps you might wear them until you get your weight down again."

Dorrie turned her flaming face toward Mollie for a minute to recover. "Thank you, Sister. I don't know why I can't stop overeating. Guess it's because Jake's in the South Pacific."

Mollie listened to the interchange, watching Sister Marie's face for signs she knew about Dorrie's real condition. The blue eyes and soft-skinned face beneath the nun's coif looked even more bland than usual.

When Sister Marie went back to her office, Mollie held up crossed fingers. "She knows, Dorrie. I'll bet a million bucks she knows."

Dorrie grinned. "Of course she does. Sister Marie has a devious streak when you get to know her. I could barely keep from laughing and spoiling her little act. I hope she keeps up the pretense or Mother Superior will find out and I'll get tossed."

Mollie returned to her room to finish a letter to Ron. She found solace in putting her thoughts down to him, now that Joe could no longer reply.

~ * ~

St. Anne's Nursing School
February 1, 1944
Dear Ron,
It was keen that you got to see President Roosevelt when he went to the Allied conference. What some people will do for an excuse not to answer letters! Dorrie's Jake will leave for overseas any day. And we haven't heard from Joe at all since that Red Cross letter.

After I wrote to you last, I enlisted in the Army Nurse Corps. It would have been Navy if I could have pulled strings to get stationed near you. With my luck, I would probably end up in New Guinea or some other steaming tropical jungle. I've fought with myself ever since February over which branch of Nurse Corps to join. Since Joe is a prisoner of war, my little brother, my dad and my conscience led me to choose Army. I feel a need to be nearer the battlefields and share our servicemen's danger.

Recently, I have learned a lot of good and bad things about military hospitals. I just returned from a disappointing six weeks at Madigan. They wouldn't let us students work with the real war victims. I spent most of the time assisting in surgery with appendectomies and tonsillectomies. And, of all the doctors I might draw, I scrubbed for Doctor Moore, a surgeon who tried to get me expelled from St. Anne's when he thought I'd told a patient's wife about his terminal cancer.

Dr. Moore joined the Army Medical Corps a couple months ago. I ignored his nasty sarcasm, but nothing I did pleased him. He threw a scalpel at me to get my attention, he said. I was lucky Captain Latke, the surgical nursing director at Madigan saw the incident. She threatened to report Dr. Moore. If I ever meet him again, I may return that little sharp scalpel to a real hurtful place on his anatomy.

Dorrie is getting fat as a barrage balloon but I've lost weight. My uniforms will be a size smaller. Guess I worry too much about the two most important men in my life. You and Joe. Gosh, I wish I could kiss you goodbye when I leave for New Jersey. All my love, really all, Mollie.

~ * ~

Mollie stared at the letter to Ron, remembering both relief and sadness when her folks received word from the Red Cross confirming Joe was a prisoner of war somewhere in eastern

Germany. A month later, they got one smeared dirty letter through the Red Cross in Joe's handwriting. He stated that he was slightly wounded, but doing well. Not good news, but not as bad as it could have been. She felt unsettled about this. It was like waiting for the rest of a "to be continued" magazine story, like part of Joe's plight lay hidden from them.

Sixteen

Mollie put the letter she had written to Ron into an envelope, licked a stamp and pushed it into the right hand corner. She'd mail it later. So many tasks had filled her last two days at St. Annie's, she needed to fight for concentration. Tonight she would share lots of goodbyes, floods of tears and a clandestine baby shower for Dorrie.

After wrapping in tissue paper a dozen scarce Birdseye diapers her mother luckily happened upon at Penney's, Mollie tied the package with a combination of pink and blue curled ribbon. Opening her door, she glanced up and down the corridor to see if Dorrie or any of the nuns were there, and then darted to Shirley and Ginger's room.

Ginger took the package and put it in a closet already bulging with tissue wrapped bundles. "Dorrie will be here any minute." She glanced at her watch. "We'd better pull the blinds in case Sister Marie is curious about why there are so many people in this little room."

Ginger and Shirley had a slightly larger corner room, but having the party there would have been impossible had not some of the girls been on duty tonight. Her classmates were working until the last shift before leaving. St. Anne's would be understaffed day after tomorrow because the next nursing class was one third smaller.

The open window offered little relief in the stifling crowded room. Mollie scanned the sidewalk below to see if the nuns were out for their evening stroll yet. "Better keep it down, gals. Can't have them checking on us tonight."

"Jiggers, here comes Dorrie," Pinky whispered from the door.

Dorrie walked in and her mouth opened. "Holy cow! Why're you all hiding in here? It must be ninety, and where the hell is the popcorn you promised?"

"Surprise!" The girls whispered. "Shower, Dorrie."

"Congratulations, Dorrie," Ginger said, placing her finger over her mouth. "Shh! Keep your voice down. This is a sneaker party and Sister Marie isn't invited."

The goal of keeping the din subdued grew impossible with that many girls making "isn't that darling" sounds at the opening of each package. Ginger's bed was piled high with the assortment when Dorrie finished. There was a gift from every one of the remaining girls in the class of '44, and Carmen had sent a beautiful woolen carriage robe.

Mollie sensed a tinge of sadness beneath the outward gaiety in the room. The girls would begin training with their assigned corps, or enter their profession as Registered Nurses, perhaps never to see each other again. Sixty had passed the rigid State Board examinations, causing Sister Marie to beam in pleasure that two thirds had made it through. Some like Carmen had left to get married, some had found nursing too distasteful, and some had flunked out. Forty of the sixty girls were going into the Army or Navy Nurse Corps. The other twenty either did not join the Cadet Corps, or like Dorrie, failed to pass the physical exam.

Dorrie lived in constant fear that Mother Superior would find out about her pregnancy. The deepest concern for Mollie had been Dorrie's Army physical. She had signed up six months ago to join the Army Nurse Corps, and hadn't canceled, for fear her secret would be discovered. Mollie and Pinky went with Dorrie to see Dr. Leeton. The grinning doctor wrote a note to the Army examiners, who rejected Dorrie as overweight. The government doctor smiled and gave no other reason or explanation. When Sister Marie heard, she gave Dorrie a lecture, a calorie chart and a list of diet foods.

Dorrie thumped the diet stuff on her bed and laughed. "I think that Army doctor enjoyed fooling the recruiters. I'm still scared St. Annie's won't let me graduate."

"They have to. You passed the State Boards. You're already a registered nurse," Mollie said, crossing her fingers. They didn't have to allow Dorrie to attend the graduation ceremony with her class.

A minute later, Mollie heard Gloria Rollins laughing at one of Dorrie's jokes. Gloria had become a model student, and though she needed to make up three months, would march in with the class and receive her black-banded cap without its pin.

A light tap at the door silenced their voices. Sister Marie peered inside. "Gatherings of this size should be held in the lounge, girls. Others are studying and you are far too noisy for the hour. I suggest you go downstairs where I believe you will find ice cream and cake waiting."

A twinkle flashed in the nun's eyes in spite of her stern voice.

"She's wonderful!" Mollie shrieked in the elevator, hugging Dorrie. "Sister couldn't have missed all those baby things on the bed."

Ginger frowned. "Will she say anything, do you think? Will she make Dorrie leave before the ceremony?"

Mollie grinned. "I doubt that very much. Didn't you see Sister Marie turn away to keep us from seeing her smile? Why do you suppose there is suddenly cake and ice cream in the lounge at nine-thirty in the evening? She and Sister Anne wanted to be part of this shower, but couldn't bend rules enough to attend."

~ * ~

The following afternoon, the class of '44 donned uniforms to attend the graduation ceremony ending three years of strenuous preparation. Those in the Cadet Nurse Corps wore their grey woolen dress uniforms with the perky berets. The rest were in their hospital white. All would be given stiffly starched black-banded nursing caps, and except for Gloria, Washington State Registered Nurse pins with their graduation certificates.

Dorrie moaned. "Another notch. I'm already big as a Sherman tank and there are three and a half months left!" She turned for a sideways view in the door mirror. "They'll all know my secret. I look a lot more than fat!"

"So what, Dorrie? You've made it. You're graduating with the class in spite of everything." Mollie remembered all the "everythings" poor Dorrie had mastered. The failing grades when she was going out on the sly with Jake and the hours spent helping her catch up, the near fatal bout with pneumonia, and then her pregnancy.

Funny how different she felt about Dorrie now, sort of protective instead of critical like she had been at first and still was with Carmen. But that too had changed. She felt sorry that Carmen Tolan would deliver any day, alone and far away from her family, while her husband served in the South Pacific. And yes, a little sad that Carmen couldn't be here to graduate with the rest of the class.

"How do you like these new nylons Ron sent? Keen, eh?" Mollie turned to view the perfectly straight seams and the sheer fit. "I don't want to know how he managed to find them. I suspect his mother helped. She's a buyer at Fredericks."

"Keen, Mollie. Wish he could have found another pair for an old schoolmate." Barbara pulled her rayons a little tighter. "But it is good to wear something besides those ugly white cottons, even if they bag."

"Lucky stiffs." Pinky peered in the door of the lounge. "Dorrie and I'll have to keep wearing white ones." Pinky had not passed the physical for the Nurse Corps. She was too small.

"They're not cotton though, thank God. I got a hole in my last pair of the damn things and chucked them in the incinerator," Dorrie said. "I'm gonna be out of uniform for the duration and beyond. Jake takes a dark view of wives and mothers working."

"And knowing Jake, you probably won't need to work unless you want to," Ginger said from the rear of the crowd gathered around the one mirror in the large room. The new gray uniform was especially attractive on Ginger. She usually had the horn-rimmed school teacher look, but Barbara had helped her do her hair and put on more cosmetics than usual. Her parents and brother had come all the way from Idaho by train to attend the festivities and to wish Ginger farewell when she left for the Navy Nurse Corps in California.

"We do have a little put away. I'm saving Jake's allotment checks to pay for the baby. Just deposit them in Seattle First National. Jake buys bonds in both our names in case I need them." Dorrie dabbed at a tear. "Today, I swore not to cry or feel so lonely and already broke my promise. Take a picture of me, Mollie," She handed over a Kodak Brownie. "From the front!"

"Okay. All of you stand over by the big windows so we'll have enough light." Mollie used the whole roll of film taking various angles of the six close friends. "Your slip shows just a teeny bit, Shirley. Definitely not military even if you're showing off a gift from Larry!"

Shirley carefully lifted the straight woolen skirt in order to keep it unwrinkled and heisted the errant lacy slip she'd received as a surprise gift from her shy basketball player. Larry Daniels, now an Army officer somewhere in the European theater, wrote dozens of letters to Shirley.

Sister Marie rustled in. "Time to put out your cigarettes and line up, girls. I have you listed in alphabetical order."

Mollie smiled. The nursing director had found a way to keep the Cadets from overshadowing those not going into the service. Another of her good lessons in humility. Mollie remembered some words Father Doran had said in a Philosophy lecture nearly three years ago: *War should not be worn like some lofty banner. War is hatred in the worst dimension. It rejects every lesson of humanity. War is failure to solve the problems of the world, the failure of love. But man is still too selfish, too immature to forego ultimate violence.* She had jotted the message down and kept the worn card in her purse.

In spite of the priest's lesson, Father Doran had volunteered as a chaplain to help those fighting to end the war, until, he said, the next one came. Now, Mollie and many in her class were following his example.

Mollie, near the middle of the long single line, moved slowly toward the auditorium. The girls grew solemn. No one spoke. Only the soft rustling of starched white skirts and sixty breathing sounds could be heard. All of us must be thinking about life before and after St. Annie's, Mollie mused. Deep in her own reflections, the clapping of the audience jerked her alert when the first girls entered the auditorium.

Searching quickly for her family, she gasped, wavering momentarily. "Ron!" she whispered to herself, causing him to grin widely that she had seen him. He waved. Tears trickled down her face and she resisted dabbing at them, fearing soiling her white gloves. She turned away to regain composure, but couldn't resist stealing a longer look when she reached her chair. Ron sat at the end of the row beside Mike, whose crutches leaned against his aisle seat. They must have all moved down one person to allow space for Ron. Mollie stifled a desire to run from the orderly line to embrace him.

Sally leaned against the arm of her young Army Lieutenant, Dave, who reminded the family of Joe. Mollie would be maid of honor at their wedding tomorrow, then in ten days, Dave would be shipped overseas for the duration. Hopefully, he would be one of the lucky who came home healthy and whole. Her mother sat stiffly erect, aware of the good posture she lectured about to her children. She looked happy and unworried for a change. Mike grinned like one of those nursery rhyme pictures of the *Man in the Moon.* Her dad's face reminded her of the pride he had shown when Joe enlisted in the Air Force, but she saw him fidget restlessly in this setting where he couldn't smoke.

Though she realized the ceremony would be as brief as possible, for Mollie it seemed endless. Sister Marie had appointed her to make announcements as the Cadets filed past, explaining to the audience which branch of the service each girl would enter and their immediate destinations. She tried to slow down. It wasn't fair to slight such an important part of the ceremony. All the girls had boyfriends and relatives here. She sipped a quick swallow from her water glass when the last one came by to receive her pin.

"Mary Zinker, Army Nurse Corps, North Carolina, she read with an audible sigh. Then laughing happily, Mollie ran to greet Ron.

The room burst into pandemonium when all sixty girls joined friends and families. Sister Marie pounded the podium hard with her gavel. "Please, ladies and gentlemen, let us rise and join in a benediction." The room stilled. Sister Anne said a short prayer in Latin and every head in the room bowed respectfully. No one in this terrible time wanted to ignore anyone's prayers. "Now, let us repeat Our Lord's Prayer." The room echoed with, *Our Father who art in Heaven.* "Looks like I don't have to mail the letter I finished last night, Lieutenant Junior Grade Van Ness." Mollie accepted another long kiss, her eyes wandering to her parents for their assessment. Approval was shining in their eyes. She touched the new band of braid on his sleeve. "New rank help you manage a leave?"

"Wasn't the rank and I'm not supposed to tell." Ron glanced about. "Loose lips sink ships, you know." He lisped through the tongue twister. "My carrier and I are in Bremerton for repairs. I'll tell you about it on our way over there. I've just been invited to a wedding tomorrow."

"If only Joe," Lou McAllister murmured, turning away. "But I should be happy for the presence of the rest of the family." She smiled warmly at Mollie.

Mollie bid a tearful goodbye to her classmates, and Sister Marie and Sister Anne. Dorrie waited for her to finish. She beamed, eyes full of suspense.

"You were right, Mollie. Sister Marie did know. She told me right after the ceremony while you were busy kissing Ron." Dorrie mimicked the nursing director. "Miss Koski or Mrs. Swartz, I understand it is now, congratulations on two important achievements. Please do not tell anyone about our deviousness, but Sister Anne and I would love to attend the baptism...or circumcision."

"And I'll have to miss both of them unless there is a miracle and the war is over by November," Mollie said, and then hurried up to her room for the last of her bags. Barbara lay across the bare mattress crying.

"What's the matter, Barb? You and I are going to New Jersey together. We aren't being separated." Mollie patted her good friend's shaking shoulders.

Barbara sniffed into a handkerchief. "It's not that, Mollie. It's just that I'm envious. Your boyfriend came and mine's so far away...and I guess I really missed Alan today."

Mollie felt her own eyes fill. "I'll see you at the wedding tomorrow. We'd better hurry. Our folks are waiting for us in the cars." Mollie took her weekend bag from the bed and Ron's letter fell out. Stamped, ready to mail, she dropped it into the waste basket, then fished it out and put it into her purse. "Might as well let him read it in person." Her other things were already in her father's car trunk. She knit her brows, puzzling still over Ron's words. He looked gaunt and pale. She patted Barbara on the shoulder. "You okay now, Barb?"

"Yeah, Mollie. Wait up. I'm coming, too." She stumbled toward the elevator on tilting heels, just like she had three years before.

Several girls from the class that started in June watched them walk down the steps of the nursing residence for the last time. A plebe said, "St. Annie's Cadets make me feel downright proud."

Mollie turned and waved to them. "Thanks and good luck," she called. Hurrying to Ron's car, she handed him the letter before sliding in beside him. "You can read this if you haven't anything better to do than kissing me."

~ * ~

St. Anne's Nursing School

July 10, 1944

Dear Ron,

The Normandy landing is the main news here. My folks have had no more letters from Joe, but we're all keeping our fingers crossed the Allies can whip the Germans quickly so he and everyone can come home. It seems like this war has gone on forever.

I am now Second Lieutenant Margaret Louise McAllister of the Army Nurse Corps. We graduated a month early so we could get right at nursing the wounded. I will leave next week for New Jersey, where I'll get overseas indoctrination.

You and I have a "by mail" love affair going, the only kind most girls here at home have. I miss you more than I ever missed anyone and this year has seemed like ten. No, sweet, there isn't anyone else. You are very hard to replace. Love, Mollie.

Seventeen

The Comrades

After parking the big Chrysler on the darkened car deck, its lights hooded because of blackout regulations, Ron pulled her into his arms. He stole an apprehensive glance in the rear view mirror when the rest of the McAllisters opened their doors and climbed out to ascend to the coffee shop. "Will your folks mind if we don't join them?"

"No. They probably trust me with you better than I trust myself." Mollie snuggled closer and felt him stiffen his arm. "You're wounded! Is that what you meant about you and the carrier?"

"Just fragments of shrapnel they picked out at the hospital yesterday. Most of it was removed by the ship's surgeon while we were at sea."

"Can you tell me where you were when all this happened?" Mollie felt suddenly chilled. "I mean, what happened?"

"The Pacific isn't exactly peaceful these days. A Zero got too close and nipped me in the shoulder. No big deal. I'm fine now, good enough to report back to the carrier."

Mollie moved a hand gently over his jacket and felt a bandage. "They didn't keep you until it was completely healed?"

"A lot of guys are in worse shape, and I hate hospitals. I wanted to see you so much, I would have gone AWOL if they hadn't released me."

"I'm glad. This may be the only time we'll have alone until after the wedding. Everything's pretty frantic for tonight." She had been looking forward to Sally's wedding, but Ron's arrival changed her attitude. She felt a little disloyal that her enthusiasm for this important family occasion had waned. To be with Ron meant more than anything else.

Mollie wiggled out of her jacket. Sister Marie had decided their summer uniforms were not dressy enough for graduation so they had suffered in wool. Ron's eager mouth found her lips, and then wandered lower to the curve of her neck and the top of her bra. Between kisses, he mumbled, "Can't you sneak away for a little while tonight? I have to report to the ship, but after that I won't be missed until morning."

"I...I don't know. There's Sally's wedding rehearsal at six, then dinner afterward. Mother prepared a buffet of chicken and salmon, lots of salads, but no beef." Mollie's mind raced. An urgent desire to spend the night with Ron dominated her thoughts. The idea of stealing a few more hours together, feeling his mouth on hers, giving in to the lovemaking dreamed of so long, erased every other consideration. Sally's wedding preparations were pushed aside. There it was again, the stab of guilt. What if it were her wedding to Ron? How she wished it could be.

Ron traced the line of her lips with his finger. "If you can break away, I'll pick you up about nine-thirty and we'll drive to the beach or somewhere for a while."

Mollie felt his questioning eyes searching for an answer, probably guessing her ambivalence. Did he experience a measure of restraint as well? She'd never felt so unsure of herself. Their own private war of conscience raged without resolution.

He tilted her chin to search her eyes. "I'm asking a lot, Mollie, probably too much."

She sensed from Ron's vague hints that he was on his way to another combat zone. Would the selfish pleasure of one night be irresponsible in times when no one could predict if there'd be another chance? Shouldn't they seize this opportunity? She watched a dim light bulb over the life preservers a long time and made the only decision in her power.

"Okay. I'll tell the folks. Mike will be in bed by then, or should be. Sally's the only one who might miss me. This is her last night to be single."

"I'd bless her forever if she could spare you a few hours, Sweetheart. God, how I've missed you!" He tilted her chin to kiss each lip, tasting her mouth with his tongue. His hands moved over her blouse and deft fingers unbuttoned it and circled the firm nipples under her bra.

Br-ank! B-r-rank! The raucous blast from the ferry whistle startled them, signaling the end of an hour far too short. Bells rang in the engine room near their car and a couple of impatient drivers started their motors.

Mollie re-buttoned her blouse and reached for her jacket, deciding to carry it to her father's car. It was unlikely anyone would know she was half out of uniform on the drive to her house. She squeezed into the front seat of her dad's Plymouth and blew a kiss to Ron, who tooted the horn and drove hurriedly up the ferry ramp toward the Navy Yard.

~ * ~

A few minutes after nine, Mollie heard the Chrysler's tires crunch on the gravel driveway, then Ron's hurried steps across the porch to the front door. "Bye, Sally. I'll see you in the morning. Get a good night's sleep. You won't get much tomorrow night." She winked at her sister and ducked a pillow.

Lou McAllister answered the doorbell and called up the stairway. "Mollie! Ron is here!"

Mollie hurried down to greet him.

"Drive carefully now. With both arms," her father teased. He rose from his old leather chair as they moved toward the door. "See you tomorrow at the wedding, Ron."

Mollie noted a special kind of arch in Ron's brows. Her dad shrugged, his head nodding with understanding. She and Ron hurried out to the Chrysler, and after he turned onto the road, she slid across the seat to snuggle under his free arm.

"Head out toward the canal. I know of a nice beach about five miles from here."

Ron drove slowly, observing the legal speed limit of thirty-five miles per hour; the regulation meant to conserve gas and tires. Mollie touched his arm. "Make a left turn here and... Oh, golly. There must have been a wind storm recently. We'll have to move that pile of fir boughs. Hope the road isn't too bad."

She directed him to drive down an old logging road to a piece of acreage owned by her uncle. Neither spoke as they bumped toward an isolated stretch of sandy shoreline at the end of the rutted lane. Here, they would be completely alone. She'd developed trust in the handsome officer holding her so closely. Letters were cold pieces of paper, yet Ron's had bridged the physical touching denied. Those fragments of stationery had recorded their deepest feelings. Spoken words were unpracticed.

It was still warm, at least seventy degrees, one of the wonderful long summer evenings Puget Sound country occasionally produced to make citizens forget all the drizzly gray days of the winters.

Ron pulled a thick wool blanket from the rear seat and took a wicker basket holding a bottle of champagne and two glasses from the trunk. The popping cork sounded too loud for the quiet setting, like a firecracker going off in church. The arches of the tall firs outlining the beach were not unlike a cathedral with stars dotting its dome.

Mollie fought a tinge of reluctance, certain that Ron hadn't forgotten his practiced plans for seduction. She found no words of protest, yet glanced toward the woods nervously. It took little effort to cast the tiny warning aside. They were two miles from any onlookers except curious animals.

Ron poured the bubbling essence into the glasses, set them on a nearby flat rock, and spread the blanket over the warm sand. Like well-trained children, they kicked off their shoes to keep the sand from the blanket. They had spoken only necessary words since leaving the house. Handing her a glass of champagne, he reached for the other one.

"This is to us, Sweetheart, for the future, for everything important in the world." The glasses clinked and they sipped deeply.

"Amen to all that," Mollie's voice caught. "You aren't coming to the wedding tomorrow?" She would not cry. Not yet. Tomorrow she would cry, sadly for Ron and happily for Sally.

"I didn't want to tell you until the last minute." Ron pulled her onto the blanket beside him. He kissed her then, tenderly, yielding like the sand beneath them. "I want you so much, I hurt everywhere, mostly in the region of the heart. It feels like it might burst when I leave you again. I love you more than when I said goodbye last time."

Mollie sat up and twisted to lean over his face, barely visible in the darkening shadows after the long summer day. "When you decided I was some kind of guardian, a saint named Mac who evidently couldn't keep the Japs from shooting at you?" Her attempt to chide deepened his solemn expression and she wanted to retract her flippant words.

"I knew you were the only girl for me then, but you weren't so sure. When you rejected making commitments that day I drove you back to Children's, I felt terrible. I worried that you might be interested in someone else. I thought I had failed to reach the most important reason for living. You." He pulled her closer and stared silently toward the top of the trees. "I tried, but I couldn't shake your image from my thoughts and dreams."

Mollie could feel his jaw twitching with tension against her cheek. She turned to take his face between her hands and kissed him. Words became lost somewhere in a jumble of emotion. She stood and took a few steps toward the water.

Ron moved behind her and circled her waist with his arms.

"For two and a half years, I've been falling deeper in love with you and fighting it," She whispered. "Admitting how much you mean to me makes it harder to think about life after tomorrow. Nuts to the damn war! For the rest of this night, I'll forget everything but loving you."

He led her back to the blanket, reached for the champagne bottle and refilled the glasses. "Now we really have something to toast." They sipped silently, entwined in each other's arms watching the breeze ripple the quiet little bay. "Are you still afraid, Mollie? Frightened of...?" He groaned and pulled her down to kiss her again.

"No, darling. I want to recall everything about you." She traced the lines in his cheeks, deeper lines than she remembered. He'd grown thin, too thin. "You outrank me, you know. You could just order me to surrender all my well-guarded treasures."

He grinned. "I have never much liked compulsion, Sweetheart. I care for it a hell of a lot less since I have been in the Navy." His hands moved over her shoulders, bared above a pink and white gingham peasant blouse. "I'd rather remember you like this than in a uniform, Lieutenant McAllister. You look so beautiful and feminine after seeing so much navy blue and khaki."

"Aye, sir." Mollie felt her blouse slip away, then the pink skirt and slip. She reached to help with the fastenings of her bra, all barriers lost in the throbbing sensations his hands sent over her body.

He struggled a little as he shed his shirt. She drew in her breath. His left arm and shoulder were tightly bandaged. "Forget about that," he mumbled. Moving gently, taking infinite care to be patient, he covered her body with caressing hands, pausing to whisper hoarsely. "Still okay, sweet?"

"Uh-huh." Mollie moaned, pulling him closer. Never in dreams had she felt sensations like these. She didn't realize just when he moved above her and she felt the presence of his hot moist erection. She heard him catch in his breath before he probed more forcibly. A small cry of pain came unbidden, lost in the passion of complete surrender. Even Ron's soft moans enhanced her pleasure.

Slowly, Ron moved her so they lay side by side. Mollie had never known such quiet relaxation. Peaceful contentment shrouded their shadowy figures prone and fulfilled on the blanket.

The moon rose, defining the shoreline and a scattering of rocks. Beside the blanket was a pile of pink gingham, and a carefully folded Navy uniform lay on the flat rock. Ron leaned on his right elbow, his shadowy face showing a mixture of love and a half hidden concern.

Mollie felt it too. So little time to pledge a commitment to each other. She must stop thinking at all. She sighed sleepily when he pushed a curl from her forehead, and kissed the spot beneath it. She touched the little curl on his forehead. "You look young and boyish, like one of those kids on the *Post* covers. You know, the Norman Rockwell ones."

"I don't feel at all young and boyish. Rrrr." He bussed her on the neck and she laughed because it tickled when his mouth touched her skin.

"I know how dreams come true," she murmured. "They begin with a handsome Navy officer, who is very tender when he makes love to a girl. Darling, if this is how you got a majority vote for Campus King." She kissed him lightly on the chin, her fingers gently caressing the back of his neck. "I'll be the first one in line for more."

"You're the only one in line, the only girl I've wanted since that frat dance, Sweetheart."

It took little encouragement to renew the passion of an hour ago and this time it was Mollie who needed patience. Ron reignited every sensation in her body with his wandering hands, the same hands she had resisted barely a year before for exploring beyond her limits. And hers, that slapped his face for being exposed to his proud throbbing manhood in the shed at the fraternity party, did the exploring.

The moon illuminated their bodies. Spent once more, they snuggled together, pulling the blanket edges around them to keep the dampness of the rising tide from chilling.

A soft splash on the rocks awakened Mollie. She jumped to her feet and nudged Ron with her toe. "The tide's in, Campus King. Join me for a swim? To keep your bandages dry, better make that a foot dip." She ran toward the edge of the water and bounced gasping through the cold ripples.

Ron leapt to catch her hand and they splashed together until her foot touched a slippery rock and she plunged face down into the water. He helped her up, laughing, coughing and sniffing the salty stuff from her nose. Both sets of teeth were chattering when they ran for the blanket and rolled inside, ignoring the gritty sand.

Soft light gradually blotted out the night when Mollie groaned and reached for her clothing. "I'm starved. Can we go somewhere for breakfast?"

"How about dessert, Sweetheart?" Ron pulled her back for another kiss, his forefinger circling a breast. He reached for his watch and twisted it to catch the dawning light. "Right. Better be breakfast." He rose stiffly, stretched and began to pull on his uniform, brushing furiously at the sand clinging to the navy blue wool serge. "Damn Navy should let us wear Suntans like we do on the ship and in the southern regions."

Mollie shook her damp hair and tried to comb out the tangles. Sighing, she fumbled in her purse for a pink silk scarf to cover it. It would take some doing to wash the salt water out of her long hair and dry it in time for Sally's wedding at three.

The all-night cafe in Bremerton's suburbs was occupied by one other couple, completely engrossed in each other, sitting in a yellow upholstered booth in the corner. Mollie relaxed, realizing scant notice would be given to the tall Navy officer and a girl hiding wet hair under a silk scarf.

Ron held her hands while they waited for breakfast. "Sorry?"

His eyes were soft jade green at four a.m. and she searched them, noting the seriousness in their depths, the bluish tinge of sleeplessness beneath. She wanted to memorize his face just like that, with the dark shadow of morning beard, the little curl on his forehead. "Sorry for what? Loving you? Never, darling." She laughed when a smile brightened his face. "One does not defy orders from superior officers, does one?"

He frowned ominously. "One had best not take these kinds of orders from any officer except Lieutenant JG Ronald Thomas Van Ness!"

"And I trust Lieutenant Van Ness will not issue such orders to any other feminine junior officer." He kissed her until the waitress carrying two servings of scrambled eggs and toast interrupted with a gravelly chuckle.

"You two want to eat your eggs or each other?"

They ate quickly, barely tasting the food, and Ron paid the check. He opened the right door, and helped her into the car, spun it around and drove toward the highway. "I dreamed of marrying you when we were together again, Mac, even if we had only one night. I wish you and I were taking vows this afternoon. Damn, there is so little time. Always in a hurry to get back to the war."

"I've been envying Sally ever since I saw you at graduation." She swallowed the catch in her throat. "Maybe fate is ruling that such binding vows shouldn't be rushed, darling. We're both going separate directions until the war is over. Be thankful we had this much time. I hadn't counted on any at all." Mollie searched for a handkerchief. In spite of her vow not to cry, tears formed.

Ron parked the Chrysler at a viewpoint overlooking a channel between Bremerton and Bainbridge Island. He glanced at his watch. "Six o'clock. Will your mother be upset that you stayed out all night with me?"

"No. These days, there are all night movies and dances. Sally has her accustomed to such things. I may have to explain about the swim because my hair's a mess." Her hand moved to the damp wisps creeping from her scarf. "I'm twenty-one years old, you know, legal age."

She sensed Ron moved conversation to lighter things to hide anxiety. Something besides his imminent departure needled him. "Are you worrying about ending my chastity?"

"Yes. What if I made you pregnant and you're left alone and unmarried?" His voice grew so low it was barely audible. "It's too late for regrets. I should have thought about that."

Ron spoke aloud her own inner feelings. "If I am, I'll join thousands of girls facing that problem. We needed something tangible, something besides words on paper to remember."

He drew a little package from an inner coat pocket. "Mac...Mollie. Right after my near miss training for carrier landing, I went out and bought these. I meant to ask you to marry me and place the engagement ring on your third finger left hand at some grand moment like they do in the movies. I had them in my pocket when you decided against making a formal commitment that day at Children's. Out in the Pacific, I almost threw the rings overboard several times. In saner periods, I'd know you were right. It was wiser to honor your concern for a pledge when we're both going to the war. Last night was so perfect..." He gulped hard, looking like a kid with stage fright. "Will you wear this?" He took a diamond solitaire from the box. "And keep the wedding band on the locket chain until we can be married?"

Mollie held out her hand and he pushed the small but flawless diamond ring on her finger. "It fits. I made a good guess." He lifted her hand and kissed the ring.

"A seal of our pledge." Mollie stared at the ring, her eyes misting. "Thank you for waiting until after the perfect night, darling. First the deep feeling, then the public expression."

The clock on the dash loomed giant sized. Its hands pointed to seven. "I eagerly accept Lieutenant Van Ness, with one condition."

His arm about her loosened, and his expression changed. "Not another one!"

Taking both his hands, she spoke softly, "If either of us decides differently when we are separated by oceans and half a world, we wait until we can tell each other in person. I've heard of sad things about Dear Johns...or Rons."

Ron whistled his relief. "A remote possibility, Sweetheart. I've already tested my passion for you a year. I do agree about rejection by mail. I promise there will be no Dear Mollie's. We have another hour if you drop me off and take the car back to your house. Did you ever get your driver's license?"

"Dad took me over to the state patrol station about a month ago. He insisted I might need a license when I'm in the Army. Why, I have no idea. I doubt I'll be driving anything but gurneys wherever I'm going."

His arms tightened around her, and she could feel the bandage on his shoulder. "Be safe. I pray God you won't be in one of those carts."

She could stem her tears no longer. They spilled over her face and dampened the blue serge on the chest she leaned so tightly against.

~ * ~

After her sister's wedding was over and her tired parents were in bed, Mollie could not fall asleep. She rose and got out her writing materials to add a note to her parents' letter. They wrote weekly to Joe, as if he were still stationed in England.

~ * ~

Home, July 14, 1944

Dear Joe,

We keep sending letters to this Red Cross address without knowing whether you are getting any of them. Our prayers and thoughts are with you every day. I'll be heading east tomorrow and probably overseas soon. Mollie

Eighteen

Mollie and Barbara joined the variety of uniformed people waiting to board planes for the European front. Mounds of baggage dotted the busy airport terminal.

Barbara paced and fidgeted with her knotted handkerchief. "Jeepers, Mollie. Airplanes scare me worse than snakes, mice, or Frankenstein movies. Why does the brass think we're so important? Don't they just send generals and admirals overseas by air?

Mollie spotted a couple of vacant chairs and nudged Barbara toward them. She sat down and pulled out stationery and a pen. "Why don't you write a letter to your folks or to Don? It'll get your mind on more pleasant things." Mollie found her own positive thoughts difficult to form. Concern for the safety of two very special men nagged at complacency at her peace of mind. "I haven't flown on an airplane, either, or even been out of Washington State by any mode of transportation until two weeks ago."

"But you're never scared, Mollie. You're always game to try anything." Barbara's voice had taken on a thin whining tone, higher with each word.

"For Pete's sake, Barbara, let's have a glass of wine or a rum and Coke. I've heard alcohol helps ease the tension of flying." Mollie packed her stationery into her bag, shifted it to her shoulder, and led Barbara toward the bar in the corner. Officers of every rank crowded the small alcove, most of them staring with interest as she and Barb pulled out two wobbly chairs at a small corner table.

Barbara, still clenching her bag tightly, managed a smile when a chorus of whistles were aimed in her direction. The attention of men didn't change her nervousness. Little white lines etched her mouth and she jumped when the waiter placed two glasses of dark red wine on the table. He stood while she searched her bag for a dollar. "Keep the change."

Mollie grinned at the waiter's bored shrug. "He got a whole dime, Barb."

"Well, that's all I had besides a couple of twenties from our last check." She took a tentative sip.

"Ugh. That stuff's awful. And you know how liquor affects me, Mollie. What if I get sick?"

"On one little glass of wine? Besides, I'll be there to hold your barf bag." Mollie grimaced as she sipped the sour-tasting vintage. It took steely resolve to swallow it herself, almost made her lips pucker. "Drink it anyway, Barb. Then I'll order another."

"One swallow of that vinegar will last me forever. How could anyone drink enough to become a 'wino?'" Her head jerked when a loudspeaker blared.

"*Transport oh-oh-five ready on runway three. Passengers please prepare to board.*"

"Golly! That's us." Mollie took a long tingling breath and felt her heart thump. Fearless? Barbara was wrong. Flying over a whole ocean wasn't exactly appealing, but she didn't plan to spend life in terror of everything different. She grimaced and marched up the ramp.

Barbara sat rigid as a post when the heavily loaded C-54 lumbered into the air. At altitude, she tensed every time the plane hit an air pocket and clamped her hands over her mouth when they approached to land for refueling in Gander, Newfoundland.

Fog held them in Iceland for twenty-four hours, and Barbara's jittery tension while they waited for it to clear kept Mollie fighting to control her own nerves.

When they boarded for the final leg of the flight, Barbara clung to Mollie's jacket sleeve. Squeezing her eyes tightly shut, she clutched the edge of the seat with her other hand. "I always had a notion to become a stewardess after the war. Right now, I envy Pinky carrying bedpans at St. Anne's. Wonder how much longer this torture lasts?"

A grinning Army Air Force crewman serving as steward brought them mugs of coffee and a box lunch just in time to hear her question. "If you take the high road and I take the low road...allowing for the stiff headwind, we'll be in Scotland in," he sang, then squinted at his watch, "about three hours." He appraised both girls and wiggled his eyebrows.

Mollie smiled. Obviously, the steward found it easy to forget respect due to superior officers, or didn't consider nurses among them. She watched him linger near each double seat. "Bet this is the most girls he has seen on Trans Atlantic flights, Barb."

He heard her and turned around.

"You're right, Lieutenant. This is the first time I've had a whole plane loaded with nurses. Sometimes we get a couple of WACs but mostly Air Corps men and generals."

Mollie nudged Barbara. "Your words a couple days ago."

Barbara's grip on the arm of her seat threatened to loosen it from the floor when the C-54 descended through thick clouds to an airfield near Edinburgh, Scotland. After the plane taxied to a camouflaged hanger, she climbed down the ramp and whistled happily. "I've an urge to kiss the ground. I'm going home by ship. Definitely no more will I travel in these flying horror chambers. Did you see the sparks from the engines?

"When did you see them? You had your eyes clenched tight most of the trip." Mollie felt as happy to be down to earth as Barbara and completely exhausted after nearly three straight days of travel.

At the base, the nurses trudged to the officers' mess for dinner, dragging their heavy duffel bags to tables before getting into the line. "I'd rather have a plate of scrambled eggs and ham than roast beef. It feels like weeks since we left New Jersey."

Since there were no women's barracks at the base, trucks took the girls into Edinburgh for the night. They saw little of the old city through thick smoky fog and hooded street lights. Mollie and Barbara stumbled up three steep flights of stairs to their room in an old hotel two blocks from Princes Street.

"Ever see furniture like this outside those historical movies?" Barbara opened an ornate drawer in the huge Victorian wardrobe. "Mirror is a little wavy, probably a hundred years old."

Mollie flopped onto one of the canopied beds. "I'm too tired to appreciate anything but the bed. Too bad they're out of hot water for baths, though. I could sure use one."

~ * ~

A bell ringing outside their door jarred Mollie awake. She shivered and ducked back beneath the warm comforter.

A Scottish-accented voice called from the corridor. "Six O'clock, ladies."

The girls washed in icy water and shivered quickly into their dress uniforms.

As they walked three blocks to the railroad station, bright sunshine raised steam from the damp, cobbled streets. Mollie stared awestruck at Edinburgh Castle looming above as they waited to board the train. The netting draped guns poking from the ramparts sent a shock of reality through her mind. The fortress made it clear this was a war-torn country.

"Guess we're where the action is, Barb. Isn't that rock castle something? And the real wonder is that it's still in use after centuries."

Barbara shuddered. "It looks terrifying to me. I read about some of its prisoners in that pamphlet at the hotel room. Reading that didn't help me get to sleep."

When they boarded the train and found seats, a girl wearing a Red Cross arm band served hot tea and crusty rolls with butter and currant jam. Signs of war grew much more graphic as they traveled steadily southward, and when the steam locomotive huffed and clanged into the station at Coventry, both Mollie and Barbara drew in sharp breaths at the devastation surrounding them. Their destination looked like a newsreel battle zone.

"Look," Mollie pointed. "That must be Coventry Cathedral, the one the German bombs wiped out early in the war. I saw it in a newsreel." She sighed at the graceful blackened arches towering above the rubble like glassless skeletons of their former splendor.

"What a shame. It must have been beautiful once. Guess Hitler doesn't care about churches. Wish I had seen it before the bombs." Barbara fished in her bag for a handkerchief. She had been sniffling through most of the cities they passed. "I guess this is the industrial section of England where the Luftwaffe drops its biggest loads."

"Funny, the contrasts. Beautiful green fields, lovely old homes, sheep everywhere and this." Mollie dabbed at her own eyes. "Think what those blockbusters would do to Seattle."

"I know. Makes me feel too smug, somehow. Isolation has benefits." Barbara lurched forward when the train stopped in the camouflaged station.

The two girls exited the train and walked past sandbags piled everywhere like banks of snow in the Cascade Mountains after a snowplow had come through. "Guess we just follow the crowd. I have no idea where the airbase hospital is or how we are supposed to get there. Oh, golly!" Mollie gasped as she passed a crater behind one stack of sandbags. What had once been someone's home was nothing but a jagged hole with a fireplace clinging from a crumbling brick wall. Assorted pipes and a battered kitchen sink poked from the rubble. The stench of death surrounded them. She shuddered, hoping some of that family survived.

Several canopied Army trucks were parked across the street from the bomb crater Mollie and Barbara skirted. A chorus of whistles welcomed the two girls and one of the drivers beckoned to them. "Going to the air base, ladies?" A smiling GI with a thick southern accent called. "We were ordered to pick up the nurses."

Mollie and Barbara stumbled across the street with their baggage, hurrying as fast as they could, hobbled by narrow khaki skirts. They had been instructed to change into dress uniforms from the comfortable pants and jackets worn on the flight. Some general's idea of a good image, Mollie had grumbled.

She puffed under her load. "Seems like we've done this a few hundred times lately, Barb. If they don't have a hot shower in the barracks, I may go AWOL to find one. I feel like an ad for *Lifebouy* soap!"

"Mollie McAllister and Barbara Andrews!" A tall thin Army nurse took long strides over to the truck.

"Shirley!" Both girls dropped their bags and screamed, forgetting officer protocol to hug her and leap up and down like school girls.

Shirley retrieved her hat, which had dislodged and settled it over her hair. "Lordy, is it good to see familiar faces in not so jolly old England. I haven't seen anyone I recognize since St. Annie's. It's been the longest month of my life."

"You could have joined the Navy and maybe stayed with Ginger," Barbara said.

"And every day of the last four weeks I've been sorry I didn't. Have you ever been to South Carolina in July? I nearly died from heat and bugs, and lost ten pounds. Did you two fly over?"

"Yeah," Mollie said, "We landed in Edinburgh."

Shirley puffed to pick up her bags. "My plane went to Manchester." She patted her stomach. "I'm starved. Hope they have something besides tea and crumpets when we get to the base."

Shirley's wish was fulfilled. The three girls joined a line at mess, and eagerly filled plates with Swiss steak, mashed potatoes and apple pie. When the nurses finished eating, they were taken on a tour of the hospital.

Mollie came close to losing that good meal several times when they walked through the wards crowded with wounded. First, they toured the ambulatory area where men in wheelchairs and on crutches packed the space tightly. Beds were so close together, their occupants could reach out and adjust their neighbors' pillows.

"Dorrie would have to slim down considerably to fit in here," Shirley whispered. "For once, it's a good thing I'm skinny."

"I doubt if you'll gain any weight either. I haven't seen one nurse who didn't look exhausted." Mollie noticed a shared expression of the hospital personnel: mask-like resignation. Would she soon have that remote detachment? Another phenomenon argued with the bland expressions of medical personnel. No matter how worn or discouraged before entering the wards, when the nurses approached patients, particularly the seriously wounded ones, they smiled and changed to light banter. Hollywood actresses could not have performed as well.

The men grinned and introduced themselves. "Hi, I'm Pete or John or Ed. Every batch of you chicks of mercy gets more gorgeous. Glad to meet you, sweetheart. How about a nice long massage?"

No indoctrination course in the States could have prepared them for the horror they witnessed in this short tour. Mollie gulped when a hole in a bandaged face gurgled. The poor man had no mouth or lower jaw at all. Tubes to nourish him ran through what was left of his nose.

But Lieutenant Porter's eyes spoke a friendly greeting, first narrowing, and then twinkling when she was introduced. She glanced briefly at his chart and smiled.

"Hello. I'm glad to meet you, Lieutenant Porter. Like you, Barbara and I are from Washington state. I'm Mollie McAllister, and this is Barbara Andrews. Our home town's Bremerton, and my cousin lives in Everett. Tomorrow, I'll be working in this ward and we'll reminisce." She squeezed his outstretched hands and turned quickly to swallow. How could the most talented plastic surgeon in the world fix that poor man's face?

The "Heads" got to Barbara. A whole ward of human flesh without brain power. One especially handsome young man, with a thatch of curly dark hair, had no visible injury, but a bullet had entered one side of his head, taking his intellect out the other. Barbara greeted him with a shaky smile. "Hello. I'm Barbara Andrews." Zombie eyes stared vacantly at the ceiling and she hurried to the corridor for air.

Odor from the burn ward met them at the door where they donned sterile masks and gowns to enter the inner cocoon. The nurse corps captain leading them felt it necessary to do a little extra briefing.

"Few of these men will recover," she whispered. "They are burned so deeply over such a large area of skin, it takes miracles to escape secondary infections. That's why we're so careful. When a man leaves this ward on his own legs, we all celebrate."

"Guess I'll have to get used to it. I'm assigned here tomorrow," Shirley said, tilting her nose to shut out the odor of decaying flesh.

~ * ~

The following morning, Mollie accompanied the doctor to Lieutenant Porter's bed. She balanced a sterile dressing tray through the narrow space, and fought to steel herself for the ordeal.

"Good morning, Andy." The doctor pulled the bandages away as if peeling a soft-boiled egg. "You have some crusting scar tissue we must remove today. I'm afraid it won't be pleasant."

The young man nodded, his eyes saying, "Okay," but Mollie noticed his fists were so tightly clenched, the knuckles grew white.

Mollie practiced detachment. It would take awhile to learn. Her heart thudded when she saw the vacancy without its covering bandage. Andy Porter looked far worse then she'd dreamed. The wound extended from his cheek bone on the right side to below his chin. The left side was a little better. Some tissue was still healthy, a cluster of whiskers sticking from the edges. She hadn't noticed the suction yesterday: tubes running from his wound to a container on the floor. Remembering Ginger's trial with a similar bottle the first day on duty at St. Annie's, she smiled.

His brown eyes stared as if he meant to say, "Thank you. You are not horrified. Maybe there is hope."

This exchange had evidently not been missed by the doctor. When they were in the corridor, he remarked.

"You've adjusted well to Andy, Lieutenant McAllister. Few do. I often do his dressings without assistance because it becomes too much for a nurse. Hope you will join us tonight at the Officer's Club."

"I...I have personal matters to attend tonight, Doctor. Sorry." She couldn't wear her engagement ring on the floor because of the constant scrubbing for dressings. Would it make a difference if she told him? Doubtful. He was probably married. Most doctors were.

"Okay, but you shouldn't miss our 'Little Hour of Comfort.' Every nurse and doctor around here who puts in twelve hours of this needs that." He smiled at her questioning brows. "It's a cocktail hour, a sort of sharing time. We all need to shed what we see all day."

~ * ~

Mollie felt exhausted by six, longing only to take a nice warm shower and don her robe and slippers. She didn't feel hungry and definitely didn't crave a drink, but Shirley and Barbara had also gotten invitations to the daily Comfort Hour. She sighed, "I'll come for a few minutes."

She followed her two friends to a low building across the road from the sandbagged hospital entrance. The room was lit dimly by red-shaded lamps, reminding her of those fancy old gay nineties hotels in Western movies.

"It's like a tomb in here." Barbara squinted to focus.

"Over here, ladies. Lots of room." The voice came from an even darker corner.

"Hello again, Captain Brown. I followed my friends, not my inclinations," Mollie said quietly. "Please meet Barbara Andrews and Shirley Britton. We were all cadet nurses at St. Anne's Nursing School in Seattle, Washington."

Captain Brown, seated at the round table covered with red oilcloth, introduced two of his fellow medical officers. "Seattle, you say? The young man with the facial injury is from Washington state."

"I know. I saw it on his chart. He's also in the Eighth Air Force. My brother who..." Mollie stammered a little..."is in that group."

"There's a big base over at Bury St. Edmund. Know where your brother is stationed?" one of the other doctors asked.

Barbara interrupted. "Captain Joe McAllister is a prisoner of war somewhere in Germany." She patted Mollie's arm, her eyes glistening.

"Sorry, Lieutenant McAllister" He paused too long. "A lot of Air Force guys lately..."

A waiter brought a tray of tinkling drinks and set them in front of the six seated around the table. Shirley raised hers high.

"A toast to the survivors. To the end of the war."

Six glasses clinked, and Captain Brown raised his again. "And to three beautiful women who are more than welcome to help us end it."

After another round of rum and Cokes for the girls and Scotch and soda for the men, Mollie placed her hand over her glass. "I'm kind of hungry and I still have to do some household chores. See you tomorrow." She rose amid their protests, hurried to the officers' mess for a bowl of soup, and then climbed the stairs to the barracks room she and Barbara had managed to share through a little trading around with the other nurses.

Barbara appeared at ten, breathless, glassyeyed and with her hair not in its usual perfect condition. "You should have stayed, Mollie. They're all very nice."

Mollie folded the letter to Ron she had just finished. "I know. I didn't mean to be snooty, just couldn't quite get into the partying spirit tonight."

"I told them you were engaged to a Navy officer," Barbara mumbled from under the slip suspended over her head. "That brought the usual anti-Gob remarks. Shirley is still out with that tall one, Doctor Alberts, even though she knows he's married."

Mollie considered the statement. Barbara's voice lacked the old moralizing tone she'd used when talking about Dorrie's, or Carmen's transgressions. Had war already pricked the solid values they shared? Would she and Barbara join Shirley and try to capture pleasure when it beckoned? To enjoy an hour when it might be the last? She stared at Ron's picture, shook her head, and picked up her pen. Paper and memories would have to be enough for a long time.

~ * ~

August 14, 1944

Dearest Ron,

Writing letters without answers to the previous ones is like talking to yourself, but I know where you are the mail isn't delivered door to door. I started this one while sitting on my duffel bag at the embarkation center. (Yes, army nurses carry duffel bags!) The war got so anxious for our services, Barbara and I, and thirty other nurses were flown over to work in a base hospital. It's nice to be needed, but I wish this war would end so we could repeat that wonderful night on the beach forever. I will mail this tomorrow sealed with a thousand kisses and praying you are safe. There are many new things to worry over now that I am really sharing the same war. Don't think it is cowardly to try and save that handsome body for me.

Love, Mollie.

Nineteen

Mollie wiped a wet smear from the stationery as she wrote a note to Dorrie. Tears came without permission these days. A choking constriction found her throat during each interval she had time to think about personal problems, like why she hadn't gotten any mail from Ron? She'd written to his mother to be sure his APO address was correct. Mrs. Van Ness's prompt answer to her letter said she believed Ron was still on a carrier somewhere in the Pacific. And his sister, Dee, wrote that he hinted he was near Midway.

She knuckled her forehead, trying to physically dislodge the hurt and doubt crowding logic from her mind. She remembered the pact they had made about not writing "Dear Johns." Anger followed that thought. She had been completely faithful, though there were plenty of opportunities to cheat. Had the Campus King's vows of love been another of his lines for conquest? Thank God, she hadn't gotten pregnant that night on the beach. During the first month after they parted, she hadn't thought about that because she was too busy traveling and too much in love to care anyway.

Mollie laid the letter atop one Barbara had written, then hurried to the place that always provided solace for her loneliness. The care of patients at the hospital served to replace anxiety about both her brother and fiancé. Each day, she found a few minutes to visit with Andy Porter while she changed his dressings. She had learned to understand his various grunts, hand signals, written notes and expressions in his eyes. He asked about Joe every day.

"No, I still haven't heard from Joe. Mom and Dad have had only one letter this whole year. The Red Cross says he's in a prison somewhere near Dresden. The Allies are a long way from there."

She watched closely as Andy's hands moved to show the sign of hammer and sickle, and then pointed east. "Yes, the Russians might reach the prison camp first."

Mollie cut the bandages away and redressed the wound. The remaining flesh on Andy's face had almost healed, but he still looked like an unfinished Frankenstein monster. The doctors had decided to keep the dressings in place until plastic surgeons made up their minds what to do about repairing the damage. Andy could have gone home a month ago, but had elected to stay a while longer. She suspected he dreaded facing his family, especially the wife he had not seen in two years. Picturing the horror of her own reaction if Ron or Joe came home looking like Andy Porter, she knew her shuddering was not from the cool air blowing through the open window. Would it be better if these young men had been killed outright?

But Andy inspired her. He hated his dependence upon others. Because most of his palate and teeth were gone, eating was a messy trial, so he preferred to sip soft thin food and liquids, even coffee, through straws. Guiding any food into his throat without causing choking required patience by Andy and the nurse feeding him. It would take an engineering miracle to rebuild his lower jaw. Mollie couldn't imagine how they could possibly design a mouth that would permit him to chew, talk, smile and kiss his wife.

Andy swung his legs over the edge of the bed and reached for his robe and slippers to go for the walks he took several times a day.

"Looks like some Harry Milquetoast to me," Dr. Albert said. "Hope he can run the war if he needs to."

Mollie listened, surprised the conversation turned to political matters. Ordinarily the men skirted anything serious. Mostly, they told Kilroy jokes or argued about who had the best chance to win the World Series when the war was over.

Doctor Brown raised a brow and smiled at Dr. Alberts next to him. "Did you and Shirley like your hop over to Ireland?"

"It was wonderful," Shirley said. "Everyone should fly over at least once while we're stationed here." She stared directly at Mollie. "Especially a certain Florence Nightingale type I know, who carries a flaming torch way too high."

Shirley had surprised her old friends by becoming the paramour of the burn specialist, Doctor Arthur Alberts. When the two had a twenty-four hour pass, they hurried out into the country to stay in little inns for a respite from war. On the last leave, they had flown over to Ireland. When Barbara reminded her Dr. Alberts was married, Shirley had shrugged and replied, "I might need to consider that when the war is over, but right now it's easier to be like Scarlett in *Gone With The Wind* and think about it tomorrow."

"So far, I haven't been invited to go anywhere more exotic than the post movies," Mollie sighed. She had almost mastered complacency; to flatten her feelings, to hide the emptiness. Worst of all, was the tinge of doubt because she hadn't heard from Ron. Why doubt? What kind of future could they have if she couldn't learn to trust? Could Ron continue to love a woman prone to jealousy? The old green monster crept into her thoughts far too often.

One of the pilots leaning on an elbow at the bar sipping scotch and soda spun around on his stool. "I'm flying over to Dublin tomorrow." He refilled his drink, strolled over to the darkened corner table and, tilting his floppy hat to the back of his head, grinned at Mollie.

"Don't I know you from somewhere, Lieutenant?" He scanned her figure, and then brightened. "Sure, I remember. You're Joe McAllister's sister!"

Mollie's brow crinkled, and then she smiled brightly. "A long time ago at the airport in Seattle, but I'm afraid I have forgotten your name, Captain."

"Major Reed." He pointed to the oak leaves on his uniform. "Terrence Reed. I-I heard about Joe. Mollie, isn't it?"

Mollie nodded. "Sorry, Major. It's either the dark in here, or I'm not very observing of rank. Most of the officers I meet are in hospital drab."

Major Reed pulled a chair from another table and squeezed it beside Mollie's. "Why not fly over to Ireland with me tomorrow?"

"You have a weekend leave, Mollie. Go." Barbara patted her arm. "You may not get another chance for a while." She shot a glance toward Captain Brown.

"I order it, Mollie. Your forty-eight hour leave is long overdue. Can't have you turning into a zombie like..." He smiled and scribbled on an order slip he pulled from his coat. "I'll get Colonel Evans to concur."

He hadn't finished the part about zombies, but Mollie knew he meant Carlin, the nurse who had broken down last week. "I don't know. I've been planning to go over to Bury St. Edmund and look up some of Joe's buddies." She had intended to go several times, but something always happened when she tried. Once there had been an air raid, another time she couldn't get on the train because of troop movements.

"You can go there next leave," Barbara insisted. "Come on, I'll help you pack." She pushed her chair back and buttoned her uniform jacket.

Mollie felt Andy touch her hand and she turned to face him. He aimed an exaggerated wink at her, making it clear he thought she should go with Terry.

"And remember, I *am* one of Joe's buddies," Terry said. "I'll pick you up at four in the morning, Mollie. We'll take off at o-five-hundred." He whistled an Irish tune through his teeth and did a little jig as he left the table.

Mollie recognized Terry's announcement of conquest, but at the moment felt only numbness. Lately she was too tired, too sad, and worse, too unfeeling, all signs of depression. Barb was right. Time to change routine before they found a padded cell for her. "Come on, Barb, if you're going to help me pack. My night is going to be awfully short. And while I think of it, don't forget to mail our letters to Dorrie."

~ * ~

Air Corps Base Hospital, Coventry, England
November 20, 1944
Great news, Dorrie!
I bought a box of cigars to pass out to the patients and doctors and when they asked about the occasion, I told them one of my best friends just had a baby boy. Jacob Joseph? You couldn't get more Jewish/Catholic! Jake probably soared right off Guam when he heard. I am glad you came through the Caesarian section without trouble.

It has been four months since I have heard from Ron. Our mail must be crossing somewhere.

~ * ~

Before climbing into bed, Mollie tried to write another letter to Ron. She felt as blank inside as the piece of paper on her desk. Like Shirley and Scarlett, she'd think about it tomorrow.

Twenty

Mollie recognized none of the six passengers on the cargo plane. While flying over the Irish Sea, she and the only other woman on board, a woman from the Red Cross, carried on a shouted conversation over the roar of the engines. Many flights went to Ireland, ordinarily to Belfast, the woman said. Dublin was in the Republic of Ireland and not in the usual flight plan unless there were special passengers or cargo.

The Air Force C-54 descended through thick clouds and landed on a rain-slicked runway, a rather bleak greeting for a vacationer. Mollie refused to wonder about irregularities today, vowing to enjoy this short respite from mangled human beings. Carrying only a small overnight bag, she climbed down the ladder from the plane and ignored whistles and raised eyebrows of the Air Force men unloading cargo.

A husky corporal in mechanic's coveralls broke her stoic expression when he winked and murmured under his breath, "Major Reed's extra baggage gets better every flight!"

So the GIs expected her to sleep with Major Reed. The nurses and even Barb made it clear they expected a romantic encounter. Mollie sighed. Detachment from feeling came easier. Major Reed hurried to catch up with her. "We're free for about twenty hours, Mollie. Have to fly this crate back tomorrow morning. I'll spring rank for one order. On this trip, I'm Terry, not Major Reed." He opened the door to an olive drab painted '40 Plymouth parked by a low building roofed with sheets of corrugated steel.

Mollie shook the rain from her coat and climbed in beside him. "Where to then, Sir Terry?"

"Ah, you are becoming enchanted by the bright surroundings," Terry quipped. "Rain is what makes Ireland so green. There's a cozy little place I know where we can warm our chilled bodies with Irish style Coffee Royals." He drove the car through the confusing tangle of streets as if he were a native Dubliner.

"Rain reminds me of home. Guess that's why I don't mind being stationed in England. It's misty like Seattle." Mollie shivered, not so much from the chill as uncertainty about the rest of her leave.

Terry parked the car in front of an ancient pub. Its exterior was brick, painted black to contrast with white window frames. A sign picturing a wooly sheep, and what she suspected was Gaelic script, hung over the door. Mollie followed Terry inside, half expecting to see James Joyce seated at the bar.

The pub owner led them to a table in front of one of the two square-paned windows facing the street and brought two cups of brandy-laced coffee. Terry leaned across the wooden table and took her hand, frowning slightly when he touched the diamond shining in the dim light. "Like the coffee?"

"Mmm, it tastes good and feels better, but I don't see any women here. Don't Irish girls go to places like this?"

"Not this time of day. They're all home knitting and tending to their *bairns*," Terry teased in a fake Irish accent.

Mollie felt uncomfortable, but three men standing at the bar seemed at ease in her presence. At Terry's signal, the pub owner smiled broadly and brought them another drink.

He wiped pudgy hands on a slightly soiled white apron. "I reserved your regular room, Major Reed, like ye asked. And we'll be having your favorite little oysters for supper."

"Fine. We'll be back around six, O'Riley. I want to show my friend some of Dublin's sights." Terry glanced at his watch. "And I'm sure Mollie will want to do some shopping."

The owner grinned, showing the gap from a missing front tooth.

"Mollie is it? A right proper Irish name."

Mollie smiled. "I'm named for my O'Halleran grandmother. I believe her ancestors were from Limerick. But my father is Scotch. My last name is McAllister."

"I tolerate a few well-behaved Scots, but for the bit of Irish, ye deserve another drink courtesy o' The Black Fleece." He brought an amber bottle to the table, splashed it into the bottom of the cups, poured black coffee to the top and spooned thick cream over it.

When they finished the drink, Terry drove through the city, stopping at charming little shops stocked with Irish handwork. Mollie caught herself briefly resenting the reminders that Ireland was not at war. She bought hand-knit woolen sweaters for herself, Sally and her mother. "Dad will love this tweed cap to cover his balding head, and I might as well get Mike one, too. I'll take the little baby sweater and cap." She smiled at the rosy cheeked sales girl. Dorrie would love that. "They're beautiful. It would take me weeks to make one not nearly as nice as this."

She searched for gifts for her friends, something they hadn't already found for themselves. "Maybe this small Waterford jam dish for Barb...and these linen hankies for Shirley." Her depressive mood faded while she shopped.

Terry stood patiently watching her, saying little. "The sun's trying to peek out. Let's drive out to the docks at Dun Laoghaire and watch the gulls argue."

He drove through the busy streets and stopped near a long pier. They climbed from the car and walked with wind blowing in their faces, down to the sea wall. Clouds fluttered high above soaring gulls and little wooden canoe-shaped boats wallowed toward the jetty opening.

"Do they actually fish in those tiny boats?" Mollie asked.

"Have for centuries, I'm told. They cut through the waves well and are a lot more stable than they look." Terry stood behind her, moving his arms to encircle her waist, pulling her closer when she didn't resist.

Mollie relished the warmth and comfort of having a man's strong arms around her. It filled a void in her life, a tenderness missing in the four months since that wonderful night. She shuddered.

"Cold?" Terry pressed his chin into her hair to shield her from the wind.

"No." She moved around to face him. "You're very thoughtful, Terry. I'm enjoying the time away from chaos."

Terry kissed her then, a sweet kiss, with none of the designs her friends had forecast for the night.

When they arrived back at The Black Fleece, linen cloths covered the tables in the pub. Terry guided her through the dimly lit room and they settled onto red-cushioned chairs in a corner alcove.

"Irish oysters are nearly as good as our Olympics." Mollie relished another morsel and took a sip of the dark ale Terry had ordered. That brew would take some getting accustomed to, she decided. "Guinness? Is that what they call this stuff?"

"Yes. Brewed right here in Dublin, has been for a hundred years or so. The flavor grows on you." He wiped a trickle of the thick white foam from his lips.

"I must say. It goes well with seafood." Mollie spread butter on a thick slice of dark grainy bread. "And this bread is delicious."

"Soda bread, the dark kind, made from rye and oats. I think it evolved from poverty and is a part of most meals in Ireland. I usually buy a couple of loaves to take back to the base, but have to eat it fast because it molds quickly." Terry motioned to the girl waiting tables during the busier meal hours at the small pub. "I'll have another Guinness and bring one of those little glasses of your best cherry brandy for the lady."

Mollie sipped the fiery red brandy. It tasted good after the meal and she vowed to try it again sometime. The girl refilled her glass. Warmth and friendliness was everywhere here, far from the bombs, yet only a couple hours flight from the destruction of England and Europe. Terry's voice made her start.

"There's a show I thought we might take in, a musical." He rose to help her with her raincoat.

The wipers fought to keep the rain from the windshield as he drove through nearly deserted streets to a large Victorian-style theater.

"Now I know where everybody in Dublin went to get out of the rain." Mollie squeezed through the crowd queued at the box office. She stared up at the marquee. "Gracie Fields, no wonder."

Terry moved toward the door. "It's a good thing I already have the tickets."

Gracie's singing of *White Cliffs of Dover* brought first silence, then cheers from the audience. This popular English song caused pure emotional response from the mostly Irish audience and brought tears to Mollie's eyes.

"Perhaps Ireland is not quite as neutral as it claims. I loved the show, Terry." Mollie dabbed her eyes for the tenth time, many of the tears from laughter. She hadn't felt much like laughing since arriving in England. The moon floated in high clouds as they drove back to their lodgings. The rain had stopped.

At the door of the rented room above the little pub, Terry fumbled with the key, unable to hide his nervousness. "Mollie, I hope it's okay. This arrangement, I mean, sharing the room."

She had not protested when they left their luggage there before touring Dublin. Her new-found friend *resignation* had ruled. That Terry expected payment for his kindness, she simply shut out. No moral thought would creep into her mind during this segment of time. At the door, she paused to survey the room, a comfortable tidy one with flowered ruffled curtains matching the spread on the double bed. "It's fine, Terry."

Terry helped her from her coat and jacket. "You take the bathroom first, Mollie. I'm going to have a drink and a cigarette." He pulled a flask from his coat and opened the cork. "There should be a glass in there if you care to join me."

"After I get into something more comfortable than this uniform," Mollie mumbled from the doorway. She scanned a questionable shower installed like an afterthought in one corner of the tiny room under the eaves. A little round wash basin with a worn rubber plug over the drain crowded beside the black painted seat of a stained old toilet, its flushing chain running to a ceiling tank. Terry had to be some kind of wonder to find this place. Shirley had reported rooms with private baths were unusual even in big hotels.

She donned the new pink silk pajamas and matching tailored woolen robe her mother had sent last week as an early Christmas present. It was the only clothing she brought along except for a change of underwear and hosiery. It felt luxurious to wear something pink after so much olive drab. She pulled a brush through her hair, loosened from the trim chignon she always wore when in uniform. The dark auburn curls settled over her shoulders. She leaned closer to the mottled mirror over the little basin. Like the peeling silver on the mirror, her steely composure fell away. The real Mollie McAllister stared back. She sat down on the toilet seat, head in hands, sobs shaking her body.

Terry tapped on the door. "Mollie? Are you okay?"

"I...I. just a minute, Terry." Trembling so that her teeth chattered, she opened the door and stumbled into the welcome arms outside.

Terry caught her sagging figure and carried her to the bed. Pulling the covers back with one hand, he eased her down onto the sheets, tucking the fluffy comforter under her chin. He sat on the edge of the bed, his hands gently smoothing her forehead.

"Ready to talk about it?" He lit a cigarette and waited patiently, blowing smoke rings toward the ceiling.

Mollie forced a weak smile. "You got yourself a real doozy for a roommate, Terry. I just remembered who I was and where I came from. Now, if I only knew where I was going, I would be fine."

"Who knows the answer to that anymore? How long since you heard from him?" He nodded toward the ring on the hand he pulled from the covers.

"Four months. He's in the Pacific theater somewhere. The last time anyone heard, near Guam." Mollie turned her head toward the window across the room, trying to escape the intense gaze boring from the blue eyes above her.

"If you love him that much, don't give up, Mollie. Mail gets real unpredictable in wars. Some guys don't hear from their families for six months at a time." He straightened and sat on the side of the bed, a sad look in his eyes. "One of mine came far too fast."

"A 'Dear John'?"

"My wife decided not to wait. She wanted a baby so bad, she got pregnant by a civilian son-of-a-bitch!" Terry crossed the room, pulled a full bottle of scotch from his valise, grabbed a glass from the bathroom and settled down on the bed.

"War distorts everyone and everything. We have to try to overlook it, I guess," Mollie said.

"Want to drink to that?"

Words flowed more easily as the pale amber liquid went down. Mollie poured out her worries, fears and the jealous anger so long tethered inside. Terry listened to her tale and she heard his. She relaxed, lying back on the pillows, drained.

"You're beautiful, Mollie." Terry leaned to kiss her lips, tasting them with growing hunger. He undressed and slipped into the bed beside her.

Mollie floated in a crescendo of sensations, conscious of his hands moving over her body and relishing the warmth, the closeness, the passion unfolding. Something caught the coverlet. Ron's ring! "No, Terry, I can't... I'm sorry." Terry groaned, sat up, and taking her hand, turned the ring on her finger.

"Oh, golly. I've ruined everything for you." Tears stung her eyes. "And you've been so kind."

Terry reached for his trousers. "It's okay. But if that Navy hero stands you up, I'll break the sound barrier flying to you," he called from the bathroom door.

Mollie heard the sound of the shower as she dozed off. She felt a comforting arm around her waist when she roused once during the night.

The odor of cigarette smoke woke her and she rolled to her side trying to focus sleep-filled eyes and a fuzzy brain. Her head throbbed. Already dressed, Terry stood by the window, the faint early morning light outlining his figure. She sat up too fast and clutched her head.

"Too much scotch?" He reached in his shirt pocket. "Good Friend Terry is always prepared for minor emergencies. I'll fix a seltzer."

Mollie heard the fizz in the glass as he held it toward her. She drank it, puckering her face. "Thanks, Terry. I'd like to try the shower if there's time."

"I'll show you how to make it work. Has a meter that turns it on for about five minutes. You may freeze, and be glad to be out by that time."

Mollie clutched her robe tighter in the chill. The room had no heat except a little peat fire smoldering in the corner fireplace. "Thanks, it's not much colder here than in the barracks. I'll be out in a minute. Did you get any sleep at all? What time is it?"

He pointed to the turned-back comforter and grinned. "The scotch put me out for at least four hours and it's eight o'clock. If we hurry, we have time for a good hearty Irish breakfast."

Mollie had no inclination for food at all. Her tongue felt dry and she swallowed a surge of nausea. After the short cool shower which left her shivering and refreshed, she dressed quickly. They descended the stairs to the pub, where Terry pushed money for the night's lodging into a mason jar on the counter. "O'Riley only rents that room to people he trusts. He doesn't open up the pub until about ten," he said, opening the door to the car. "We still have time for breakfast at a little coffee shop near the river before heading for the airport."

Mollie nibbled a slice of soda bread, and forced down a second cup of vile-tasting black coffee. "I think I might live awhile after all."

"I am glad you have decided that." Terry's eyes had a strange look. "I want to apologize, Mollie. For last night, I mean."

"Apologize? It's I who am sorry, Terry. And regretful... no, that isn't quite the word either. I didn't plan to lean on you so hard." Mollie stared into her plate, trying to sort out a mixture of feelings. The night was still fuzzy, but undeniably real. "I'm sorry I disappointed you." She couldn't blame the liquor for wanting Terry to make love to her. If Ron's ring hadn't reminded her of a solemn commitment... "You're a sweet man and I spoiled your leave."

"Promise me something." He leaned across the table and took her hands. "Promise me you'll try not to feel guilty and that you won't confess what did or didn't happen between us last night to the man you really love."

"But, I..." She felt his finger over her lips.

"Stop! I know you feel like a cheat right now. I also know how it feels to learn about infidelity, however incomplete. If your fiancé is the kind of man who deserves you, he won't expect to hear about a brief encounter with a near stranger in Ireland."

Mollie saw a curtain of sadness draw over his eyes. "I hope you aren't sorry you brought me along."

"Believe me. I never enjoyed a date with a girl more. How I envy that lucky Navy stiff." He smiled then, and rose from the table, glancing toward the car parked outside. "And I probably got off lucky. If Joe learned I tried to seduce his sister, he'd deck me. Guess we must get going."

Mollie tugged at his arm before he entered the pilot's compartment of the airplane. "Why didn't you get angry at me last night? I know I led you on, then pushed you away."

"Baby, your face is a map of honesty unlike any other girl I've ever known. You are definitely a one man woman, as the saying goes. Remember our promise." He raised two fingers for a "V" sign, slid into his seat, and clamped the ear phones on.

~ * ~

The flight back to England went smoothly and Mollie hurried to her room. On her bunk was a pile of mail. Her bag thudded to the floor and she plunged into the stack of letters eagerly. Twenty-four were from Ron. Tears spotted the V-mails while she read every one twice to be sure they were real, that she wouldn't wake up and find them a pleasant dream. She was still reading and blotting her eyes when Barbara burst in at six.

"I couldn't wait until after Comfort Hour for your reaction to Ron's letters. Wish I could have been off duty to see your face. Where is he?"

"On a carrier near a place called Saipan," Mollie said, "and he wrote in a sort of code we figured out before he went overseas. I know he got shot down and spent some time in the water before being rescued. He just said he had gone for a long swim. I suppose that is why I didn't get any letters. He spent a month in a hospital in Hawaii catching up on writing."

"Oh golly, is he okay?" Barbara's hand flew to her mouth, revealing her regret she had asked.

Mollie understood. If Ron was in the condition of some of the guys in the hospital, maybe she wouldn't want to talk about it.

"After reading between all the lines, I figure he broke his arm in the parachute landing and got a touch of pneumonia from the exposure. Says he lost twenty pounds, but is gaining it back rapidly."

Barbara grinned. "I trust your leave turned out to be fun."

Mollie sighed, fighting the very feeling Terry made her promise against."Yes. Major Terry Reed is a guy you can really talk to. Reminds me of Joe in that respect. Guess I miss being able to have confession sessions with my brother. I know I needed to get away."

"So Major Reed is the brotherly type. Probably one of the only loyally married guys around here."

"He got a 'Dear Terry' from his wife. She found a substitute to father her baby." Mollie jumped from the bed and pulled packages from a bulging shopping bag. "I bought this for you, Barb. Hope it's not too fragile to hold your bobby pins."

Mollie followed Barbara down to the Officers' Club, feeling a little nervous about the round of bawdy jokes bound to fall to her and Terry. She relaxed when she spotted him at the bar. He turned with a quick "V" sign, raised his glass, and strolled over to join them.

When Mollie returned to the barracks, she sat for a long time trying to make the pen write the things she needed to say to Ron. It wanted to spill out the whole story to cleanse her conscience. Yes, it was there, the guilt Terry warned about.

The door burst open and Shirley came leaping into the room.

"Guess what? We leave tomorrow morning to air lift wounded from France." She hugged them. "We will be close to Paris, gals. Paris!"

"Oh, no!" Barbara buried her head in the pillow. "That means we'll be flying!"

~ * ~

November 23,1944

Darling, at last I got your letters and have read each one at least three times. They were here when I got back from a twenty-four hour leave in Ireland. What a wonderful green land it is, and a lot like Washington state. I hope we can go there sometime together. Do you know what the guys say about me? That I am a "one man woman." I hope you know how high you rate when there are thousands of men to each girl around here.

Love, Mollie

Twenty-one

Since moving to a base at Dover, Mollie and her friends saw little of each other between flights. The Hour of Comfort enjoyed at Coventry was a distant memory. Medical Evacuation nurses were always so exhausted. Their layovers were spent catching up on lost sleep. Swiping a hand over the moisture covering the small barracks window, Mollie saw that it was still raining and blowing. Her flight had been postponed until the weather cleared enough to take off. She stretched out on her bunk to read, and dozed off. When Barbara woke her, she forced open reluctant eyes, wishing she could have had a couple more hours of sleep.

"I checked on our flight. The latest weather report says it's clearing. We take off in an hour."

Mollie noted that her friend's face had turned nearly as pale as the chalk cliffs below the airbase. She watched as Barbara reached into her foot locker to pull out a bottle of cognac. Poor Barb, still terrified of flying, but she had discovered a couple of stiff drinks put enough strength into her shapely legs to mount the steps to the plane. Once airborne, she practiced steely stubbornness and worked diligently on nursing the gravely wounded.

Rarely did Barbara and Mollie fly together, but today their rotations coincided. Because of the late start, they would return after dark or possibly stay overnight in Belgium. Interrupted schedules had become as routine as missing meals and sleep.

The two nurses hurried out to the C-47 and up the loading ramp. Mollie usually read on flights to the Continent unless the plane was full of talkative passengers headed for the war. Today, she and Barbara shared the company of several American newspaper and radio correspondents, who lounged on the litters smoking and making passes at the two nurses.

The balding guy from Associated Press, without pausing in his conversation, did a juggling act with a mug of coffee through a pocket of rough air. "You gals must find these flights routine now that the coasts of France and Holland are in Allied hands."

Barbara's fidgeting hands showed anything but calm routine. "Wrong. Weather like we have today gives me nervous shakes even if flak is missing."

"Ordinarily, EVAC crews fly over to Belgium or France and back the same day so we can sleep for a few hours in our own nice, noisy barracks," Mollie added.

The handsome N.B.C. announcer staggered across the aisle and crouched close to Barbara's jump seat. He placed a hand on her knee. "Your duty must not give you much time to see France. If you get a chance to stay over in Paris, I'd be more than happy to show you the city." He squinted to read her name badge. "Lieutenant Andrews."

"Paris? All I've ever seen is from the airfield. We barely have time to use the john and grab a sandwich before the wounded are loaded aboard and we head back across the channel." Barbara glanced at her watch. "We're going to be very late today. May have to stay over if the ambulances aren't waiting for us."

The newsman scratched a number on a slip of yellow paper. "I'll be in Brussels for a couple of days, so if you do layover, you can reach me at this number. Just tell them you have an important message for Richard Charles of N.B.C."

Dusky shadows hovered over the bomb pocked field in Belgium where the plane landed. As the newsmen walked toward waiting command cars, two of them aimed cameras at Mollie and Barbara, then at medics hurrying the stretchers into the war-worn C-47.

"If that film reaches the newsreels at home, Mom and Dad will have a heart attack," Mollie said, nodding toward several severely wounded men. "Looks like we won't get dinner tonight."

~ * ~

Barbara and Mollie climbed back aboard the cargo plane. The C-47 had been stripped bare except for necessary medical supplies and tiers of brackets on each side holding litters for the wounded. As soon as the plane was airborne, the girls unstrapped themselves from jump seats and began their emergency nursing chores. If the air stayed this rough, half of their patients would be sick.

Mollie reeled from side to side to grasp the swaying litters, and struggling to keep gear in place. She searched for comforting words to calm the injured men, and glanced anxiously toward Barbara, who was stoically concentrating on doing the same thing. They exchanged "V" signs.

In the tail section, Barbara held a paper bag over a green-tinged face, placing her hand on the GI's chest wound to keep the stitches from pulling loose. "Okay, Corporal, just urp in here." She turned away to swallow the surge in her own throat, scrambling for a handhold when a loud thunk sent her stumbling to the bumpy floor. Plasma bottles and pillows sailed over her head. Flak thumped precariously close to the fuselage, its bursts flashing through the tiny window slits. Barbara gnawed her knuckles, cowering momentarily. She craved nothing more than to cover her face and ears and succumb to terror. Forcing herself to her feet, she stumbled over the cluttered assortment covering the floor, and grasped a litter support to keep from falling again.

~ * ~

"Better strap yourselves in back there, girls. This might take awhile," Lieutenant Jordan reported calmly over the speaker like he was piloting the plane through ordinary air turbulence.

Barbara staggered toward her little jump seat at the narrow end of the tail section. "Oooh!" her cry of fright swallowed her breath and voice, when metal screamed beneath her. She stumbled aft barely in time to avoid falling through a gaping hole midship. Smoke from the explosion filled the compartment and the dim cabin lights blinked off. Groans of pain from the wounded and the roar of rushing air sent a deafening chorus through the plane.

"Judas Priest!" In the smoky dimness, she caught a nightmare image of a loosened stretcher sliding slowly toward the jagged opening on her side of the hole. She grabbed wildly for the handle, her screams for help swallowed by the din. Holding on to the litter took every measure of strength. To pull the litter backward would be impossible without help. She grunted with pain when turbulence slammed hard against the floor onto her stomach. Still she hung on.

The soldier's head lay near her desperately clinging hands, his feet dangling over thousands of feet of empty space. Another lurch and Barbara grappled to keep the tenuous hold. The litter slipped inches farther. Her arms felt as if they would pull from their shoulder sockets as the plane angled downward, nosing slowly toward earth. Another lurch. She forced strength enough to lodge her toes beneath a metal brace. The stretcher and its burden slid another few inches into the hole. Minutes seemed like hours as she clung as if frozen in place.

Air rushed like a giant blower, loosening her long blonde hair to tangle over her eyes. Bursting shells flashed all around the plane.

All Mollie could do from her side was gasp and pray. Helpless, to get to Barbara's side of the hole. She knew that three litters had been sucked into the gap.

After the plane outran the antiaircraft batteries, Mollie aimed her flashlight from the cockpit side to assess the damages. Brackets that had held three litters hung empty. She spotted Barbara. "Oh Lord! Hang on, Barb." She searched wildly for something to cover the jagged chasm before it claimed Barbara and the fourth litter. Rushing air from the ruptured metal muted her voice.

Rolling one of the wounded men out of a cot, Mollie handed him a strap for holding the bunk to the frame of the plane. "Hold onto this, soldier. Tight."

The C-47 lurched sideways and she thudded to her knees, clinging to the billowing canvas cot and praying she could cover the yard-wide hole in time to keep everything movable, including passengers, from sliding through. She lay flat on her stomach to push the cot forward and over the torn metal edges. It took half a dozen tries to jam it into a jagged notch in the other side. She lay on her stomach, searching frantically for a way to secure it from blowing around or out.

"I have it. Hang onto your end while I find some way to tie it," a male voice shouted from Barbara's side. "The problem is I can't see." Mollie's flashlight outlined a soldier, his eyes bandaged and one leg in a splint. He fumbled along the edge of hanging cots until a soldier in one of the litters placed a belt in his hands. Looping it over a support frame at the end of a cot, the wounded occupant helped him fasten the buckle. Mollie secured hers the same way.

Mollie could see the stretcher being held by her friend only when shells burst nearby. From her point across the chasm, she watched in helpless terror as the plane lurched them close to the edge again. She held her breath when the blinded soldier crept close to help

~ * ~

The air was freezing, and Barbara tried detachment to keep her grip on the litter. Rough air tilted the plane, and the patient's litter skewed sideways and another six inches toward the opening. She clenched her jaws tightly, her hands like empty rubber gloves. She screamed over the turbulence when another set of arms grasped the litter, just as her perilous grip loosened.

"Got it. Can you roll a little to the side so I can get a better hold?" The soldier nudged her over until she could slide backwards. "Get one of the straps around it and we'll pull him back." Crouching, she struggled with shaky stiff fingers, until the belt was buckled and another secured over the litter handle.

Turbulence knocked Barbara hard against a post at the edge of a cot. The blow sent her tumbling sideways. She lay crumpled and unmoving.

Mollie's breath caught when the patient's foot, still hanging out of the hole in the fuselage became wedged under a metal groove, temporarily halting his progress toward eternity.

"I can't hold him much longer or see how to bring him back in," The blinded man yelled. "There's no one else over here that can move."

Several heads leaned from the sides of their litters. One of the men pulled Barbara's flashlight from her pocket and aimed it toward the hole. He shouted directions."There, his foot is free. Pull his leg to the right."

"There's a bottle or something to your left," another called.

Slowly the blinded soldier inched backward, tugging the litter. After tying it to a support post, he dragged Barbara's limp figure until they were both wedged into the narrow space in front of the jump seat.

~ * ~

When the plane finally leveled, Mollie ran her tongue over her lips, tasting salty blood from cuts where she had been biting them. She screamed when a hand touched her arm.

"Little excitement back here, huh?" The co-pilot, Lieutenant Hoffman, bundled to his chin in his fleece lined leather jacket, shouted over the noise of rushing air. "Did we lose anyone?"

"Six GIs on the litters that were located over that hole. Another poor guy and Barbara were hanging mighty close to oblivion until someone over there rescued them. Barb is hurt and I have to get across somehow." Mollie moved toward the billowing canvas cot covering the crater.

"Hold it, Mollie!" Lieutenant Hoffman hurriedly untied the two metal boxes filled with medical supplies and dragged them one at a time to the edge of the hole. He secured them with webbed straps. "I doubt these will strengthen the edges of the damaged brace, but let's hope." He crossed his fingers.

"Phew!" Mollie whistled when she aimed her flashlight and could see the bracing struts, dented and torn, hanging under the fuselage. The thinnest of metal skin was all that had been holding Barbara and her two patients. Minutes before, she'd leaned over that weak spot. Shuddering, she recalled the badly damaged planes she had seen land, some with but one engine, some without landing gear; some with holes in fuselages. How large would a crater need to be to send the plane crashing into the channel?

As if testing her thoughts, a piece of metal ripped off and took the hanging struts. Forcing deep breaths, she managed to conquer panic.

Lieutenant Hoffman grasped the framing on top of the sloping fuselage and swung across the gap. "Barbara has a nasty cut on her head. Toss me some compresses," he shouted over the din.

Mollie understood and grabbed her little bag of supplies. "Be right over." She climbed onto the box, stretched on her toes to reach the handhold, and leapt to the other side.

"You Tarzan, me Jane!"

He grinned. "You're crazy, gal!"

"Hold the flashlight. This needs a good hefty compress or it'll keep bleeding." Mollie cleaned the two-inch gap in Barbara's scalp and pulled little pieces of tape over it, then covered the wound with a bandage. Barbara's eyes responded to the flashlight by a narrowing of the pupils. Mollie sighed with relief. The head injury was probably a concussion and a bad cut, not a fractured skull.

Barbara moaned.

"She's coming around. How are you guys?" Mollie moved her flashlight across the faces of the frightened men, then settled it on the one Barbara had rescued. He was unconscious, surely in shock. She pulled a bottle of plasma from her bag, braced herself against a support pole and after a couple of tries, plunged a needle into his arm. "I thought Belgium was in Allied territory."

Lieutenant Hoffman shrugged. "We must have missed a few antiaircraft batteries. Ike will burn some asses. We'll be back to Dover Airbase in about thirty minutes. Cold, Mollie?"

"Frozen, now that I have a minute to dwell on it."

"I'll scrounge all the covering I can for the wounded. We're flying low over the channel to keep this crate together and that should help keep us warmer." Lieutenant Hoffman swung across to the front of the plane and was soon back with several extra blankets. He removed his coat. "I'll donate this to Barbara. She needs it a hell of a lot more than I do." He knelt and put the jacket backwards over Barbara, who opened her eyes, blinked in confusion and then closed them again.

The patient, who had played such a heroic part in the rescue, crouched beside Barbara in the cramped tail section.

He cleared his throat as Mollie secured the plasma bottle on the edge of a litter. "Will she be okay?"

"I hope so. Thank God you were there." Mollie choked a little and turned to kiss him soundly. "Thank you, sir. I don't know your name or anything, but thanks a lot for Barbara."

He touched the little cross on his collar. "Captain Howard Price, Chaplain, Hundred and first Airborne."

"Oh, golly...I should've guessed we had a pipeline to God. Thanks even more, sir. I'd better secure things back here to keep you from scattering during the landing. Send up a few more petitions that this piece of battered metal will reach the base in a few minutes, Captain." She crawled around tightening straps and tying Barbara and the chaplain firmly to the support posts.

Mollie gathered up her case, slung it over her shoulder and reached for the bracing strut. "Better check the rest of the guys. See you in Dover." She swung neatly over the chasm.

Ten minutes later when the plane approached to land, Mollie watched through cracks in the torn fuselage as a fire truck raced to meet them. She gripped the post beside her, and stopped breathing until the wheels touched the pavement. Hanging metal scraped sparks across the runway and she clenched her eyes waiting for an explosion.

One of the patients spoke relief for everyone aboard the plane. "Thank God. We're home!"

~ * ~

Barbara felt fine in a couple of days and went back to her duties. "Know what, Mollie? Something odd happened on that flight."

Mollie jerked her head to get a better look at her friend. Maybe Barbara wasn't over her head injury after all. "That's an understatement. It was terrifying, a lot more than odd."

"Of course! But that scare changed my attitude. Today on our trip over to France, flying didn't scare me at all. It's the first time. In fact, I almost felt good about climbing aboard the transport. Merry Christmas."

"Ditto, Barb. Guess our poor GIs are having a very bleak one in Belgium. Things are really terrible, according to the latest news." Mollie remembered the poor condition of the wounded they had brought back today. Some were suffering from frost bite along with their wounds. Two GIs had died on this EVAC trip.

"Just when we thought we had the war going our way, too." Barbara brushed her hair carefully over her scar. A little patch was missing where they shaved to put in the stitches. She sighed and crawled under her blankets. "Richard Charles from N.B.C. called it the 'Belgian Bulge' in his broadcast tonight."

"He's sure a good-looking guy. Sorta fell for you, Barb."

"One problem. He's married and has two kids." Barbara covered her head to shut out the noise.

The barracks room shuddered from low flying transports headed for the war front. Barbara soon slept undisturbed, but Mollie had never quite got used to them. They reminded her too much of Joe and Ron. Still no word from Joe, and only a couple more letters from her fiancé. Everyone was moving around. Everyone but prisoners of war and those poor guys who dropped through that flak hole last week.

She rose from the bed and squinted at her watch. Midnight. Pulling a woolen overcoat over her shoulders, she slipped silently into the hall and down to a window at the end. Across the blacked out base, a thin beam of moonlight reflected in the moisture on the cobble stones below the barracks.

Why did God allow His special creations to play such destructive games, to practice such hatred? She couldn't remember really hating anyone in all her life, except maybe Hitler. Disliked, disagreed with, but never hated anyone enough to kill...and to kill those we don't even know, have never seen at all...and babies, and old people and...the chain of war's death seemed endless. She shivered. This war wasn't started by the United States. But was her country an innocent bystander?

A strange screaming whistle sent her crouching to the cold floor, a reflex action since coming to Dover. Rockets without accurate aim, heading for any target, assuring more casualties. This new weapon destroyed without seeing its destruction.

She stole quietly back into her room and pulled out Ron's unfinished letter, tilted her flashlight to cover the page, and wrote.

~ * ~

Dover, England
December 25, 1944
Dearest,
The Air Corps guys sing, Off we go into the wild blue yonder, but the song wasn't written about one of our recent flights. The blue yonder was not only wild, but more black than blue and the heavy clouds stalled at our base. We are now assigned to a Medical Evacuation team airlifting the most seriously wounded from Belgium and France on a stripped-down C-47. I admit it's exhausting, definitely not pleasant duty, but we do feel appreciated when we bring the guys back. (Hope you can decipher this) It's Christmas Day, my darling, but there's no Peace on Earth. I wonder if our world will ever be free of war. We must try to get this awful thing over before much more killing and maiming happens. Keep faith for that someday future. I love you.
Mollie.

Mollie closed her fountain pen and clicked off the flashlight, wondering if she had fooled the censors.

Twenty-two

Mollie stopped writing her letter to Ron and chewed the end of her pen. Since his mail came more regularly, she suffered a feeling of remorse that she'd doubted him. It had been three months, yet the short interlude with Terry Reed in Ireland still pricked her conscience. Cheating on Ron and using a really nice guy like Terry to accomplish it, filled her with guilt. She ignored the dozens of opportunities for other romantic alliances, and to be honest, had no inclinations for anything but friendly relationships. That Dublin weekend had served to ease her inner turmoil and to tumble the facade of the stoic Lieutenant Mollie McAllister. Shirley loved to refer to her as an indefatigable Florence Nightingale of World War Two.

As if called by her thoughts, Shirley burst into the room, her habit any time day or night when she had exciting news to tell.

"Mollie, guess what? We're going to Paris!"

Mollie blotted at an ink smear from the letter. "What's different about that? We go over to France every other day."

"Not on flights like this one. We're flying to Allied headquarters to receive citations." She clapped her long fingers together. "And the best news is we'll have three whole days to see Paris. I mean a three-day pass to really see Paris."

"Who are we? You and me and Barbara, or are there a few other people in on this big shindig?"

"The whole Evac unit. I haven't told you the best news. Our group is being transferred to a hospital there. We're to be in the order room in fifteen minutes." Shirley hurried out, shouting the news to Barbara and half a dozen other nurses in the corridor.

After their briefing, Mollie and Barbara hurried back to their quarters.

Barbara read the orders. "It says U.S. Army Field Hospital, Paris, all right. We'll be close to General Eisenhower's headquarters."

"And we have only two hours before boarding the transports. Guess we'd better do double time." Mollie snatched her uniforms from hangers. "Darn, I meant to get my dress uniform cleaned." She felt a tingle of excitement. The move might mean she would be a little nearer to Joe when he was released. Everyone predicted the war was winding down at last.

Barbara scratched at a smudge on her dress blouse. "Shirley's got some spot remover. Maybe we can fix them up with that and a good pressing. It's been so long since we had them on, they probably won't even fit." She scurried out and up the stairs to Shirley's barracks room.

~ * ~

Mollie had paid scant attention to the Eiffel Tower and the Arc de Triomphe on previous flights into Paris. Today, the lacy tower etched on the city skyline in thin February sunshine reminded her of prewar travel posters. The Seine below wove like a silver ribbon through the city. The transport plane banked and landed smoothly, the tires squealing as it braked.

She hefted her shoulder bag and stood in the doorway a minute, waiting for Shirley and Barbara. "No medics running to the plane with the litters. Am I dreaming?"

"Paris does improve without ambulances lined up for miles." Shirley took a deep breath. "Smell that air. No bombs."

"Guess those are the buses to take us to our new barracks." Barbara lifted her bags. "Hope we drew good quarters."

As she rode through the streets of Paris, Mollie noticed the city lacked the bomb craters and piles of broken buildings common to London. The scars here were in the condition of the inhabitants. Children wore tattered clothing, too large or too small, thin limbs poking from sleeves and trouser legs. Months after liberation, many of the housewives carrying long loaves of bread looked too thin, their eyes sunken. But they all smiled when the American nurses passed by.

Mollie drew a sharp whistling breath. "Look over there, Barb. See the three women standing by the iron fence? They're wearing scarves because their heads have been shaved. Remember the correspondent guys telling us about the German collaborators, the whores?"

"How awful!" Barbara's hand moved over her mouth."I mean for French women to do that." She touched the shimmering blonde curls over her forehead. "Guess they must have been terribly hungry to let Germans make love to them."

"I doubt love entered into their thoughts. During wartime, lots of people lose moral values fast," Mollie muttered, hoping Shirley hadn't heard her preachy little speech.

~ * ~

The next morning, the nurses, dressed in neatly pressed uniforms and spotless shoes, lined up in front of Allied Headquarters. The gold and silver bars on their caps glinted in benevolent sun. "There he is, Barb. It's really General Eisenhower," Mollie whispered from the side of her mouth. That the Supreme Allied Commander had found time to participate in giving citations to nurses and medical personnel increased her excitement.

"And General De Gaulle. No one else around here is that tall." Shirley flashed the look of admiration she always had when she saw anyone more than five feet ten.

"Isn't that Dick Charles?" Barbara eyed the correspondents gathered on the wide steps to the headquarters. "Probably covering this for bond drives back home."

General Eisenhower read a short speech of welcome to the medical group, stumbling several times, but smiling so infectiously no one noticed. He looked like everyone's favorite uncle, his neat uniform with a unique short jacket emphasizing a trim figure. Beside him stood General De Gaulle, who Mollie thought looked like one of Mike's toy soldiers, in his high stiff hat and red shoulder epaulets. She smiled, remembering her little brother's long ago reference when he saw her in the cadet nurse uniform. It was a quite honest comparison.

An aide opened a case and spread papers out on the podium for General Eisenhower, who thanked him and returned his salute. The general cleared his throat and read:

"While flying seriously wounded men to England, enemy antiaircraft flak opened a large hole in the floor of their Medical Evacuation transport plane. Lieutenant Barbara Andrews held a wounded man's litter, keeping her patient from dropping through the hole in the fuselage until an ambulatory patient helped her pull him to safety. I take pleasure in awarding her a Bronze Star for extraordinary bravery, and the Purple Heart for the head wound she received in the same operation." The general waited for Barbara to step forward and salute. He handed the citations to Barbara and shook her hand.

"Lieutenant Margaret McAllister, the other nurse on the crippled transport, managed to partly cover the opening in the fuselage with a cot, then at great risk to her own life, swung over it to aid her comrades. She also receives a Bronze Star." He saluted sharply then, his sideways smile crinkling pleasantly.

Several other citations for bravery in line of duty were given to nurses and doctors in the unit.

As they walked back to their quarters, Shirley chided Mollie and Barbara, "Okay for you, gals. I may not speak to you ever again. Why didn't you tell us about that trip? Barbara said she bumped her head in air turbulence."

"Gets to be routine, I guess." Mollie shot a glance at Barbara and laughed. "There was one positive benefit. It cured Barbara's fear of flying." She felt lighthearted and hugged Barbara tightly.

Barbara grinned. "Nothing could have been any scarier than that flak hole in the fuselage, but I wouldn't recommend it as a treatment for any kind of phobia."

~ * ~

That evening, the three girls accepted invitations from three officers from the headquarters staff for a dinner dance and floor show at *Moulin Rouge.*

Mollie felt fairly secure going out with a graying, admittedly married, colonel but soon found he wasn't elderly at all below his belt. She pulled his hands from beneath her skirt and tried humor. "Sorry, Colonel, that happens to be private property!"

"You're kidding. All nurses like body rubs." His speech had become slurred from too much good wine that magically appeared when American officers dined in French cafes.

"This one's a bit selective about who does them. I would like to dance." She pulled the officer to the crowded floor and found him a capable dancer even in his state of insobriety.

After midnight, Mollie pleaded weariness and the colonel escorted her to the hotel where the girls were staying while on their leave. "I gather you aren't going to invite me up to your room."

"You gather right," Mollie patted him on the arm like she would her uncle John, then pulled his face down and kissed him. "But I do thank you for the lovely evening."

"You wear some lucky stiff's ring. Hope he's scored better than I have."

"There are lots of nurses in Paris. Maybe next time you'll have a better draw," Mollie called as she skipped up the stairs, leaving the colonel shrugging his shoulders.

Tonight, she found it easy to be true to Ron even in the tattered glamour of Paris. The colonel just didn't compare well at all. She had been the one to make an issue of living independently during the war and taking events and days as they came. Her decision had been well meant when Ron slipped the ring on her finger, yet she had almost cheated once. She twisted the diamond, thinking sadly of the many broken romantic promises among the nurses.

A tiny doubt needled as she tried to push Ron's part of the agreement aside. He must have found opportunities while in the hospital in Hawaii to test their relationship. The nurses would flirt like everything with such a handsome patient. She must stop such foolish notions. Jealousy ruined love. Pulling the faded coverlet aside, she climbed into bed, only to toss fitfully. The day's excitement and thoughts of a future after the war nudged her from sleep.

Barbara crept into the room and slid into the twin bed beside hers. Soft breathing announced she fell asleep quickly. Mollie sighed, envying Barb's gift for forgetting the war.

~ * ~

Their three-day pass over, the girls returned to graphic reminders of the conflict half a day's ride from the hospital. Shirley and Mollie hurried toward surgery and Barbara to the Psychiatric unit.

After reading the printed schedule posted on the bulletin board, Mollie's hand covered her mouth. "Not again. Not Doctor Moore! Dozens of nurses here and they assign me to the knife thrower!" She turned to appeal to Shirley. "Trade?"

"Can't. See the note. He requested you. How lucky can you get?"

Three hours later, Mollie pulled off her mask and wiped the sweat from her face with a piece of gauze. She'd assisted Doctor Moore through a gruesome abdominal operation to remove putrid gangrenous tissue from an old wound. The patient was a German prisoner of war, an officer in the S.S. He would live, but not comfortably, with most of his lower intestines replaced by a colostomy. Doctor Moore might be a disagreeable tyrant in the operation room, but she had to admit he was a skilled surgeon.

Doctor Moore tossed his surgical gloves into a receptacle and moved beside Mollie at the scrub sink to clean up. "Christ, McAllister, I should have let the son-of-a-bitch die. I'm a Jew! Have you heard what they are finding in those camps?" He took the towel she handed to him, dried his hands, and moved to the chart desk.

"I do commend you for remembering your oath, Dr. Moore."

"Well, it does say something about doing no harm, but it was tempting."

Mollie's spirits fell another notch. "I try not to dwell on the prison camps. My brother is a prisoner of war. We think his camp's near Dresden."

Captain Moore turned to face her. "Sorry. Guess you've heard what our bombs are doing to Dresden."

"As I said, I try not to think about it." Mollie reached in her pocket for a handkerchief. "The latest radio broadcasts sound like we're winding the war down. Wonder why it's necessary to do saturation bombing?"

"Right now, I don't give a damn if they slaughter every last German on earth! I plan to find a full bottle of booze and get snookered. Want to join me?"

Mollie shook her head. She couldn't think of anyone she would care less to share a drink with. "Can't. Too busy looking after your German S.O.B., Captain Moore."

"You're a good nurse, McAllister." Doctor Moore slammed the chart into its notch and stomped down the corridor.

"Your belated compliment didn't raise my mood, Doctor," Mollie mumbled mostly to herself.

A medical corpsman stood at attention at the chart desk, his face creased with a broad grin. "Lieutenant McAllister, there's someone in Ward A who wants to see you."

Mollie wiped an ink smudge from her fingers and walked numbly behind the corporal. Probably some patient who remembered her or one of the jokes the girls were constantly pulling, or that wolf of a colonel trying another ploy.

She followed the medic to the end of the long ward without recognizing a soul. Working in surgery did that. You saw only carefully draped parts of human beings. The patient in the last space was sitting on the edge of the bed with his back to her. Something familiar about that neck.

"Joe?" Laughing hysterically, she ran to him. "It is you, not a mirage?"

"The very one." He hugged her so tight she caught her breath. "Golly, Mollie." The funny old family expression stuck in his throat and tears made shiny paths across his face. "Couldn't believe my luck when the doctor said you were stationed here."

"When? How did you...? It's wonderful. Let me get a look at you." Mollie began to giggle. "What happened to your hair?" His head had been completely shaved, and he looked skeletally thin. Dark hollows framed his eyes, emphasizing their brightness.

Joe grinned widely as if he couldn't quite get his mouth to do anything else. His brown eyes twinkled and teased just as Mollie remembered and treasured. Her own were blurred with tears.

"The goddam Germans have a corner on all the lice in the world. I suspect they grow them for protein supplements. I learned a thousand ways to squash 'em. Still, they managed to multiply for two years into flourishing colonies over my miserable body."

Mollie realized how much Joe had been through when he began to unravel the story of his escape. He hadn't waited for liberation from the Russians.

"About two months ago, when allied bombs dropped so incessantly, the Germans started acting scared, almost panicky. We noted the change in attitude, and the difference in the age of our guards. There were no young ones, just old duffers. Real old, in their seventies."

"I want to hear all of this, Joe, but first I must check in at the charge desk." She kissed his freshly shaved cheek. "I'll be back as soon as I can get away."

Mollie ran to the charge desk to ask first to see her brother's records, then for leave the rest of the day. Both requests were quickly granted. She was happy to learn Joe was in good condition except for malnutrition and three frozen toes that might need to be amputated. X-rays of his arm showed it had healed well. The Germans had done a good job setting it.

She led Joe to the day room where they sat for hours over coffee while he poured out his story.

"My radio operator and I were the only survivors when our B-17 was shot down. The gunner and bombardier were killed before we jumped and the co-pilot got machine gunned on the way down. Jim and I landed a couple miles apart. I broke my arm. He twisted his right forearm in the parachute landing. Jim got a broken left leg the same way. We met at the prison hospital where the Germans set the bones." Joe's hands tapped nervously on the table as he talked.

"Ron broke his arm in much the same circumstance as you, only he landed in the Pacific Ocean and the Americans found him before the Japs or sharks. Where were you captured?"

"About forty miles south of Berlin. We were returning from a raid on the Ploesti oil fields in Romania." Joe grimaced at intervals throughout the story, revealing graphically where the most painful memories dwelt.

"I can't believe you made it all the way to Paris," Mollie said.

"Jim and I had tried to escape before. I haven't the faintest idea why they allowed us to remain in the same Stalag unless they wanted an excuse to shoot us if we tried again. That night, a bomb crumbled the command post and wiped out a hundred yards of fencing. The flood lights were knocked out and we simply ran through the opening." He showed her a deep, unhealed cut in his thigh. "Got this from the goddam barbed wire we didn't see."

"Did the other prisoners get out?"

"Some of them, mostly Russians. They headed east and we went west. Jim and I stuck together. We traveled only after dark and damn near finished freezing and starving. We survived on a couple of frozen cabbages and one skinny half raw chicken during the two weeks it took to reach Czechoslovakia. We didn't know we'd crossed the border. That night we scared a lovely old lady half to death. Anna lived alone in a rundown farmhouse. When she heard us speak, she knew we were Americans. She kissed us like we were her own sons and fed us the most wonderful eggs and sausage. After dressing the cut on my leg like an expert medic, Anna hid us in her hay loft and let us sleep for twenty-four hours. That respite gave us the strength to push on."

"And you say you caught up with the Americans at Strasbourg. My God, isn't that hundreds of miles from Dresden?"

"Anna, the blessed Czech lady, had a lot of connections. She got us hidden in a coal car on a train headed west. It was bombed and strafed several times, but by then, both Jim and I thought we were immortal." Joe coughed and blotted his eyes with a big G.I. handkerchief. "We were wrong. Jim got it right by my side. Through those piles of coal and from our own guns."

Mollie, silent and drained, stared at the table. It was five p.m.. They had talked more than four hours. She rose stiffly and reached for her brother's thin arm. "I guess we had better get you back to your room. Supper will be coming in half an hour and you look as if you could use all the food you can get."

"But we haven't talked at all about you, Mollie. They tell me you got a Bronze Star. You had to be doing something besides carrying bedpans for that."

"Just my part in this miserable war, Joe. Barb and I had our own bout with Ack Ack, which blasted a big crater in the floor of the C-47. Lieutenants Hoffman and Jordan deserved all the medals for landing the crate on English soil instead dumping it in the channel."

"And that stretch of water is too damn cold for swimming," Joe said with a catch in his voice. "Too many guys who ditched there never made it."

Mollie led Joe back to his bed and grabbed a folding chair for herself. She pulled the chain holding Ron's rings from under her uniform shirt. "These represent the most important decision I have ever made." Her eyes filled. "Oh golly, Joe, I nearly broke that promise once with an old acquaintance of yours." She poured out the story of her weekend with Terry Reed. Now three people knew.

Joe tilted her chin and stared into her eyes. "Are you still in love with Ron?"

"Yes. I never stopped loving him, even though I enjoyed my leave with Terry. We didn't really make love. I sort of let the poor guy down." Mollie felt a flush in her face, surprised she hadn't lost all her sensitivity to the animal instincts of war. She dried her eyes, feeling immensely relieved. "Did you know his wife sent him a Dear John? She got pregnant with some civilian."

"I never got much news, good or bad, where the German's kept us. Never had any mail at all."

"Terry said I shouldn't tell Ron we spent the night together in the same room."

Joe's grin revealed he guessed it had been in the same bed.

"Terry's right, Mollie. Consider that incident but a tiny speck on your conscience. The trip to Ireland probably kept you sane." Joe smiled broadly as the dinner tray appeared and grabbing a glass of milk, drained it without breathing.

"I'll get you a full quart." Mollie turned and almost collided with Shirley and Barbara.

Every patient in the ward smiled when the three girls and Joe hugged each other, sharing laughter and tears.

~ * ~

Paris, France
February 14, 1945
My Sweetest Valentine,
These lipstick kisses are the closest I could come to a real valentine. I'm still dreaming of repeating that wonderful night on the beach. It has been only nine months, but I'd swear it's nine years. Your last letter was the most up to date I have had. It took only three weeks to find me! You say you are now a communications officer on your ship, yet you still fly?? A little puzzle for me, huh? Barbara, Shirley and I are clocking a lot of air miles too.

The Russians have liberated Warsaw, so I hoped Joe might soon be released. He surprised everyone by escaping and making his way here. Right now, Joe is on his way home. I wish all of St. Annie's Cadets were traveling on the Queen Mary with him. But, there are still a lot of GIs who need nursing so we'll stay on awhil.

War has changed all of us. Can you believe I got a veiled compliment from that jackass, Doctor Moore? Remember he's the one who threw a scalpel at me? Turns out, he's Jewish and we ache for them since we heard what happened in the Nazi concentration camps. Last night I dreamed you and I were together and woke up hugging myself. What a disappointment!
Love and kisses,
Mollie

Twenty-three

The Victory

"Owee!" Mollie flapped her hand over her mouth in her old high school cheerleader mode. Laughing, she pointed at the remnants of stockings draping over her shoes.

Barbara, tugging hard with a comb through the tangles in her champagne-soaked hair, pulled a sticky strand from the mass of flattened curls. "To heck with it! Today I'd just as soon swim in champagne. Where's Shirley? Didn't she go out with you, Mollie?"

"Lost her somewhere around the Arch. Last time I saw her, Shirley was being carried flat like a log on the shoulders of half a dozen GIs. Her feet were kicking like a Can-Can girl's, and the crowd was cheering her pink lacy panties." Mollie slipped off her shoes and peeled the shreds of torn hosiery from her legs.

Shirley burst through the door, holding her blouse front closed. Every button had been torn off. "Lordy, I'm lucky to be alive!" She moved her tongue over her lips. "But isn't this fun? I must have been kissed a hundred times in half an hour. Whee!" She turned a somersault on Mollie's bed, popping the tightly tucked blanket corners apart.

A full bottle of wine rolled into the room, followed by half a dozen nurses, who emptied it in one round.

Barbara held the bottle to her lips for the last drops. "Let's go find another one, gals." She raced down the steps of the barracks, nearly toppling a tall officer wearing dark glasses.

"Sorry, sir." She moved around him, but a long arm tugged her back. Somehow it felt familiar. Trying to focus her eyes in the bright sunlight, she gasped, "Captain Price?"

He laughed. "Haven't had it changed, Lieutenant Andrews. I heard your unit was here and I certainly picked an exciting time to look you up."

Barbara covered her mouth with her hand. "I...that is...we were celebrating with a bottle of wine."

"Looking for a refill?" He pulled a long-necked bottle from his rumpled raincoat. "Happened onto a bottle of *Calvados*. A French waiter had hidden it in his cellar for a special occasion. He donated it to me and I hoped to share it with you, Lieutenant."

"It's that potent apple brandy isn't it? But you're a priest!" Barbara sobered. "Aren't you?"

"I'm a chaplain in the Hundred and first Airborne, ordained in the Episcopal church. Neither discipline prohibits me from succumbing to a dash of spirits on special occasions." He grinned down at her rumpled uniform and tangled hair. "Must I drink this whole bottle by myself?"

Mollie was close behind Barbara when she met Captain Price. She turned quickly to stop Shirley from running after them. "Let her go, Shirley. He's a chaplain, the one who saved her life on that C-47."

"Guess she owes him, but I can't imagine anyone wanting to spend today with a preacher," Shirley said.

"I have a hunch this one might be rather entertaining, Shirl. He flashed a bottle of Calvados, which is not exactly holy water. They deserve some real time together if they can find a place quiet enough to talk." A special expression on the chaplain's face caused Mollie to suspect he had more on his mind than conversation with Barbara. She watched Barb, with the captain's arm tightly around her, weave through the crowd.

~ * ~

Barbara and Captain Price, clinging tightly to each other, made their way slowly across the crowded park. He led her down an embankment and into a tunnel, nearly hidden by vines, under a garden path. She hadn't stopped laughing the whole way. Nothing today was surprising. Leaving bright sun, she squinted in the dimness. An old automobile seat leaned against the mossy stone wall of the culvert.

Captain Price pulled the seat down, took off his raincoat and spread it over the moldy upholstery.

"Excuse the condition of my parlor, Lieutenant, but it is not crowded under here, and quiet enough for conversation. I stumbled upon this little haven on the way to your quarters." He helped her down beside him, uncorked the bottle and handed it over.

Barbara gasped as the essence reached her throat and sent burning warmth through her body. She felt safe and comfortable, leaning against his shoulder. "What did they do about your eyes? It's evident you can see."

The captain removed his dark glasses and turned normal-looking hazel eyes to the light from the tunnel opening."For a while, I feared I'd need a guide dog. My eyes are still sensitive to light. Specialists in the States will remove some scar tissue when I get there. I leave for home tomorrow."

He tipped her chin and his lips moved over hers in a long, probing kiss.

It seemed so natural, so tranquil to be in this near stranger's arms, as if destiny tightened the bond that began when he rescued her from falling to death. "You are sweet, Captain. I liked that kiss, and I like you very much," she mumbled sleepily, curled like a kitten with her head on his chest. The war was over, far away now. She would forget everything gruesome this wonderful day.

"My mother calls me Howard, my friends, Howie." He leaned to reach her lips again, his eager mouth moving down and over her throat and neck. Trembling fingers fumbled with the buttons on her shirt.

Barbara dreamily assisted him, slowly removing each item of clothing, caught up in delightful sensations as his hands soothed every inch of her body. She became lost in a world of love, deaf to the chaos of the celebration roaring above them in the streets of Paris. Moving as one, passion soared above mere noise to a concerto of their composing, erasing four years of fear and pain in a few moments.

Losing all sense of time or place, she cuddled close to him. With their coats pulled over bare bodies to stave off the dampness of the culvert, they dozed.

Stumbling steps and uneven breathing outside woke them. Barbara searched frantically for her scattered clothing.

A grinning bowlegged little man bent to enter the tunnel, and then stepped back. He mumbled, "Pardon" and something about a boudoir, shook his disheveled head, and turned away. They could hear him laughing and talking to himself as he climbed on unsteady feet back up the embankment.

Howard chuckled. "Probably wants to sleep off his wine on this disreputable bed. I confess it's a bit cramped for me." He struggled to his feet, bending from his waist to reach his clothing. Shifting comically from foot to foot, he struggled to pull his wrinkled trousers over his legs, his head bumping against the ceiling of the low tunnel. He tipped the brandy bottle to his lips, draining the last drop. "Shall we try to find another bottle and get something to eat?"

Barbara pulled on her clothing, suddenly aware of her surroundings and that the wonderful man who made love to her wasn't a genie loosed from a bottle of Calvados. It had happened like a long pleasant dream. A dream she regretted was ending. "You're some sort of Svengali, a magician, Howie." She pulled him back down on the rickety seat and kissed him, welcoming the strong arms tightening around her once more.

"You're the magic one. Do you believe in love at first touch? I couldn't see you in that transport plane, or in the hospital afterwards, but I remembered the shape of your body and the smell of your hair. I couldn't forget that fresh clean odor, like rain on a spring day. You're more beautiful than I imagined." He pulled a blond strand from her tangled mass of hair and rubbed it between his fingers. "And your hair, even when mixed with champagne, feels like spun silk."

~ * ~

After numerous cups of black coffee to regain a measure of sobriety, Mollie and Shirley spent the rest of V-E day assisting in the hospital emergency room. The alarm kept announcing accidents from the wild scene on the streets and all medical personnel within reach were called back to duty.

Mollie laughed when a very tall Army captain with carroty hair was wheeled from the casting room. He'd broken his right tibia when surging crowds toppled him from a balcony. "I think you ought to look at this one, Shirley. His face seems downright familiar."

"Lordy! It's Larry Daniels," Shirley shrieked. "How in hell does Larry from Seattle manage to be here?" She ran to plaster his face with kisses. "What are you doing in Paris?"

Larry smiled weakly, still a little fuzzy from the anesthetic. "Came here to break a leg, I guess. Got through the whole damn war without a scratch until today when that mob of wild Frenchmen toppled me off the edge of a balcony."

Shirley forgot her wartime paramour from that minute. The following six weeks, she spent every spare hour with Larry. Their romance became public in the crowded ward, the folding screen around Larry's bed giving the couple scant privacy. The nursing staff made a habit of rattling pitchers and clanged bedpans to warn them when they approached.

~ * ~

Mollie grew more restless each day. She had watched her two best friends fall in love and make permanent alliances, but she hadn't heard from Ron in nearly two months. The war of the Pacific was not over.

"You worry and he always writes, Mollie. You'll get a whole batch at once like before." Barbara donned her jacket. "Stop staring like a zombie and come out with us for one last dinner in Cafe Francois before we go home."

"Might as well, I suppose." Mollie buttoned her blouse, refreshed her lipstick and hurried to join Barbara and Shirley.

The three girls walked across the park to their favorite cafe. It was dark and crowded, but a friendly waiter remembered them and found a small table in a corner.

Mollie speared an artichoke heart from her salad. "We're like three widows with faces as long as Larry's pant legs."

Shirley grimaced. "Lordy, don't remind me of his pants. Larry should just about be home in Seattle."

"Do you realize today's the third of July? In just half an hour, it'll be Independence Day. Let's drink to that." Barbara raised her glass of wine high, then reddened as diners in the whole room joined her.

At midnight, the girls saw their waiter whisper a message in the ear of the Cafe Francois band leader. He bowed to them and raised his baton high. The *Star Spangled Banner* then *God Bless America* brought the uniformed American soldiers, sailors and nurses to their feet to join hands in a huge circle.

The little waiter dressed in a worn tuxedo climbed onto a table to lead *La Marseillaise* while the owner of the Cafe Francois watched anxiously, probably remembering the wild celebrations of May 8th. Shrugging, his eyes filled with tears, he began to sing louder than the Americans.

Not to be ignored, a British sergeant major with a roaring bass voice bellowed *God Save the King*. It became an allied thing then with each country represented leading their national anthem.

"Guess we just started our own United Nations. I heard Edward R. Murrow reporting they held a meeting on—June twenty-sixth to organize the real one." Mollie remembered the date because it was Joe's birthday.

"I suppose I'd better get some sleep. Gotta get up at seven for my shift, then pack my gear." Shirley led the way, her tall figure towering above the short French waiter as if she walked on stilts.

~ * ~

The following afternoon, Barbara and Mollie spread their clothes out on the bunks and began to stuff them into bags.

Barbara laid out fresh clothing for tomorrow's trip. "It will be good to see Dorrie and Pinky and everyone again. Let's see. Little Jacob will be nearly a year old. Wonder if his daddy is still fighting the war?"

"Jake is stationed on Guam and doesn't expect to be home until the whole shooting thing is over." Mollie tossed an envelope to Barbara. "Here's Dorrie's letter. I just picked it up from the mail room."

But none had arrived from Ron.

"Our orders give us thirty day leaves, and then heaven knows where they'll send us," Shirley said from the doorway. "If Larry or I go to the Pacific theater, we plan to be secretly married on that leave. We'll wait for the whole white gown bit until after the war's over or I get pregnant. Mother sort of counts on inviting all my relatives to her only daughter's wedding."

Barbara turned, smiling. "Howie and I aren't waiting, either. I'm stopping in Connecticut to visit his mother and brother and we plan to have our wedding then without any fanfare at all. As soon as his eyes are operated on, Howie will be discharged."

Mollie felt an overwhelming twinge of envy. It came too often lately. Tears moistened her face as she hurried into the corridor, down the stairs and across the street to the park. There were lovers on some of the benches, with arms of French girls moving over various uniformed shoulders. She walked to a little pond and settled down on a damp rock, staring into breeze dappled water.

Soul consuming thoughts of Ron crowded everything else into faraway corners. His face loomed when she closed her eyes, the little curl dangling from his forehead appearing as if spotlighted. Some of the girls said they forgot what their loved ones looked like, and she couldn't remember any other men she had dated. Ron erased all their faces. His green eyes, so full of mischief and love, seemed to stare from the pool.

Two figures moved to the grass beside her.

"We're real dopes, Mollie. Sorry, we should have thought about you," Shirley said.

Barbara pushed a thick letter into Mollie's hand. "Our commanding officer said this came in a courier's satchel with the dispatches."

Mollie ran back to her room to read the pages over and over.

Later, while awaiting a truck to take the comrades to the boat and home, she puzzled over why Ron's letter had come to her in this manner.

"He must be in some kind of special intelligence service," she whispered to Barbara. "There have been several odd things, like his being at a meeting of the Allied leaders." Smiling, not caring at all about his Navy career, she clutched his letter, full of closeness and love, to her heart.

~ * ~

After a ten day cruise on the Queen Mary, Mollie and Barbara were at the home of Captain Price's mother in Connecticut.

"If you keep moving, your hem will be scalloped." Mollie tucked another pin in the unfinished edge of Barbara's white rayon taffeta dress. They had been lucky to find the fabric for it in the spare stock of yardage in the small town's only department store.

"I'm thankful Howie's mother had a sewing machine or my uniform would have been my wedding dress like it is for most of the service women." Barbara twirled around in front of the mirror to get the effect of the full skirt. "It looks beautiful, Mollie. Thanks."

"We still have to make the veil and find you some sexy lingerie to dazzle Howie with." Mollie mumbled, crawling around the floor picking up scattered bits of thread and material from the carpet.

Barbara turned, tears shining in her eyes. "Isn't Mrs. Price sweet? Did you notice how she treats me like a real daughter already?"

"When's your dad's train due to arrive?"

Barbara glanced at her watch. "This evening at eight. I can't wait to see him."

Mollie nodded, watching Barbara thoughtfully as she helped her pull the nearly finished dress over her head. Barbara's mother had died of a heart attack shortly after they were stationed in England. But her dad would be there to give her away. She had not mentioned her stepmother.

Feeling anxious about her friend's future, she decided to be practical and bring it up. "Have you considered what you're getting into? Do you have any idea what is expected of a pastor's wife?"

Barbara spun around sharply. "It scares me almost as much as flying did, Mollie. I love Howie, but not his profession. How I wish he was a mechanic, a plumber, anything but an Episcopal priest!" Tears filled her eyes. "And I'm not even Episcopalian, at least not yet."

"Have you spoken to Howie about your fears?" Mollie moved to a low window seat covered in flowered chintz. Mrs. Price's home, very old, sparkled with colonial charm. She rubbed the satiny material, waiting for Barbara to answer.

"To be honest, not much. He keeps trying to warn me about the important things I'll need to know and has introduced me to some of his parishioners." Barbara buried her head in her hands. "Jeepers, Mollie, everyone in this town knows Howie and no one knows me at all. They stare at me as if I'm some blonde floozy like those down on skid row in Seattle."

Mollie took a long time to reply. Barbara still had an innocent look, not hardened like a lot of the nurses who had been through the scars of war. Her clean, well-scrubbed face needed little make up and what she used was tastefully applied. Her honey blonde hair was its natural color, aided only by the lemon juice rinse. Under strained conditions, Barb's language could get rough, but she had a good sense of when to keep quiet and the right things to say when she spoke. Barbara's work had always been well organized and she was fastidious about her appearance. The ladies of the parish should appreciate that.

"A lot of people in the east think we still have cowboys and Indians shooting at each other in our streets, Barb. I'm sure you'll be a wonderful pastor's wife. I've tried to think of another girl who could, and you're the only one."

Mollie went to the bedroom she shared with Barbara to finish the letter she'd started to Ron in Paris, add to it, then write a note to her folks.

~ * ~

Paris, France
May 8, 1945
Darling, this is an excerpt from my diary. Thought you might like to know how I spent V.E. day.

At last! On this glorious day it's over in Europe! Paris is absolutely wild with joy. I joined the celebration on the streets for a brief time and nearly got my uniform torn off. I could throw away the rest of it, if your section of the war would end. I read your last letter a dozen times and still wonder how it happened to come to me in a dispatch case. Oh well, there are many more questions than answers about your tour of duty and I hope to hear them when we all get home. Right now, I'm at Barbara's fiancé's home in Connecticut. She's getting married tomorrow. After the wedding, I'll head to Seattle. Love and kisses, Mollie

~ * ~

Connecticut, U.S.A.
July 14, 1945 (Bastille Day in France!)
Dear everyone at home,
We crossed the Atlantic on the Queen Mary and I can barely believe I am here in the good old U.S.A. even if it is Connecticut! Poor Barbara prayed to come back by boat a year ago when flying scared her so much, but she got so seasick, she begged to be off that luxury liner if it meant swimming home!

I planned to go directly to Bremerton, but I simply couldn't turn Barbara down. She needed a true friend for her maid of honor, and since I already have experience from Sally's wedding, I volunteered. Mr. Andrews is arriving tonight and Barb is happy about that. See you in a couple of weeks.

Loving you and impatient to be with you all, Mollie

~ * ~

Mollie sealed and stamped the letters, donned her uniform jacket and opened the door. "Barb, I'm going down to the post office and mail my letters. Want to come?"

Howe winked at Mollie as he moved from behind Barbara. "I have better plans for her time, Mollie." He nuzzled Barb's neck. "One more day."

Twenty-four

Northern Pacific Starlighter
Somewhere in Indiana, I think
August 5, 1945
Dearest Ron,
My homecoming would be perfect if you were there to meet me. I keep having this feeling our real life together might begin soon. Hope I'm right.

I said goodbye to Barbara and her new husband when they boarded a train for a honeymoon in the Catskills. I hope Barb isn't disappointed by those mountains. Compared to Mount Rainier, they're just little hills, not that she will see them with Howie around. They make a wonderful couple.

It will be great to see the folks. All my love,
Mollie

~ * ~

Soldiers, sailors and marines either going home or being reassigned, filled the seats and crowded the aisles of the train traveling west far too slowly to suit Mollie. She patted the folder in her purse and smiled, still unable to believe her luck in getting assigned to Madigan Army Hospital just forty miles from home. Waiting for Ron would be so much easier with her family nearby.

"Extra! Extra!" A paper boy waved the *Sun* bearing two-inch headlines at the train passengers when it stopped in Chicago. "Bomb equaling 20,000 tons of nitroglycerin dropped on Hiroshima!"

Mollie drew in her breath sharply, tapped on the window to signal the paper boy and raced to the door to buy a paper. "Dear Lord! How awful! but maybe it will end the war," She murmured aloud.

An elderly woman seated next to her blotted tears from her eyes. "Yes, but think of the destruction. Think of the thousands of innocent lives."

"They haven't exactly been missing our guys with their bombs and kamikazes, lady," a husky marine snorted. "We ought to wipe out those crumby islands and every living thing on 'em." He stalked down the aisle. "I'm gonna get drunk."

Mollie fidgeted, wishing the train would hurry and get to Seattle. She had tried to get a seat on an airliner without luck and had only another ten days of leave before going to work at Madigan.

~ * ~

The outline of Smith Tower and the big clock on the King Street Station sent her heart thumping and the eager faces of four McAllisters brought rivers of happy tears. Laughing almost hysterically, she hurried down the steps to hug them all. Sally, due to deliver any day, danced up and down on her toes, and her mother cried.

"Mike!" Mollie kissed him soundly on both cheeks like the French and he hugged her tightly, tears sparkling in his eyes. He had grown taller and his voice cracked. Was that a beginning

257

beard? Little Mike, could he be fourteen? She swallowed hard when she saw him shift his balance with his crutches to ease the pressure on the brace encasing his right leg.

Her dad looked like he had aged more than a year. He coughed hard and blew his nose. "Dad, you ought'ta cut down on smoking. It always makes your asthma worse," Mollie chided. "You haven't changed at all, Mom, pretty as ever." But there was a sprinkling of gray in her mother's dark hair she hadn't noticed before. Mollie searched the platform. "Where is Joe?"

"He left yesterday for Kansas to get checked out on those new B-29s. He's training for the invasion of Japan, but I don't think he'll need to go. They are the bombers that did this." Ian opened the newspaper in his hands to reveal the headline, *Atom Bomb Dropped On Nagasaki.*"

"I hope they end it soon, Dad. Those monster bombs can't be limited to just destroying military targets..." Mollie saw a figure approaching at the edge of the crowd. "Dorrie!" She dropped her bags and ran to hug her friend, nearly crushing the curly haired baby she carried. "And this is little Jacob." She kissed him, surprised that he didn't pull away and cry. "He's beautiful, Dorrie, much more handsome than his pictures."

"Want to go to your Aunt Mollie, Jakie?" Dorrie handed the chubby baby over and he clung to Mollie's neck, quickly pulling her hat from her head. "I'm afraid he is a little spoiled. He is the only man around my house...still."

"Where is Pinky?"

"She had to work this afternoon. Can you come up to St. Annie's before you head home?"

"Better not today. But I'll be over before I report to Madigan." Mollie glanced over her shoulder to wink at her father's beaming face. "I was keeping that for a surprise. I can't imagine why the Nurse Corps decided to be kind and station me so close to home."

~ * ~

Mollie slept until ten o'clock the following morning, then enjoyed the luxury of lounging in her old red chenille robe to read the paper and have a third cup of coffee. Her mother chattered excitedly about Sally's approaching motherhood and everything else that had happened in the neighborhood during the past thirteen months.

The doorbell rang and Mollie jumped for the stairs. "I'll be down when I'm more presentable, Mother."

She quickly slipped on a pair of gabardine pants and pulled a sweater over her head. Probably just one of her mother's neighbors. It had been ages since she had lazed around in her robe until eleven a.m.. She ran a brush through her hair and rubbed her lips with scarlet. A masculine voice murmured in the living room, a very familiar voice. She leapt down the stairs two at a time.

"Ron?" Her voice rose to a high squeak when arms trimmed in gold braid engulfed her. "When? How?" He kissed her again, ignoring her sobbing questions.

"My ship arrived last night. I came as soon as they would let me off." He held her face between his hands and stared a long time, as if memorizing every pore. "You have changed, sweetheart. I don't know how it is possible, but you are even more beautiful than I remembered."

Mollie touched the curl in the center of his forehead. Its short length lessened the spring, but it was the same one she had treasured all through the months they were apart. The lines in his face had deepened and he looked thinner, his eyes circled with fatigue.

A clatter of china turned their heads toward the door. Lou McAllister entered carrying a tray of coffee and butterhorns. "I thought you two might enjoy a little brunch while you catch up on the past year."

"Thanks, Mom." Mollie couldn't keep her eyes from Ron's face and her voice sounded remote.

They nibbled the pastry without tasting it and sipped coffee in silence, their eyes searching each other for sameness and change. Ron pushed his cup away and kissed her deeply, his reluctance to stop at the barrier the surroundings dictated causing his arms to tremble.

"Can we go somewhere?" He glanced around to see if her mother was near. "I noticed my car is still in your dad's shed."

"Right where I drove it that morning, darling." Mollie frowned. "But the battery is probably dead."

"I'll check." He started out, then came back to take her hand. "I'm not going anywhere without you, though, even to the garage."

He slid into the car and twisted the key in the ignition. The engine turned over immediately. "Someone has kept this charged up, Mollie. Your dad is my friend, bless him."

Mollie ran back for a jacket in case it got windy at the beach. "I don't know when we'll be back, Mother. We're going for a drive."

When they arrived at the turn to the beach road, she stared in disbelief. The rough logging track was a paved thoroughfare with a white line down the middle! Six new houses and the bare bones of several others had ruined their private destination.

"I wonder when all this happened? I guess Uncle John must have decided to make some money from the Navy Yard workers." She frowned. "I forgot about gas. Do we have enough to go somewhere else?"

"The same good elf who kept the battery charged must have put in half a tank." He leaned for a quick kiss. "Where to, sweetheart?"

Mollie giggled. He sounded flirtatious, yet there was a hint of seriousness, as if such light banter no longer came easily. "I know a nice place out on the canal we could try."

"Just so it's not too far. I'm impatient to catch up on kissing the girl I love."

Fifteen minutes later, he pulled the car into the parking lot of a log inn with the sparkling blue water of Hoods Canal peeking through a grove of tall firs behind it.

"We used to have picnics here when I was in high school. An elderly couple owns it. Mother read in the paper that their only son died at Guadalcanal and they're trying to run it by themselves. Maybe I should have gotten dressed up a little more." Mollie smoothed her slacks. "They have a nice dining room."

"Do you really want to eat?" Ron leaned to peck a quick kiss, then took her hand and walked boldly to the desk. "We would like to rent one of your little cottages, please."

The woman's brows barely twitched. "Your name, please."

"Commander and Mrs. Ronald Van Ness." He grinned and signed the book. "Can we reserve it for a couple of days?"

"Two days?" Mollie smiled happily, but somehow his expression revealed doubt. She feared asking the whole question in her mind.

"Don't think about time, my darling." Ron opened the rustic door and pulled her inside. "Let's forget clocks for awhile." He pulled the bar on the door and led her toward the bed. "Should have carried you over the threshold, but that can wait until we sign the piece of paper saying we're married."

Mollie loosened his tie and slowly unbuttoned his shirt, soothing the soft hair on his chest with her fingers. She sighed when his mouth moved over her bare shoulders after he slipped her green sweater over her head. They forced themselves to stall, to enjoy each sensation, deep emotion flooding every sense. Complete fulfillment proved impossible to stem more than minutes. Their moans of anticipation came in unison.

The memory of her Irish weekend flashed in Mollie's subconscious mind, but she was too busy with the present to heed it. She gasped with his entering and the rhythm of the thrusts sent her quickly into newly experienced, uninhibited wonder. All doubt dissolved. The only man she would ever love was the dreamy one nuzzling her breasts and holding her so tightly.

"Just like I remembered, only better," Ron mumbled into a half-buried ear.

Mollie touched his cheek, laughing. "Maybe beds are better than sand and daylight better than darkness." Mollie glanced at her watch. "Only four p.m.."

"Damn." Ron slid from the bed and reached for his clothes. "I hate to tell you this, Mollie darling, but I have to be back on the ship at six." His voice trailed. "Some kind of briefing..." Mollie showered quickly and dressed, her throat tightening until she couldn't be certain her voice would work. It had been such a brief interlude. Again they must hurry to finish this war. But he had paid the lady at the desk for two days...

"I'm sorry, sweet. I must stop keeping things from you. I shouldn't have even come to see you today because it's like tearing out my guts to go back." His voice came in a hoarse whisper.

"It's okay. I just forgot for a few hours there is still a war on." Mollie stared straight ahead at the highway curving around the canal. At the gate to the Navy Yard, she moved over to the driver's seat. Ron leaned to kiss her sweetly through the open window. "I'll call you when I can break free. I hope it won't be long, but..." he paused, "it could be all night..."

~ * ~

Mollie tossed in tangled sheets during the warm, humid August night. Ron had called at ten to say he wouldn't be off until dawn. She finally fell asleep only to be awakened by her mother shaking her.

"It's Sally. She is going to have her baby. Her pains are four minutes apart. Dad's backing the car out. Will you come with us?" She hurried out and down the hall.

Mollie reached for her clothing. Why did babies always come at night? She opened the door to Mike's room. "Mike, if Ron calls, tell him I'll be back after Sally delivers," she called toward the sleeping red head.

"Delivers?" Mike sat up, mumbling.

"Has the baby, you nut." She patted his head. "Don't forget to tell Ron."

Mollie sat with her parents fidgeting in the stuffy waiting room. Sally had been dilating when they arrived, but progress of labor had stopped for nearly an hour. She peeked at her watch. Four a.m.. Working at relaxing, she dozed until a portly nurse swished into the room.

"We took her to the delivery room. You can watch if you want, Mollie. I brought you a gown." She turned to Ian. "It won't be long now until you're a new grandfather."

Mollie frowned because Sally was so completely anesthetized. She had seen too many sleepy babies delivered this way. Twilight sleep, they called it; painless childbirth. Vowing never to allow it when she had a baby, she smiled at a sudden thought. She and Ron hadn't considered preventing pregnancy. The thought had not entered either of their minds during three loving hours. She counted days. Should be a safe time.

Would her mother and dad be shocked if they knew she was no longer a virgin? Did they suspect how few of her friends were? She nodded her head absently, causing the doctor to glance over his mask and smile. He thought she was approving his work! Her attitude toward lots of things had changed in four years. She couldn't imagine not making love with Ron. A thing as wonderful as that should be relished any available time when there was such chaos on the world.

She watched a wet dark head appear, then shoulders and buttocks. A boy! She was an aunt... Were there more males born during wars? Dorrie and Carmen had had boys, too. The doctor held the baby high and slapped it gently on the behind. The lusty cry made Mollie breathe easier. She glanced at her watch...four forty-five.

After they were certain Sally and the baby were all right, Ian drove home. Mollie assured him Sally wouldn't wake up for hours, and he had to go to work at six. He phoned a telegram in for Dave.

Mollie decided to try to get a little sleep on the living room couch to be near the phone. She felt drained from the day's frantic pace.

The ring jarred her awake.

"It has been a very complicated night, sweetheart. I...I have to leave in a few minutes on a special mission to Washington D.C. I'll fill you in when I see you."

"When, darling? How long this time?"

"I can't be sure," He whispered hoarsely, sounding hesitant. "I don't think I can stand being away from you more than another week."

"A week?" Mollie strained to hear over the sound of aircraft revving near his connection. "You are in a very public place, I gather." She cleared her throat to stifle a sob. "We had a few precious hours, darling. Remember them and hurry home. I am planning a wedding next week for Lieutenant Commander Van Ness and Lieutenant Margaret McAllister. You had better be there. I'm not sure proxies are legal!"

She ran up the stairs to her room and buried her face in a pillow. Her heart felt frozen, so numb she couldn't even cry. She tossed the pillow violently against the wall, sending a wastebasket clattering when it slid to the floor.

"God damn this stupid war!" She pounded hard on the mattress with her fists.

"Mollie?" Lou McAllister stood in the doorway, a worried, questioning look on her face. "What is it, honey?"

She slid onto the edge of the bed and Mollie welcomed her mother's arms.

Twenty-five

Mollie had planned her leave for months and the shortened version even more carefully. She wanted to savor all the things of home she had missed. Now, she felt stifled, confined like effervescence in a Coke bottle. Everything at home was so quiet and calm, changed, yet the same. She faced no compulsion, no deadlines, no disfigured bodies and minds. From habit, she woke early the day after Ron left and tried to force time to pass by being too busy to think.

After laundering everything she owned and taking her uniforms to the cleaners, she visited Sally to ooh and ahh over her new nephew and give him a silver cup with "Ian Michael" engraved on it. Everything she had planned for the day was finished by four.

After dinner, she leaned over the back of her dad's old chair, her arms around his neck, patting his collar bones. He worried her, being so thin. "Dad, I'm going over to St. Anne's tomorrow to see everyone. And I plan to visit Mrs. Van Ness and Dee. Since they won't be off work until five, I may just stay overnight with them."

Ian leaned to turn the radio down. "Okay, Mollie. I'm sure they're looking forward to seeing you."

"If...never mind..." She almost said if Ron calls, but he wouldn't. His veiled message had indicated it would be a week before he returned, if he got back home at all. They had allotted barely three hours for love in more than a year. A coldness settled over her heart. That could be all they were ever destined to have! "I'm going up to take a bath, then listen to the ten o'clock news on the portable in my room. See you in the morning."

~ * ~

Sun poured through her mother's crisp organdy kitchen curtains when Mollie came to join her father in the breakfast alcove. Although she had slept fitfully, she felt better, more relaxed.

Ian sipped his coffee and glanced over the top of the *Post Intelligencer.* "Is there still gas in Ron's car?"

"Probably only a couple of gallons after my trip in to see Sally."

"I have saved some ration stamps since I got into the ride pool." He opened the coupon book, tore out two four-gallon stamps and handed them to her.

"I hadn't considered taking Ron's car, but it would be nice not to have to ride buses all over town. Thanks, Dad. See you tonight or tomorrow if it gets too late to make the last ferry."

~ * ~

Mollie's heartbreak and her restlessness waned while visiting her old friends and the nuns at St. Anne's. She cautiously asked Pinky about Gloria. "Dorrie said she got her degree, not just an R.N."

"Gloria works at Children's. She is happy since she became engaged to marry an Air Corps captain. He's a doctor, a psychiatrist." Pinky flashed her own engagement ring. "Chuck's on his way home. You're invited to our wedding. We plan it for Thanksgiving week."

"I wouldn't miss it for anything, Pinky." Mist filled Mollie's eyes. "Guess I'd better get going. I'm meeting my future mother-in-law for dinner."

Mollie met Ron's mother and sister in a restaurant downtown. She picked at her roast chicken, fighting to keep her mind on Dee's gossipy chatter and Mrs. Van Ness's quiet comments.

Dee laughed. "No question about it. You are pining for my brother or you wouldn't ignore that chocolate mousse!"

Mollie patted Dee's hand after the chiding. "Sorry, I'm terrible company tonight. And you're right, my thoughts are three thousand miles away. You are both good sports for putting up with me."

"I hate to break this up, girls, but it's ten o'clock and I have to go to work in the morning." Mrs. Van Ness slipped coins under her napkin for a tip and reached for the ticket before Mollie could.

"Me, too. Did Ron tell you I'm doing my apprentice pharmacy training at Guys downtown drugstore? Mother and I go to work on the same bus."

"Yes, he did, and said you passed your State Boards."

Mollie parked the car and entered the ivy covered brick house. The porch light revealed peeling paint on the door framing. Paint and painters were among the things in short supply. She followed Mrs. Van Ness upstairs, cursing herself for drinking that last cup of coffee at the cafe. Dee and her mother had looked disappointed when she suggested going back to Bremerton on the twelve o'clock ferry so she'd decided to stay over.

"Hope you won't mind sleeping in Dee's other bed, Mollie. I still have two girls living in Ron's room," Mrs. Van Ness apologized.

Mollie had become accustomed to unfamiliar sleeping quarters, but the soft twin bed ensured insomnia most of the night. The phone startled the silent house at four, and Mollie leapt from bed before she remembered where she was.

"Mollie! It's Ron calling long distance. Hurry," Mrs. Van Ness called.

"Darling? That's wonderful." She wiped tears with the back of her hand. "Tonight? I'll be there with bells on!" She hung the phone on its hook and turned to hug Mrs. Van Ness. "He called from Chicago. Caught a ride on a transport that is flying into McChord Airbase sometime this evening. They stopped to refuel and he doesn't know what time he'll arrive. I'll drive over and pick him up."

Mollie heard a soft sigh from Mrs. Van Ness. She hadn't seen Ron for more than a year and guilt tugged at Mollie. It was selfish to keep Ron to herself. How would she feel if her son rented a room in an inn to make love to his fiancee` instead of visiting his mother? She followed the slender woman to the kitchen to make coffee.

"W-would you like to come with me to McChord?" Her squeaky inner voice forced itself out. "I'm sure he won't be there until after you are off work."

Mrs. Van Ness carefully measured the scarce brown grains into the percolator, turned on the gas and faced Mollie with tear-rimmed eyes. "Thank you for inviting me, Mollie. You and Ron need the time to make plans for your future together. I had him twenty-two years, now it's your turn." She kissed Mollie and hugged her tightly. "I only hope he knows how lucky he is to find a girl like you."

~ * ~

The sergeant at the gate reported that Ron's plane wasn't expected to arrive until at least eight, so Mollie decided to check out Madigan while she waited. It would give her a preview of her duties and where she would be billeted.

Captain Eloise Scott, the nursing supervisor, took her on an extended tour of the maze of camouflaged one-story wood buildings connected by covered walkways. Noise from planes landing and taking off at McChord disturbed thought and speech.

Mollie paused while a low-flying transport passed overhead. "This is an odd place to build a hospital."

"I believe the hospital came first, Lieutenant McAllister." Captain Scott led her around another corner. "Let's have a cup of coffee so you can see our typical G.I. hospital cafeteria."

"Lieutenant McAllister? Mollie?" A muffled emotionally broken voice turned her head.

"Andy Porter!" Mollie hugged him tightly, and then summoned courage to look at his face. It was swathed in fresh gauze bandages. "Golly, I'm glad to see you. I'll be stationed here next week and we'll get re-acquainted." She started, realizing that he had spoken words! A little garbled, but real speech, not sign language and eye contact. "Looks like there is already vast improvement, Andy."

"They made me a jaw bone and false dentures, Mollie. As you see, I have this funny lisp and my smile isn't exactly like Cary Grant's...but then it never was like Cary Grant's," He mumbled through the opening, his eyes gleaming. He took her arm, ignoring Captain Scott. "Come on, I'll treat you to the best dinner Madigan Army Hospital offers. Sorry about that. Wish it was at the Olympic Bowl."

Captain Scott tugged at his arm smiling. "You two go on. I have to make my report."

"Thank you, Captain. I met Andy in Coventry." Mollie saluted and turned back to Andy. "How long have you been at Madigan?"

"Since March. They're doing some skin grafts, little ones, but my behind is already beginning to look like a red and white checkerboard!"

Mollie watched Andy cut his meat in fine pieces and chew it slowly.

"Another improvement. You aren't restricted to soup, eggnogs and milk shakes."

"And I'll never touch cream of wheat or lime gelatin again!"

Mollie told Andy about Joe and Ron. She listened to his account of his medical history, waiting nervously for him to mention his wife. She felt pain tug her heart. The sadness in his eyes didn't match his light banter. Glancing at her watch, she rose.

"Ron will be arriving soon, sorry to rush out, Andy."

"Bonnie...my wife...couldn't quite get used to my handsome face..." Andy made a coughing sound. "Wasn't sure I was the Lieutenant Andrew Porter she married. I guess she's right." He fumbled with a paper napkin. "I've seen quite a few guys worse off..."

"Bonnie must be nuts, Andy. We would all look alike with our skin peeled off." Mollie hugged him again and hurried out, unable to stem tears another minute.

~ * ~

It was midnight when Ron drove the Chrysler into his mother's garage. He and Mollie crept softly into the house, but not silently enough to keep his mother in bed.

After a tearful hug, she produced steaming cups of cocoa and they sat in the living room to talk.

"I have three days," Ron said, like an apology. "Maybe it is enough time to get married. We could get the license in the morning. Dee and Mother can come to the courthouse as our witnesses."

"Isn't there a three day waiting period?" Mrs. Van Ness asked.

"Sometimes you can get a waiver. Dorrie and Jake got one." Mollie grew excited over the prospect. "Maybe Sister Marie can help us."

Mollie felt light-headed when the laughing group met to sign the forms. Sister Marie and Sister Anne smiled like girls when the waiver went through, delighted to have a part in arranging for the marriage license.

After driving his mother and sister back to their house, Ron hurried into the car beside Mollie. "We have to make the two o'clock ferry," He called to his mother. "I'll phone you after Mollie makes the arrangements with her pastor. But the wedding has to be tomorrow."

Mollie and Ron watched the seagulls dive after crumbs a sailor threw from the deck of the big streamlined ferry. They relished the hour on Puget Sound warmed by the sun and the joy in their hearts.

When they parked at the Navy Yard gate, Mollie traced the cleft in his chin with her forefinger. "Dare I ask your agenda for tonight, Commander Van Ness?"

"I have exactly half an hour to report, but I'll be back in time for a wedding tomorrow if I have to jump ship." He stretched for a hurried kiss, and then climbed from the car and Mollie slid to the driver's side. He leaned an elbow on the open car door. "Sister Marie seemed delighted with the idea of you being married, but said she was worried you may have to resign your commission. Does that bother you?"

"A little, because nurses are so desperately needed for awhile. I'll have to report to Madigan Monday and see what the Army says." Mollie frowned. "It's utterly wasteful for married girls to leave the Corps unless they're pregnant, especially when their husbands are...are overseas." She swallowed to stop this dark thought from marring their happiness.

"Another thing, sweetheart. Can you drive out to the canal and reserve that cottage for tomorrow night?" Ron reached in his pocket and pulled out several bills. "You'll have to use the gas coupon Mom collected from that girl for partial payment of her room rent. The tank is breathing vapor now."

After leaving Ron at the base, Mollie hurried home and picked up Mike to take along for company, then drove toward Hood canal, stopping only to put four gallons of gas in the tank.

"But you have a day's credit, Mrs. Van Ness. Your husband paid for two nights. See." She turned the register around.

"He...we didn't think you would honor that. Thank you."

The woman smiled and handed over a key. "We've become quite used to changed plans. We'll look forward to having you tomorrow night."

Mollie turned to see how much of the conversation Mike had heard or understood. Her young brother was making a concentrated study of a flock of ducks, but he had a knowing look and his mouth twitched up at the corners.

Twenty-six

Ian and Lou McAllister scurried frantically to make arrangements for another daughter's wedding. "Twenty-four hours, Ian, barely a day to do everything. I'm afraid it will be a very Spartan affair."

"Won't be the first such wedding, dear. Remember ours?" He squeezed her still-narrow waist.

"Just you and I, my brother and sister started all this twenty-seven years ago at the home of Reverend Wilkes." Lou pecked him affectionately on the cheek.

"We will just do our best for Mollie." But Ian frowned. "There's something very mysterious about Ron's assignment, Hon. The carrier is badly damaged and will stay in the Navy Yard three months at least. Yet Lieutenant Commander Ronald Van Ness is leaving. Very puzzling."

"Guess they need him back at the fighting." Lou reached in her apron pocket for a handkerchief. "Joe can't be here, or Sally...but I'm happy for Mollie. Ron is very special."

~ * ~

Mollie buttoned the placket of her sister's wedding dress. "Good thing Sally and I are almost the same size." She gathered in a half inch at the waist. "This little bit won't show at all with the satin sash pinned tighter. What time is it, Mother?"

"You have just about five minutes to finish dressing. Dad is already in the car. You know how impatient he always is to get going." Lou shrugged and pulled her blue linen jacket over the rayon print dress she had chosen as proper "Mother of the Bride" attire.

Mollie hugged her. "You are the most beautiful grandmother in the country. I spent a lot of time overseas thinking about the love you have given me the past twenty-three years." She kissed her mother, eyes brimming. "Thanks."

Gasping in surprise when she entered the nave, Mollie sniffed to be sure the flowers were not artificial. She stole a quick look into the sanctuary. It was almost full. Sprays of fragrant roses and stocks stood beneath broad candelabra at the altar. Pink satin ribbons saved from Sally's wedding decorated the pews.

Dorrie moved behind her and put her hands over her eyes. "Guess who?"

Mollie laughed. "That's easy, Dorrie. You smell like baby formula! Thanks for everything. I couldn't have anyone else for matron of honor."

Dorrie wore her own wedding dress, a soft blue rayon taffeta, which fit a little snugly after the birth of little Jacob. She tugged at her old friend, the tight rubber girdle.

"Don't bridesmaids rate?" Shirley hugged her. "Pinky and I ran into another very important person and brought her along."

"Ginger!" Mollie danced around hugging her four good friends from St. Annie's Corps. "When did you arrive in Bremerton?"

"Just this morning. Starting tomorrow, I am stationed at the naval hospital here." Ginger whirled around in the sweetheart-necked pink dotted Swiss dress matching Shirley's and Pinky's.

"I'll never know how your mother managed to get this dress altered so I could surprise you."

"And someone put lace on all of them so mine would be long enough and still match." Shirley lifted her skirt hem.

"Ginger's didn't need much altering or they wouldn't have been ready." Lou McAllister pulled Mollie's corsage from a box and fussed with the ribbons. "And the lace was Sally's contribution. She sewed it on this morning from her hospital bed."

"You are all spoiling my make up." Mollie fished for a hankie to dab her eyes, thinking only one of her close friends was missing and Barbara had a good excuse...

Mrs. Van Ness brought out corsages for the bridesmaids. Dorrie, Shirley, Pinky and Ginger carried bouquets of white and pink carnations outlined with baby's breath. They stifled giggles as they waited for the ushers.

Mollie held her small white leather Rainbow Girls Bible covered with a spray of gardenias and ribbons, her head bowing slightly with the flood of memories it brought. She wavered on her father's arm, drawing in her breath when the music started. Wearing carefully pressed dress blues, six officers from Ron's ship served as ushers. She hadn't expected the Navy to co-operate!

The ribbons dangling from her bouquet rippled as she walked slowly down the aisle to meet a very pale Ron. His hand in hers shook when they knelt together at the altar.

Pastor Dean's words were brief and traditional. Mollie and Ron parroted his instructions, smiling with relief when he said, "You may salute your new wife, Commander Van Ness."

Ron grinned and snapped a quick military salute before leaning for such a long kiss the audience laughed. Mollie felt her face flush when she heard Mike, who had stood proudly on his crutches as Ron's best man, whistle through his teeth and whisper.

"If you don't let her up for air, she'll need Gaspy Gertrude!"

When the Navy officers raised ceremonial sabers high over the heads of the new bride and groom, Mollie felt a path of tears moisten her face. Only in fairy tales were there such weddings...

"I can't believe anything so perfect could be arranged so quickly, darling. We must look like Snow White and Prince Charming," Mollie whispered as they stood in the receiving line. "How did they find time to buy gifts?" She glanced toward the pile of packages on a table in the foyer of the church.

"Credit goes mostly to our mothers, darling," Ron whispered. "They will be as exhausted tomorrow as the two principals in this affair!"

After cutting the small cake made mostly of fruit, Mollie tossed her bouquet to a beaming Dee, and ran out to the car under a curtain of rice.

"One stop, darling, before we go to the cottage. I have to let Sally see me in her dress." Mollie created quite a stir walking down the hospital corridor in a white wedding dress and veil, dripping a trail of rice.

Sally cried just as if she had been at the ceremony. "If you could have waited another two days, I would have been there, Mollie."

"Would you and Dave have waited if you had so little time?" Mollie watched her sister digest this statement.

"Of course not. I'm sorry, Mollie. It's only...we haven't even had a chance to talk." Sally blotted her eyes. "I feel fine. Can't understand why they make you stay nine days when you have a baby. I will go home Saturday. See you then."

~ * ~

At the cottage, Mollie removed her wedding finery, pushing away Ron's helping hands. "Just wait until after dinner so we can finish what we start, darling." She slipped into an aqua blue suit made of rayon linen. "You wouldn't want Mother to find out I didn't wear my *going away* dress. How else could she report it properly to the newspaper?"

The inn was full of diners when the newly-weds moved to their table in the most secluded corner.

"The baked salmon is delicious. It has been over a year since I tasted it." Mollie ate with relish, hungrier than she had been for months. Everything today was perfect, the wine, and the ice cream...the arm so tight around her waist.

"At last!" Ron whooped happily at the door of the cottage when he lifted her over the threshold. After closing the door with his foot, he kissed her and turned the gold ring on her finger. "It's real. This is really our wedding night, Mrs. Ronald Van Ness. God, how can I be so lucky?" She felt moisture from his eyes when he buried his head in her neck.

Mollie felt like crying for happiness herself because their lovemaking came like a bonus, a fulfillment of desire without guilt or fear, a promise of a contented future. She cuddled into the arms she had dreamed about so long. Too soon the summer night passed.

~ * ~

She felt Ron move from the bed slowly, trying not to disturb her lying half under the sheets. When she opened her eyes and smiled, he slipped back down beside her to watch her with renewed hunger. "Every day since we spent the night on the beach, I planned our honeymoon. Sometimes it was in Hawaii, other times Victoria, a number of exotic places. I pictured each little detail hundreds of times this past year. When the world gets back to normal again we'll try them all, sweetheart."

A knock at the heavy cedar door turned his head. "Yes?"

"Ensign Knox, sir. I have a car waiting. You have half an hour."

"Dammit!" Ron shouted. "Go on back to the base, Ensign. My wife will drive me." Ron leaned for a remembering kind of kiss. "I won't be late."

"Don't, darling Ron. Don't think about what might have happened. We had three wonderful days and one and a half nights. Remember them." She rubbed her hand against his prickly cheek. "You had better hurry. I wouldn't want to get into trouble with your commanding officer our first day of marriage!"

Ron scraped at his tough beard talking between strokes, forcing light teasing words and trying to make his voice sound normal. He slammed the razor into his toilet kit and came from the bathroom with a white towel around his neck, wearing only his jockey shorts. "I... sweetheart," he whispered. "I am not supposed to tell anyone about this. The carrier is here for repairs, but the war is over except for the signing of treaties. The Japanese will surrender in a couple of days." He glanced toward the door.

"Then why must you go?" Mollie felt the old tight hurt squeeze her chest.

"Hell, I could be shot for telling you. But you know how to keep silent better than those stupid government types. I am assigned to the group who will accompany President Truman to the peace signing. That's why I was sent to Washington for briefing." He sighed. "It's supposed to be an honor, Mollie, and I am assigned to assist in writing the report for history, but I would trade the whole damn thing for another night like this one."

"They're flying you over?"

"By way of Hawaii. Wish I could sneak you aboard."

"I'll be pretty busy while you are gone, darling, and relieved you won't be dodging Zeros. Remember, I have to report for duty at Madigan day after tomorrow." She felt thankful for that, too. Giving nursing care to guys like poor Andy would make excellent use of the waiting time...

~ * ~

September 2, 1945

Dear Joe,

Today it is really over; the killing, the insanity, the fear and the rationing. Dad filled his gas tank and splashed a couple of gallons on the ground! Ron is over there on the Missouri watching the whole ceremony. You can't know how much I would like to be beside him. He writes wonderfully descriptive letters, but he should have learned something as a journalism major. He plans to try to get a job on a newspaper when he gets home (which is soon, I hope) and maybe write a book one day.

Mother is excited about your call. She told everyone in Bremerton you would be home by the fifteenth. I haven't told her you plan to make the Air Force a career. Good thing they saved those toes. I know we must be prepared and keep a strong Air Force for guys like you to fly in, but I hope we also remember the reasons leading to the war and try to live together as a world, to learn to appreciate our differences, not destroy each other because of them.

Since they changed the rule about married nurses, I'm staying in the Corps until Ron gets out of the Navy, then I will be just plain Mrs. Van Ness and hopefully Mommy in a year or so.

Love,

Mrs. Ronald Thomas Van Ness (have to practice writing my new name!)

~ * ~

Mollie closed her eyes, thinking sadly of the thousands of families whose sons and daughters would not be coming home at all, or those like Andy Porter, barely recognizable, so altered their loved ones might wish they hadn't. Yet Andy gave her hope. His will to live and adjust inspired everyone he met. Andy planned a future, a healing of the horrible scars of war.

She walked slowly down to the mailbox, watching the sun set over the bay, so peaceful without the silhouettes of barrage balloons...

After dropping the letter into the box and raising the flag, she chased the big German Shepherd up the driveway. "Come on, Casey. We have a lot of living to catch up on..."

Epilogue

Fiftieth Reunion of St. Annie's Class of '44

The women gathered around tables in the lounge to celebrate the golden anniversary of their graduating class. The reunion was bittersweet because they were saying farewell to their alma mater. St. Anne's no longer would maintain a school of nursing. Now a large research hospital, its only original building after extensive restructuring was the nursing residence, which would serve as living space for relatives of cancer victims.

Though Mollie and her close friends had been meeting each decade, she sipped a glass of white wine, noting both sameness and changes in her former classmates. She turned to her table mates at the gathering in the lounge of their old nursing residence. "My memory isn't as sharp on some things, but I'll always remember our St. Annie's years. Weren't we innocent before the pill? Had to be, of course."

Barbara Andrews Price pushed the back of her short champagne-tinted hair. "If I didn't keep passing mirrors to remind me, I wouldn't believe it has been fifty years."

Dorrie Koski Swartz patted her generous bosom, reminding them she retained her infectious sense of humor. "And scales! All my life I've fought my own private war with fat."

Shirley Britton Daniels thumped her boyish chest beneath a tailored white silk shirt. "Lordy, Dorrie, I'd still love to have about twenty of your pounds. After six kids and six grandchildren, my bra size hasn't grown an inch!"

"We may be a bit tarnished by years, but you gals sound like we still live in rooms three-ten, three-thirteen and three-twelve." Ginger King Rossi, looking like she always had except for white hair and expensive clothing, removed her stylish tinted glasses and wiped moisture from them with a tissue. "Only Pinky's missing."

The graduates of St. Anne's Nursing School class of 1944 sniffed and blotted tears. Pinky had died of cancer three months before the reunion.

Dorrie munched a potato chip. "World War Two had one redeeming grace. We all met our husbands while it raged and have produced..." she counted with her fingers, "...there's Pinky's daughter. My two, Molly has two boys and a girl, ditto Ginger. And Barbara twin sons and Shirley, three of each! That's seventeen! And we all have grandchildren. You can tell we didn't have the pill. My God, we *are* the population explosion."

Mollie grinned. "Remember the Forty-two New Year's Eve fraternity party when Shirley, Ginger and I met our future husbands? I still bless Gloria for inviting us." She nodded toward Gloria Rollins Norberg chatting at another table. Evidently Gloria still didn't drink anything alcoholic, an oddity in the society circles she frequented.

Turning back to Ginger, Mollie asked, "Since you became a professor of nursing education, have you learned to drink champagne, Ginger?"

"That's one party I wish you had forgotten! I still can't drink the bubbly stuff without feeling sick."

Barbara had a thoughtful expression. "If there's another war involving the whole world, no one will survive."

They all nodded, aware that Barbara's clergyman husband, Howard, had been jailed in several anti-nuclear demonstrations, and against the Vietnam war. One of her sons had gone to Canada to avoid being drafted.

"We have changed, yet we are the same, we and the world," Mollie said, feeling a sting in her eyes with the reminder of the anguish war had brought to her own family. Joe had fought in Korea and afterward became an airline pilot. He had married his English girlfriend and brought her to America. Now retired, Joe and his family lived in Arizona near Kingman where he had done his basic flight training. Mike, after several operations on his legs, was able to walk with the aid of a cane. He'd become a pediatrician, married a school teacher and had two red-haired sons.

Mollie and Ron were still friends with Terry Reed, who had married Pinky after her first husband died in the last days of the war. They had all consoled Terry when Pinky died. The Reeds had a lovely daughter and two grandchildren.

Andy Porter became a respected psychologist and married a nurse who saw beyond his scarred face to the spirit inside. He was on the staff of Veterans' Hospital.

In Vietnam, Mollie and Ron's oldest son had lost a leg. Jason's injury had been a desperate trial for Ron, a television newscaster, who had to report his own son's wounds while viewing the war in close-up vivid color. Jason had recovered from that unfortunate war more quickly than had his father. Ron's healing came by writing a well-received book about the war.

Mollie sighed. "World War Two didn't end wars, religious wars, political wars, civil wars." She laughed wryly. "Who coined that term? There's nothing civil about any of them. We did a lot of crying, loving and coping. Now we remember."

Meet Mary Brockway

Mary Brockway has been writing and publishing for thirty years and has conducted two writing critique groups for much of that time. Her book, Persimmon Bayou was published in 2010. She is married and has five children, eleven grandchildren, and one great grandson. Nursing school was the inspiration for St. Annie's Corps, and where she met her husband when he was a patient.

VISIT OUR WEBSITE

FOR THE FULL INVENTORY
OF QUALITY BOOKS:

http://www.wings-press.com

**Quality trade paperbacks and downloads
in multiple formats,
in genres ranging from light romantic comedy to
general fiction and horror. Wings has something
for every reader's taste.
Visit the website, then bookmark it.
We add new titles each month!**

www.ingramcontent.com/pod-product-compliance
Lightning Source LLC
Chambersburg PA
CBHW061017120726

47910CB00006B/1979